PRAISE FOR *THE PAYBACK GIRLS*

"This book is best for fans of thrillers like Karen McManus's *One of Us Is Lying.*"

—*Forbes*

"A thrilling and suspenseful journey. . . **a definite must-read!**"

—*Parents*

BLACK GIRLS DON'T CRY

ALSO BY ALEX TRAVIS

The Payback Girls

BLACK GIRLS DON'T CRY

ALEX TRAVIS

sourcebooks fire

Cover design by Corina Lupp/Sourcebooks
Cover images © MIRRORstudio/Shutterstock, Lithiumphoto/Shutterstock
Internal design by Diane Cunningham/Sourcebooks

Published by Sourcebooks Fire, an imprint of Sourcebooks
1935 Brookdale Rd, Naperville, IL 60563–2773
(630) 961-3900
sourcebooks.com

Cataloging-in-Publication Data is on file with the Library of Congress.

Printed and bound in the United States of America.
PAH 10 9 8 7 6 5 4 3 2 1

To Riley: It's okay to cry, especially when Mama is writing a book while snuggling you. I love you.

CHAPTER 1

MY BEST FRIEND SIMONE HAS BEEN LAUGHING FOR THE last ten minutes, with tears streaming down her face. Her foundation doesn't even budge, and I make a mental note to ask her what powder she's using when she catches her breath. Should she be laughing? Probably not, but what else can you do in the face of complete ridiculousness?

Banneker High has been almost entirely paperless for two years—until this morning. Someone decided to litter the hallway with the paper of at least three trees. But something tells me the assistant principal, who is also our resident environmental activist, won't be taking much time to address this one.

Simone tips her head back, trying to will the water back into her eyes. She flips her braids behind her shoulder. Like I said: The situation's not actually funny, but we might as well get in our laughs now. As members of the Black Student Union, we're going to have to address this. As vice president of said Black Student Union, I am *really* not looking forward to that.

"Taped to a locker though? Is it the seventies?" Simone says.

"Which seventies?" I reply, pulling the paper from my locker. I glance at it and wince.

"Eighteen," Simone says. "In the 1970s it would have been a telegraph."

"Pretty sure they had fax machines, but go off," I tell her.

Simone snatches the paper from me and scans it. She raises her eyebrows as she flips it over. Then she crumples it into a ball and, in true state-champion-basketball-forward style, launches it into the nearest trash can at the end of the locker row. The cerulean-blue beads on the ends of her braids click, and she winks at me, her golden-brown sparkle eyeshadow temporarily blinding me as the light hits it.

"Point for Banneker High." It's Jason Miller, captain of the lacrosse team and six foot four inches of blond, bacchanalian blandness. His best friend and lieutenant of loser-dom, Grayson Davis, trails behind him.

Jason holds a stack of papers, which he flings above his head so they rain down the hallway like a gender-bent Regina George in *Mean Girls*. His teeth are slightly too big for his mouth, so when he grins, it looks distinctly animalistic. Considering his non-school-related extracurriculars, I'm pretty sure he's more the Big Bad Wolf than the hunter. That would make Cassidy Burke, number three on the list, his Little Red. I say a silent prayer for her to dump his ass.

Simone clears her throat. "He definitely did it."

I can't tell if she's disgusted or slightly envious. As a star basketball player, she should be one of the most popular girls in school. She should be ripe material for a list like this, but because she's a dark-skinned Black girl, none of those guys look twice at her. She's had to fight for a date to the homecoming dances when most of the non-Black freshman JV girls get asked by dudes in our grade without a second thought.

"Probably," I reply. "Nothing we can do about it now."

Simone snorts. "Tell that to JJ at the meeting later." She's visibly gleeful at the thought.

I roll my eyes. JJ is BSU's president and, for the past several years, a constant thorn in my side, though until a few weeks ago, I really liked the prick. "I shan't be doing that."

I didn't get the best look at the list before Simone snatched it from me, but I got the gist. Class rankings are typically held for the end of the year when there're actual grades to rank. I thought maybe it was someone's prom court campaign, since nominations open in a few days. But then I saw the subsections. Oh, the subsections.

Bridget Lewis, captain of the field hockey team was ranked number ten. Nothing too questionable there. She's in mostly Advanced Placement classes and a solid B+/A– student, extrapolating from last year's academic rankings. I figured she'd bumped up the extra credit and secured that 3.7 GPA. Except class rankings don't usually have a strengths and weaknesses section, at least not one that's publicly available. Still, Bridget's were, and they had absolutely nothing to do with her academic performance.

Strengths: blond, flat stomach, flexible

Weaknesses: a little hippy, could use a nose job

Numbers nine through three are variations on the same—an interspersing of blond and brunette female athletes, who are a size four at most and whose physical features were mined for jabs at their perceived positive and negative qualities. All were white.

"As treasurer, would it be irresponsible to use club funds to make shirts that say: *Sorry I don't fit your standard of attractiveness?*" Simone asks. "Would Amayah approve?"

Amayah Murphy, BSU's publicity chair, walks over to us and leans against the lockers. Her twist out is as well-defined as her cheekbones and her arm muscles. She's holding a copy of the list, and her top lip is curled upward, so I just know she has an idea brewing. After college, she wants to become a political campaign manager and someday help the first gay president get elected. She always has a plan.

"Do they charge by the letter? If so, yes, it's irresponsible, and no, Amayah would not approve." I reply.

"T-shirt ideas?" Simone asks Amayah.

"I'd go with *hot-slash-not* with *hot* circled. Black shirt, silver writing. Calligraphy, of course," Amayah replies. "We can all wear one." Amayah has literally taken calligraphy classes so she can design invitations. How cool is she?

"Simple. Brilliant," Simone says. "I will personally donate"—she digs in her pocket—"twenty-three cents."

JJ, BSU's president and Banneker High's most persistent protester, has never been the biggest fan of slogans. His argument is typically that something too catchy distracts from the actual message and often gets distorted by the other side. Is he entirely wrong? No. Is he insufferable when he makes his case? Yeah.

"JJ brought jollof rice and chicken for lunch. Maybe we can sell samples for ten dollars a pop to fund our clothing budget. Say it's 'African and magical.' Neither is technically a lie," Amayah says.

"JJ would never give up jollof rice," I tell her. "And he'll be eating in study hall while plotting BSU's response."

"Well, you'd know," Simone says.

Amayah takes a long, loud sip from her iced mocha, then smacks her lips.

JJ and I rather notoriously were a thing for all of last year, after two years of ferocious buildup. He started plotting his tenure as BSU president two months into freshman year and tapped me to be the Betty Shabazz to his Malcolm X not long after. Not that I was complaining; JJ, though sometimes overbearing, is six foot three, a well-regarded poet, and he does this thing with his tongue when you kiss him... Let's just say, he's got some pluses.

"He is president of the *esteemed* Black Student Union and deciding which HBCU deserves the honor of his presence next year. It's common knowledge that he's never in the cafeteria," I say.

"Where he *goes* to plot, though, only a close associate would know," Simone says.

"Like a vice president?" I shoot her a look to will her to silence. Amayah doesn't need to hear all of this.

"Like an ex." Simone waggles her eyebrows.

Ex is a strong word. Technically, despite the very public nature of our relationship, we never put a label on our time together. We were sort of exclusive but didn't actually talk about it. I didn't hook up with anyone else, and I assumed he didn't either. I knew he'd occasionally flirt with other girls, and once took our class president on a date, but he implied that it never went beyond that, and I believed him. I could have gone on dates too; I just didn't.

Amayah bites her bottom lip. Something about her face strikes me as bothered, but that may be wishful thinking on my part.

"As much as I love this drama," she says, "I'm more intrigued by who is number one. Why keep the mystery, especially if this is going to blow up?"

"Maybe there isn't one," I say.

"Of course there's a one. I bet it's Lauren Buckley," Simone says.

Lauren Buckley is the swim captain and editor of the school literary magazine. She looks like a CW teen drama's idea of a popular high school girl. A real-life classic Barbie, though as editor of the lit mag, she has shown an impressively acerbic sense of humor.

"She's definitely the type," Amayah replies. "Her ranking of literary characters from the AP English reading list who would appear on right-wing podcasts was inspired."

"Who would *you* pick?" Simone asks, smiling at me. "Who's the hottest girl in school?"

I could never pick only one, even if we were purely going on physical attractiveness. There's no way to nail down my physical type. I don't think I have one. I'm frequently wowed by a new girl at least once a week. Simone knows that, but she won't say it in front of Amayah or anyone else.

"No one, because it's objectifying," I say.

Simone turns to Amayah, who shrugs. "After that, I can't answer. But it wouldn't be anyone they'd have the astuteness to choose." She looks over at me.

Or maybe I imagined it.

"Boo, you're both no fun. The answer is obviously Ashley Beckett," says Simone.

"The Ashley Beckett who refuses to join BSU because she says she's *a woman of the world* and not Black?" Amayah says.

"The Ashley Beckett who said she's from all the continents, not just Africa?" I add.

Ashley Beckett is the co-captain of the girls' tennis team and is never seen without a fifteen-inch sew-in or in pants. She even does her morning runs in a Nike skirt to manifest her future athleisure line. If our AP lit teacher would let her, she would write every book report on *The Feminine Mystique*. She dresses like a character from *Mad Men*, her self-proclaimed bible, and only publicly dates the WASPiest, palest white boys our school has to offer.

"She's my problematic fave. Leave me alone." Simone shrugs. "Plus, she pulls some of the hottest guys in school. Call me jealous."

We have different definitions of the hottest guys in school. I love Simone, but she finds the most generic guys attractive, and it grinds her gears more than a little that they don't look her way.

"She wouldn't pass the paper bag test, so there's no world in which she's making number one for the likes of Jason Miller," Amayah says.

She's not wrong. As stunning as Ashley is, Jason Miller would never give her a second glance. It's ironic. She's too Black for someone like Jason Miller but too interested in absorbing whiteness for someone like JJ, who has called her, and I quote, "emblematic of our collective oppression."

JJ, a.k.a. Jeremiah Johnson, arrives in a whirlwind powered by his own indignation. Per usual, he's wearing a dashiki shirt and black pants. He keeps his red-tinged afro combed out for full impact, meaning he gets frequent complaints from whoever sits behind him and then calls them racist. He refuses to sit in the back of the classroom, "due to history," and wears a bracelet with a simple gold *X* every day. Sometimes it feels like he's cosplaying someone he hasn't truly figured out yet. He wants to be a radical and frequently quotes *The Autobiography of Malcolm X*, but he tends to revert back to his own idea that he's the most important person in the room. We lose the communal nature of BSU because a seventeen-year-old boy is grappling with both his racial identity and masculinity on a stage of his own creation.

"Sixty seconds after last period. Room 104. Much to discuss," he says.

The bell rings, and he catapults himself down the hall toward his homeroom, each step hitting the ground like he wants to cause an earthquake. He probably will at our meeting later. I wonder who he'd vote for, not that he'd ever tell us. *It would be irrelevant to the mission*, he'd tell me, giving me a look that reminded me how superfluous I was.

We were supposed to be a partnership, but it's hard to be a *we* when you're fighting the ego of the *he*.

"That intensity," Amayah says. "Did he bring it to everything?"

Simone bursts out laughing. "Can you imagine?"

"Well, not with him," Amayah replies. "Not interested in the parts. But the intensity..."

"Girl, shut up," I huff.

He did. That's why I still imagine ways to end up in a locked room or stuck elevator with him. Our parents never left us alone, for good reason, meaning we could only make out in his car or under the barely used science staircase in the back of the school. Maybe I could camp out in the parking lot. Not that he believes he can be tempted. Especially not by me. Not anymore.

"What are we working with here? Like, how badly are you compromised for him?" Amayah asks.

Amayah and I are newer friends; we connected over this past summer despite having been in BSU together for years. We have an absurd number of favorites in common, almost identical Spotify Wrappeds, and serve the same signature dish when we host parties (chicken parm). I'd avoided her previously, mostly because I found her terrifyingly attractive and didn't want to admit it. But now, we're friends. She's into girls but probably not into me, which I can respect.

"I'm not compromised. It's been three months. We've been cordial at the meetings," I tell her.

That's true. We haven't bickered in front of anyone, except

for the first meeting after Thanksgiving. But still, there are whispers. The rest of the board is desperate to know what happened to break up the first couple of BSU, and I'm not particularly inclined to tell them.

"You back in the saddle?" Amayah asks.

"I have options."

"Of course you do," Amayah replies. "But are any of them actually happening?"

"No," Simone answers for me, and I reach over to swat her arm. She knows about my crush on Amayah, and I need her to rein it all the way in. She shouldn't have too much of a problem with that. While she accepts my sexuality, she's not encouraging me to head a pride parade. She clears her throat and nods toward another group of lockers.

The fallout from the list continues all throughout the hallway.

Cassidy Burke, the soccer team's star defender and number three on the list, walks by with her eyes trained on the floor. For the first time since freshman year, she has her hair down, seemingly to block her face. I still can't believe her own boyfriend insulted her in front of the entire school.

"Hey, legs," a sophomore on boys' junior varsity basketball calls out to her.

"Don't hide your butterface!" another guy shouts.

Cassidy Burke's strengths were, in order, her body, her legs, and her C cups. Her only weakness was, and I quote, "her face." The fact that there's nothing wrong with her face is beside the point. All of it is made worse because her boyfriend, Jason, is probably the one who made the list. At the very least, he's distributing it, quite literally throwing it in her face.

"Hey, assholes," Amayah calls. "She'll never look at you, talk to you, or acknowledge that you exist. Neither will anyone else. Shut the actual fuck up, and leave her alone."

"You wouldn't even make the list," JV Basketball replies. "None of you would."

"Yeah, that's a statement on the list, not on us. We've got some real knockouts in this group," Amayah says. "You're dismissed. Shoo."

She fixes them with a look so heated, I'm surprised it doesn't scald their skin. When she flicks her hand at them, they raise theirs and shuffle down the hall. They don't dare to peek back at her.

"Thanks," Cassidy says, tucking some of her hair behind her ear.

"'Course," Amayah replies.

"You didn't have to... I appreciate it." Cassidy turns visibly red.

"No problem," Amayah tells her.

Cassidy pulls out her phone and begins typing so quickly that her thumbs practically blur. She glances back at Amayah and flushes again, then keeps walking.

Simone turns to Amayah. "So is she your hottest?"

"No, I just like to cause trouble." Amayah gives me a pointed look. "You should try it. You need to step out of JJ's shadow."

Simone whistles. She's been telling me that for the past two years, and I resent the accusation. I'm behind the scenes of almost every decision he makes, supporting and shaping the mission. It only *seems* like I'm hiding.

"I'm *vice* president. I'm not a shadow, more of a trampoline."

"So he steps on you either way," Amayah says. "Like in your breakup."

I lock eyes with Simone. Did she say anything?

She shakes her head. Well, rumors are rumors. Even if they're true, how much can anyone really know?

I turn back to Amayah and feel myself growing hot. The way she's looking at me... she can't be far off, and it's making me sweat.

"What do you have against JJ?" I ask.

"Nothing. I'm just *for* you," Amayah replies. "I respect your vision. I want to see your methods. That list doesn't impact him. It impacts us. That's why we have to change the culture."

"How am I supposed to disrupt a school's perceptions of beauty? Get a Black person on the list?"

Simone and Amayah exchange a glance. Amayah moves her coffee to her lips, and I frown. They have way too much faith in me.

"We could try," Simone says. "But..."

"But?" I ask.

"Is the list the cause or a symptom of the issue?" Simone asks.

A fair question. There wouldn't be a list if Banneker culture didn't prize whiteness, athletics, boys, and the intersection of all three more than anything else.

"So what's a comparable cause?" I ask.

"There's never been a Black prom queen here. Ever. Hell, only two people of color have had the balls to run. Even running would be radical," Amayah says.

I'm not expecting that to change in the current prom cycle. But it's a goal.

"Okay, so what do you think that would take?" I ask.

"We'd have to run the right candidate. Someone who appeals to the guys and can still bring the girls together. Someone who, theoretically, could make a terrible list like this if the list was less racist," Amayah says.

I'd love to see Simone make a play. She's a star athlete, stylish, and an academic powerhouse. She's a perfect emblem of what a prom queen *should* be. But could it really work?

As much as I'd love to stick it to whoever made the list, we're facing more than an uphill battle. Personally, I'm Black popular, a.k.a. popular with the relatively small number of Black kids and basically invisible to all the white kids. It'd be a real coup if I could mobilize the different factions at the school around a candidate, especially the mainstream—read: white—majority. Trying to court the same people who don't see me or my friends as attractive? Scaling a mountain.

Still, it's been a while since I've seen Amayah so jazzed about a publicity idea. I love her excitement, but it feels futile. How would we infiltrate the ultrawhite ranks of the prom court *now*? Two BSU members tried to run for prom queen a few years ago amid another racial reckoning, and they couldn't even get on the official ballot.

"Why does it seem like you've been thinking about this?" I ask.

Simone grins. "We've been talking about wanting to see a

different kind of prom queen. Not the usual head cheerleader, soccer team captain, blond, with an asshole boyfriend. And we might have a better shot this year."

"Who would you run?" I ask.

"Open question," Simone says, but she and Amayah exchange another look. Clearly, they have an idea they're not telling me.

I sigh. If they want to float their plan at the BSU meeting, I'll support them. They're my friends. "I guess we can discuss it at the meeting."

"To see if the esteemed Jeremiah Johnson approves?" Simone asks.

"To put it to a vote. Come on, we're about to be late," I reply.

Our boot heels click on the floor as we fast walk down the hallway. If we're going to try to get a student body that has never looked twice at a Black girl to vote one on the prom court, getting BSU on board with the idea should be a piece of cake in comparison, right? Ha.

CHAPTER 2

JJ HAS WRITTEN *THE GALL* IN DARK RED BLOCK LETTERS on the whiteboard of our meeting room. As we file in, he underlines it eight times in quick succession.

Simone hides her face behind her water bottle, but I can see her shoulders shaking with silent laughter. It's a shame JJ left theater club. He really has a flair for dramatics. Dark red symbolizes the blood of our ancestors, spilled in favor of the oppressor. And here we are, being oppressed by the beauty standards of a few. Or at least, that's what he claims this means.

I kick Simone underneath the desk, and she coughs a few times before taking a long drink of water. We always fought over JJ. She never thought he was good enough for me; I thought he was the sun. One of us is right, but I'm still trying to decide which one.

"I asked you all not to be late," he says. "The bell rang one hundred and eighty seconds ago."

Just say three minutes, dude. No one is going to die if we start our discussion after the clock strikes three. This isn't academic Cinderella.

"Harrison's calc class ran long," I say. "Sorry."

"I didn't ask for excuses, Ida." He glares at me. So much for keeping it civil.

"Lighten up, man," Amayah says.

JJ throws the marker onto the tray under the board. "*Lighten?*"

The list isn't about him; this is about us Black girls. He should be deferring to me, as his second-in-command, as a female. But he'd never do that. And now, we're getting drama about semantics for what? Because outrage is fun to perform?

"Oh, come on." Amayah rolls her eyes. "Is all of this really necessary?"

"She just means that this is a . . . charged situation and we want to formulate the best strategic response to get our point across. One that addresses the intersection of feminism and Blackness," I reply.

Amayah raises her eyebrows. Ever since we've become friends, she has made her position on JJ's and my dynamic quite clear. Apparently, I cover for him too much. Basically, I turn the sometimes-outrageous things he says into palatable policy positions.

"You don't need to translate for me," JJ says.

Well, actually I do. This whole thing should be pretty cut-and-dried. We condemn the list and write a statement about the Eurocentric beauty standards it perpetuates by tomorrow. Then we figure out how to disrupt the beauty binary the list conveys. Done. Intellectually, he knows this. At least, I think he does.

"This doesn't impact you," Amayah replies. "Maybe let a Black woman talk for once, Brother?"

JJ throws his hands in the air, which is more for effect than from actual frustration. I know him well enough that I can see in his eyes that he knows he's wrong; he's just loath to admit it.

"Fine. Ida. What's our response then?" JJ asks.

Paul Bailey, BSU secretary/notetaker, tennis team equipment manager, and Mathlete extraordinaire, scooches his chair to face me with his laptop. He nods at me, then to his computer. Great, now everyone thinks I'm going to say something profound.

No pressure.

Simone kicks me under the table, and out of the corner of my eye, I see Amayah giving me a thumbs-up. I swear Amayah is staring at me harder than everyone else.

All the pressure.

Or maybe simply my imagination, yet again.

"Um… We have to…" I take a deep breath. "We have to address the racism behind it publicly, of course. Maybe through a statement to the school paper. Or…um…we could…"

"A statement to the school paper?" JJ repeats. He grimaces. *The school paper is an instrument of the institutionalized discrimination we face*, I can practically hear him shouting.

"Let her finish!" Simone says. "Jesus, you're determined to step all over her ideas."

I hear Amayah choking on her iced mocha a few feet away, and Paul slaps her on the back until she coughs up what sounds like a hairball. Everyone else is uncharacteristically silent. JJ tends to suck the oxygen out of a room, but this quiet from the rest of the organization is on another level.

"We could write out our statement in a list format and tape it around the school, the way they did with their list," I offer.

JJ bites the inside of his lip and looks at the Spanish grammar rules poster on the wall behind me. When he breaks eye contact, it usually means he's trying to reconcile that someone else's idea is better than his. I fight the urge to smile. Finally, a win.

"I like it. You and Amayah can arrange it. Get a Google doc to everyone by ten p.m. We can meet tomorrow morning to tape up our response. Seven thirty?" he says.

"Sounds good," I reply.

Simone clears her throat. "*And?*"

Maybe she *is* angling to make a run for queen. The investment she has in this idea is only rivaled by her dedication to a 3.9 GPA and a thirty-plus-point-per-game scoring record.

All right, let me get her set up. Queen Simone, first of the Black prom queens.

"We have to address the elephant in the room: how the student body perceives beauty standards," I answer.

"Agreed," JJ says. "How do you want to do that?"

I close my eyes. He's not going to take this well. He thinks prom is stupid. If there's anything worse than me speaking over him in a meeting, it's reminding him I'm a girl who can galvanize people around ideas. Even if those ideas aren't mine.

"Infiltrating one of the favorite exhibitions of that standard," Simone replies.

JJ scrunches his forehead. "A protest? A takedown?"

"A takeover. With Amayah's help, and BSU's support, we'd run BSU members for prom queen with a sharply coordinated campaign," I explain.

JJ blinks several times. "Okay...who?"

I look to Simone and Amayah, who are both practically vibrating with excitement. Simone, obviously. Amayah? Definitely not, only because there's no way she'd do it, but I know she'd organize a killer campaign. A couple other girls in BSU might be open to trying.

"Anyone who's willing," I say, looking at Simone.

At the same time Simone says, "Ida."

Wait. What? They never mentioned me, and I am not interested. Sure, I love the idea of breaking the tradition, but I'm a behind-the-scenes girl. We all know that, especially JJ.

JJ has always been the face of BSU. He's always made sure of that. And if he can't be the face in this, I know he'll want a say. The idea of me being attractive enough to other people to be a credible candidate... I don't think that fits his self-narrative. He was always the leader, the catch. I was the supporting character. I sort of liked it that way, or at least, I was used to it. I *am* used to it.

"No," JJ says. "No way."

"Ida is one of Banneker's top students, she's been a BSU leader for years, she has that unique cool-casual style that's in vogue right now, and she's objectively a stunner," Amayah says. "Wouldn't you agree?"

I feel my face growing hotter and hotter. I know she's just

saying it to make a point, but part of me really hopes she means it. I'd love to be a stunner in Amayah's eyes, screw the objective. Subjectivize me, please.

"It's a terrible idea," JJ insists.

His tone makes me think his opposition isn't to the overall idea, just me. What about me, the girl he dated and called gorgeous, is so difficult to accept as desirable to other people?

"Well, at least put it to a vote," I tell him. "Running for prom queen is not my favorite idea either, but if everyone thinks it has merit—"

"I said no," JJ replies.

Paul is typing furiously, like he's making a full transcription of every comment, which knowing him, he is. He'd make a killer court stenographer. But this is about to devolve into a verbal battle across our warring factions, and the idea of being able to revisit this conversation word for word makes me want to melt into the floor.

"I didn't realize this was an autocracy," Amayah says. "The vice president can call a vote. Can't she?"

Everyone looks to me for a response, and Paul's hands hover above his laptop keys. Amayah's eyes widen as they meet mine, as if she's not the one who suggested this. It's tantamount to a coup, at least in JJ's perspective.

I'd be proving myself to be the unsuitable partner JJ already thinks I am.

I clear my throat. "Uh, yes. The vice president can. All those in favor of me, or anyone, running for prom queen...raise your right hand."

Everyone except JJ raises their hand. I can feel the steam from JJ's ears charging at me, and part of me wonders how much worse this is going to make things between us. Another part of me doesn't care. He's being a jerk.

"All those opposed..."

JJ raises both hands. "The white man will often try to mount symbolic victories—"

"Okay, Brother Jeremiah. Let's take it down a notch," Simone replies. "It doesn't matter if Ida wins. What matters is the visibility of our movement and our ability to communicate our mission to a wider audience by utilizing a traditionally white event to make a statement. But for the record, I think Ida might win. She has my vote."

Oh, thank God. They don't expect me to win, just be the figurehead for the visibility of our movement. That I can try to do. Especially if it means that someday someone like Simone, who deserves to be in the running, actually could.

"I'm not against it because it's shallow," JJ says. At the arch of my eyebrow he adds, "Not that Ida is shallow. Prom is shallow; the title is shallow. I'm saying no for Ida's safety."

What does he think our classmates are going to do, try to kill me? Worst case, someone says something nasty and gets a slap on the wrist. It'll suck, and it'll hurt, but I can handle it. How fragile does he think I am?

"Please elaborate," I say.

"Maybe we should talk privately," JJ says.

Oh, *now* we get to be private. This is BSU business; he can put me on blast in front of everyone and face the repercussions. Safety. *Please.* That's such bullshit.

"There's no privacy between us anymore, at least if recent actions are to be believed," I reply.

JJ smacks his lips together, and I can practically see the calculations running in his head. *What to do…what to do…*

"I was already planning a protest of prom because of the legacy of racial injustice at this school," JJ says.

I restrain the urge to roll my eyes. Is it really a protest if you were going to boycott prom anyway? JJ doesn't engage in school-sponsored events in the first place.

"Why were you planning a BSU protest without consulting publicity?" Amayah asks. Amayah really isn't taking her foot off JJ's neck today, and it is much appreciated. And hot. It's very, very hot.

"I was going to consult publicity when I formulated my ideas. And talked to my VP. I'd like to propose an amendment to the decision regarding prom," JJ says. He smiles at me for the first time in months. I try to push down the little tug in my chest. We had some good times together and really good chemistry. We fought hard but made up harder.

I swallow. "You can't revoke the decision via an amendment. It's in the bylaws."

"Not a revocation," JJ says. "A stipulation. Anyone is free to run for prom queen. I'll vote for them, one hundred percent, and throw the full weight of BSU behind them."

It's such a marked shift on his part that I know a pretty big *but* is coming. One I'm not sure I'm ready for.

"You can't make someone go to prom with you," Amayah says.

JJ glares at her, and I feel my face heating up. That was never where this was going.

"Very funny. I don't need a date," JJ replies. "The actual stipulation is that BSU can put someone up for prom, but I don't want it to be you. There are already group chats popping up about the people on the list, and you're at risk, as an intersection of thr—*several* marginalized groups. Plus, we can't afford to lose our VP to prom planning."

JJ has seen group chats about the list, and he's not divulging what's in them? Talk about being complicit. Besides, what do those have to do with me anyway? I'm not in danger of being called hot by the likes of Jason Miller.

JJ caught himself before saying *three,* but it's clear enough. I'm not only a girl and Black; he basically confirmed my sexuality for the entire BSU. And somehow, that's about to make its way out to the guys of Banneker? Who the hell has he been talking to?

"That's a bullshit excuse, JJ," Amayah says.

"No, it's not." He turns to Simone, who blanches when he makes eye contact. "You know what I'm talking about. You know why she shouldn't run."

Oh, screw him. All of these innuendos, and *someone* is going to pick up on what he's implying. Simone's face practically screams that something is up. Like she's scared for me too. She was supposed to be on my side. Screw her if she's going to agree with him!

Simone pulls out her phone and starts texting. Who, I have no idea. She's an athlete; she has connections. There are other basketball girls on the list. But why would that have anything to do with me?

"Who do you propose instead?" Amayah asks.

"Ashley Beckett," JJ replies. "She's more palatable to them, and she has had no involvement in BSU. There's nothing that can be used against her."

Unlike you, he doesn't say. How would he know what skeletons Ashley has in her closet? I don't think they've exchanged two words. He's acting like I'm secretly a murderer, and Ashley is the dedicated agent who's going to bring me down.

"What does Ida have that can be used against her?" Amayah asks.

"Amayah, leave it," Simone says, looking up from her phone. "JJ's right."

"Why, Simone? What would someone want to use against Ida?" Amayah presses.

I'm at a loss. Simone was just extolling my virtues, and now my *best friend* is looking at me like I'm a leper. Simone, who has been raised intensely Baptist, has been supportive when it's the two of us but has been weird about any public displays of my bisexuality. She balances it with a verbal pride parade when we're alone, and I'm starting to see how that isn't enough. Especially right now.

"Some things should be kept private. Which is difficult when you're running for prom queen," Simone replies, avoiding my stare.

What do I have to "keep private"? The only thing about me that was semi-private was my sexuality, but that's basically out the window. What's the difference if the rest of the school finds out?

Amayah narrows her eyes. "What does any of that have to do with Ashley Beckett?"

I refocus on what JJ said. He'd rather run *Ashley Beckett* than me. The same Ashley Beckett he's never said anything nice about. What is the logic? Why would he even think she'd be willing to run for *us*? Why would we put our weight behind her?

"Ashley has no involvement in BSU by *choice* because she doesn't actually care about being Black," I say.

JJ shakes his head. His voice softens. "There's more to her than you think."

It takes me a few seconds to stop shaking. He's always been snarky about her and the we're-all-better-off-being-colorblind schtick. Until today. Until this very moment.

I feel sick to my stomach. Is this the real reason he didn't want to be with me anymore? Forget my sexuality. Did he dump me for someone else? Or maybe it was because of my sexuality. Ashley is more traditionally feminine because she eschews pants *and* other girls. She's a better fit for his particular male ego than I ever was.

"You've got to be kidding me. *You're* with *her*?" I say.

A gasp ripples through the room.

I'm horrified. Obviously, JJ can make his own decisions, but to reject me because of my sexuality and then accept someone whose racial views are diametrically opposed to his? It says a lot about what JJ prizes.

"*That* definitely should have been run through publicity," Amayah adds.

"We're keeping it low-key, friendly. But she already has inroads with the different factions at school. Ashley's less likely to be treated terribly, and if she is, that says a lot about the student—"

I hold up my hand to cut him off. "Nice try. Another vote, then. All in favor of running Ashley Beckett as the BSU candidate?"

JJ, Simone, Paul, and three other members raise their hands. Paul, I understand, since he's affiliated with the tennis team. But Simone? Seriously?

I motion for Simone to put her hand down, but she only has eyes for JJ. She's been convinced that, despite the purported liberalness in our school, me being Black and bisexual is going to be a bigger deal than I think it will be. She has wanted me to keep it as close to the vest as possible, for what she calls "safety." She's not homophobic, but she's so certain other people will be that she wants me to stay halfway in the closet. And she's playing right into JJ's stupid narrative, even though it was her idea for me to run for prom queen in the first place. What the hell is going on with her?

"All opposed?" JJ asks.

Amayah's hand shoots up, as does mine and one other person's. Amayah nods toward me, and I smile weakly.

"Amendment passed," Paul says.

"Seriously, y'all, come on," I protest.

"I'm doing this for you," JJ replies.

"I can handle myself, JJ. You made sure of that. I need some time to think." I swing my backpack over my shoulder.

Simone stands up next to me, and I shake my head. She's complicit in whatever this is, and I want no part of it. She backed off the second JJ said *jump, even* knowing what he did to me.

Unfortunately, since I don't have my own car, Simone is supposed to be my ride. So now I have to wait outside for an Uber, hoping not to run into anyone from BSU before they stop talking about me. I order the car as I half sprint out of the meeting and down the hallway.

As a deterrent, I head toward the gym entrance, which is off to the side of the school. Senior parking is a bitch to get to from there, and I hope none of them will take the time to come look for me.

I sit down on the nearest bench, scrolling through my Instagram while I wait. What the actual fuck is Simone's problem? How could she vote with JJ, especially knowing he's with someone else already? And given who that someone is—

Amayah slides beside me, holding a bunched-up candy wrapper. She hands me a square of dark chocolate and gives me a sad smile.

"I appreciate you being in my corner," I tell her. "Doesn't feel like anyone else is."

"Well, here's hoping we make a good team. I don't necessarily think this fight is worth it, but if you want to stick it to JJ, I'm here."

"How much do you think you know?" I ask. "About me and JJ."

She sighs. "Enough."

I nod. Who told her, and who else knows? Or does that even matter anymore? Ugh, my thoughts are starting to sound like Simone or, God forbid, JJ.

"I'm not embarrassed," I say. "I have nothing to be embarrassed about. I was coming to terms with it myself, and he reacted so negatively, I—"

"So have you...come to terms with it?"

"Yeah. I just wish it wasn't a big deal. I don't know how people will react. Especially if I run for prom queen. Like, what's the real level of progressiveness here?"

"Let's find out together. A queer Black prom queen? I want her. And by the way, screw JJ for dumping you over it. So much for his sterling masculinity," she replies.

I snort. JJ is more sensitive than any of them know. His reaction was less outright homophobic and more offended that I could be attracted to someone who wasn't like him. And to be attracted to a girl was the biggest possible insult to his masculinity.

Technically, after our last fight, I was the one to dump him. And in this moment, I don't regret it. Even if she didn't mean it that way, and I *know* she didn't mean it that way, hearing Amayah say "I want her" about me as prom queen...

Well fuck, I want that too. I want *her* too.

My Uber pulls up.

"There's my ride," I say.

"We'll figure this out," Amayah says. "I'm in your corner. We're going to run the best goddamn prom campaign this school has ever seen."

"Thanks, girl." I stand and wave to the driver.

Amayah clears her throat, and I turn back to face her.

"Earlier," she begins.

"Yeah?"

"Simone asked who'd be my number one."

I think my heart has stopped beating. I'm going to need

resuscitation on the sidewalk, and I'm almost certain Uber won't cover that.

"Yeah?" I ask.

"Let's see if she wins prom queen." Amayah smiles.

A rush of adrenaline makes me feel like I can fly. Either that, or Amayah has somehow brought me back to life right after taking my breath away.

"You'd better not be talking about Ashley Beckett," I say.

"You know I'm not."

The Uber driver honks, ruining the moment that will haunt my dreams tonight. Here's hoping my subconscious can replay it uninterrupted.

When I get into the car and look out the window, she's gone. Almost as if I imagined the whole conversation.

CHAPTER 3

MY MOTHER PULLS INTO THE DRIVEWAY AT THE SAME time as my Uber, and I watch her eyebrows raise to her exceptionally low hairline. She's going to have questions, since she knows I usually ride with Simone, and she and Simone's mom are also best friends. I've already ignored four calls and ten texts from Simone. At this point, I'm shocked she isn't waiting outside my house.

But if Simone were waiting outside, then she'd have to answer questions from both me and my mother, which I assume she's also trying to avoid.

Mom waits until the Uber pulls away before getting out of her car. She gestures to the street. "What happened between you and Simone? She's supposed to drive you."

Geez. I can't get a moment of peace today, and coming off

the high with Amayah, I'd really like to avoid the Simone of it all for a few hours.

"Nothing. What did her mom say?"

Mom shoots me that mom expression that tells you she knows you're lying. But if we're letting the moms in, then we should let them know everything, right? *My* mom wouldn't take kindly to the insinuations that I'm a bad figurehead for a movement because of my sexual orientation.

"She didn't say anything, but you just did. What happened?" Mom asks.

"I don't want to talk about it. It's fine," I reply.

I start walking to the front door, with Mom following close behind me. I can sense that she wants to push but is holding back, at least for now.

Mom's ringtone—a harsh church bell–sounding toll—goes off. She glances down at the screen. "Speak of the devil."

I groan. Moms have some kind of radar, a secret communication system that operates over vast distances without words. Either that, or Simone *did* tell her mom what happened, and they want to get my mom on their side. Good luck.

The phone continues to ring, which is almost worse. I can't tell if Mom is trying to play coy, pretending she won't answer only to call back later, or if she's making me sweat it out before telling her what happened. The latter isn't really her style, but who knows? Everyone seems to be breaking character today.

JJ, shockingly, hasn't tried to contact me. To be fair, I did block his number after we broke up, telling him that he could use our school emails for BSU business, but it's not like he couldn't figure out other ways to get to me. Plus, I did unblock him, though maybe Ashley has put a moratorium on him reaching out.

I still can't comprehend how the two of them got together. I'm not jealous. I'm confused. JJ gave me so much shit about how I was supposed to be as his partner, both romantically and in the movement, and now he's with someone who, as far as I know, stands for none of that. If she knew half the things he'd said about her…

Well, then they probably wouldn't be together. And it's none of my business, any of it, until it impacts BSU.

Mom's text alert goes off. She lets out a small shriek.

"You good?" I ask her.

"You want to run for *prom queen*?"

"Thanks for sounding so horrified."

Mom sighs. "I'm not. I mean, I am, but not because you're not perfect. Your dad told me that when a Black girl tried to run for prom queen back in his day, they wanted to *Carrie* her."

I don't need to ask who "they" were in this equation. They're the same people who made the list this year. The status quo is rarely ever challenged, and isn't that the problem? Ashley reinforces that problem by kowtowing to the status quo and rejecting those of us who try to push back against it. Except JJ apparently. No pushback for him. The thought makes me grind my teeth.

"Yeah, Mom, that's what protest is for, to make a point."

"And what is that point?" she asks.

Mom is the diversity, equity, and inclusion coordinator for the closest state university, and she had only been around a handful of white people before moving here with Dad. She wasn't thrilled to send me to a predominantly white school, but it was the public school their dream house zoned into, and it's ranked in the top ten in the state. She's become markedly less thrilled over the years as it has become apparent that the school hasn't really changed much since Dad was a student there.

"That there's been no racial diversity among prom queens, ever. Hell, there's barely even hair color diversity. And those kinds of standards lead to the non-white girls being treated as less than," I reply. *As we saw today*.

"And what does JJ think of this?" Mom asks.

"Who cares?"

She snorts. "JJ not being reasonable after the breakup?"

I shoot her a look. She knows what he's like. She went to an all-Black high school in the 1980s. Most of the guys were like JJ. She dated at least three wannabe Panthers and warned me what being the first lady would be like. I should have listened.

"It was Simone's idea, and I'm running with it, no matter what she thinks," I reply.

"Your dad is going to have a lot to say. And what do you mean, 'no matter what Simone thinks'?"

I'm sure Dad will. Dad and Banneker have a complicated history, despite him being one of its most prominent alumni. And I am certainly not ready to answer questions about Simone. Then I'd have to admit to my very politically active, walk-the-walk parents that I've stayed friends with someone I think could have homophobic tendencies, for what? Loyalty?

Her phone starts chiming again, but this time, Mom answers. It's clear from the smile on her face that it's Dad. She puts the phone on speaker.

"You want to run for prom queen at *Banneker*?" Dad's voice booms. "Have things improved that much?"

"What's the harm in letting her find out?" Mom asks, her tone teasing.

The harm is Dad's street cred, of course. He's a prominent civil rights analyst who was the only Black kid to graduate from Banneker until ten years ago. Banneker High "integrated" when it was legally mandated to, but that doesn't mean Black kids stayed through all four years. It took a major overhaul in the early 2000s, of the administration, the school board, and the local leadership, to make the school more hospitable. I think Mom and Dad only sent me there to prove a point: Their hard work made a difference. I can make a difference by simply being there.

No pressure.

If you ask him about any other institution, Dad's happy to give a rundown of all its past structural problems and how they were addressed. But Banneker High, however problematic, helped shape him. It's his big blind spot, even though he's the one who helped effect change.

We'll see how much change has occurred.

"It's an idea, to find out how far the student body has come, and if we can push the envelope," I reply.

Dad pauses. "There could be backlash. Actually, I'm certain there will be. You're Black, you're bi; it's going to be a whole situation."

"Absolutely counting on it," I reply. There's no need to mention the list, in all its sexist glory, that came out right before prom campaigns are due to start. The only question is how much of a wave that backlash is really going to make.

"Was this JJ's way of winning you back? Making you the face of Banneker beauty?" Dad asks.

I try my hardest not to laugh. Dad's always liked JJ and has a habit of giving him, and teenage boys in general, a lot more credit than they're due. JJ is one of the smartest people I know, but he'd never come up with flirting via high school rituals.

"He wants to run someone else actually," I say.

Mom's eyebrows shoot up, but she has the good sense to not ask follow-up questions with Dad on the phone. Dad is absolutely not the face of toxic masculinity, but I'm willing to bet he'd lose his cool if he knew the real story. He's always been overprotective, with a bit of a complex around respect, and this whole situation has been pretty disrespectful.

"So, what's your plan? How are you going to make this happen?" Dad asks.

"Obviously, we want to help. And are uniquely positioned to do so," Mom adds.

"Are you looking to harken back to previous campaigns? I can contact the Black alumni group and see if anyone is willing to go on the record about their runs," Dad says.

Here we go. They'll have everything figured out before I put down my backpack. They're both so good at what they do, and this is their arena. I'm already the second-in-command to JJ and whatever his mission is for BSU. They're well-intentioned, but something feels like it's burning up inside me.

"I'm working on it. I'll keep you updated," I say. "I've got it handled, and I have homework. We'll talk later, okay?"

Before either of them can get out another word, I start up the stairs. Why is there a pit in my stomach?

I know I have to chart my own path, which is something they don't fully understand yet. How can I go to college next year and be who I want to be if I'm cosplaying as my parents? They just want the best for me. Does that make me wrong?

I take my phone out of my pocket and glance at the screen. Amayah is texting me, which makes me smile.

She's already mocking up BSU's response and wants me to help her hang posters tomorrow morning before school.

I'm there, I reply.

I'm not particularly looking forward to running for prom queen. It's not really my thing, beyond making a point. But hanging out with Amayah one-on-one? That I'm definitely interested in.

CHAPTER 4

THE NEXT MORNING, AMAYAH STAPLES HER VERSION OF BSU's list, decorated with slogan stickers, on the bulletin board outside the principal's office. Most of the slogans are ironic, like #whiteally, but she also threw in #believeBlackwomen so admin would look terrible taking the list down. Plus, as publicity chair, she had to make JJ's straight-to-the-point black-and-white list a little more exciting.

We're brainstorming other places to hang posters, but Amayah keeps going back to one location. Sure, it would gain a lot of traction and eyeballs, but at what cost?

"It has always been my *dream* to storm into the boys' locker room," she says.

"For..."

"The drama of it. Plus, I assume it's a cesspool of potential blackmail. You know, in case we ever need that," she replies.

I snort. In addition to being our resident creative mind, Amayah is also BSU's designated shit stirrer. Whenever we need someone to drop a strategic piece of information discreetly, she's our go-to. Despite her being one of the most dynamic people I've ever met, she somehow fades into the background to a lot of people at Banneker, making her perfectly positioned to find out anything we could ever need to advance our mission. I don't really know how you develop that skill set, but I am interested in finding out.

She'll make a killer political campaign manager someday. Though, for now, I doubt either of us are making it into the boys' locker room without a fight.

"Are you talking, or are you stapling?" JJ asks, appearing behind us.

I nearly jump out of my skin. Where the hell did he materialize from? And is he wearing Axe body spray? This is not my JJ. *He's not your JJ anyway; he's Ashley's.*

"Jealous? We can do both." Amayah somehow knows exactly how to push JJ's buttons, and I'm loving it. She's seemingly unflappable. As someone who constantly feels flapped, I find her aspirational in a way that makes me question whether I want to be her or be *with* her. At the moment, the answer is firmly both.

JJ sucks on his teeth. It's one of his many frustration tics, as if he has any right to be upset.

"This was *your* idea, Ida," he says.

Technically, it was Simone's idea, but we're all pretending *that* didn't happen.

I slam the stapler into the nearest bulletin board, leaving one of Amayah's lists swinging in the breeze of the air-conditioning vent above it.

"And I'm doing it. Now, are *you* talking or stapling, Jeremiah?" I ask.

He hates his given name, especially since his parents have veered more toward the just-blend-in, don't-ruffle-too-many-feathers brand of Black activism. It's a low blow, but not lower than any he's struck recently. It's not clear who he's trying to prove himself to, but whatever standard he's trying to meet seems to be eternally out of his reach.

"That's"—he swallows—"fair. Do you have a moment?"

He's asking, but not really. His head is angled across the hall, where there's an empty classroom. There's an expectation that I'm going to agree. If I don't, can I take the balance of power in our relationship back from him? Or does even considering that mean I can't tip the scales either way?

I follow him.

He holds open the door, and I stay put in the hallway. I motion for him to enter first, which seems to cause him physical pain. He wants to be the chivalrous one. At least I can needle him a little.

"Is this BSU business?" I ask.

"Well, as the leaders of BSU, our business is BSU business."

"Or did you make it that way?" I sit down at the nearest desk.

He leans against that desk, and the edges of today's dashiki brush against my leg. His breath tickles my nose, and I try my hardest to remember that I'm mad at him. I also want to angrily kiss him against the nearest wall, just a little. Pheromones are stupid. As is my heart's eternal quest for validation.

"You're the one who dumped me," he says. "Or have you forgotten that in all the accusations?"

"What exactly have I accused you of? Besides making private parts of our relationship public to the whole BSU which is true."

"Ida, I never told anyone why we broke up. I swear to you. Why would I do that?"

No one else knew I was bi. He was the first person I told, because I thought I could trust him. I thought he'd still love me. It turns out he never did. After years of professional partnership, and months of romantic connection, I'm amazed at how little he cares.

"You told me I was an untrustworthy partner because I'm bisexual," I reply. "So what am I supposed to think?"

"I was surprised! I obviously didn't mean it."

"Well, that wasn't obvious to me."

Crap, why am I tearing up? I wipe a rogue drop from my cheek. He's the one who implied that if I liked girls, I'd end up needing to physically explore that side of my desires, betraying him and our relationship. Not that we had fully defined our relationship anyway.

JJ reaches out across the desk. He puts his hand over mine and squeezes it.

"I am truly sorry. I was jealous, of whoever else you might be into. My ego got in the way," he says.

"It does that often."

"I'm just trying to look out for you. You're a queer Black girl, in a world that refuses to protect every single one of those identities. If you're going into the line of fire, I want you fully briefed on what you're up against. There's only so much I can shield you in this," he says. He's softened his tone, like he does when he wants to sway me against my better judgment.

It almost always works. But today, something stops him from plucking at my heartstrings.

"Well, you're off base," I say.

Amayah bursts through the door. She focuses on me, her gaze darting to JJ.

"Posters are up; the first buses are pulling in. Time to scatter," she announces.

I take the out and scurry into the hallway. Neither of them follows me, and honestly, it's better that way. I have a lot to think about regarding BSU and the position I'm putting myself in by running for prom queen. Plus, if I'm about to try to be the face of BSU against Ashley Beckett, I can't be caught hanging illicit posters, can I?

Maybe if I act squeaky clean, JJ and Simone will fall in line. After all, I don't actually have anything to hide.

CHAPTER 5

AT LUNCH, I'M PUSHING MY BARBEQUE TOFU AROUND the plate when she approaches. I hear her beads clacking before I see her. I'm already pissed off. She *still* hasn't told me what changed her mind. Her texts last night were all platitudes or excuses, and I want none of them. Is it religion? Or because she wants to run for queen herself?

"JJ wanted me to check on you," Simone says, sitting next to me.

"So now when JJ says, 'Jump,' you say, 'How high?'"

"Ida, come on. I'm genuinely worried for you, and he made some good points for once. I'm on your side. But your side needs to be safe, and I have questions."

I roll my eyes. *She* has questions? As if she's the one who has been wronged here. Screw this. I take my plate and stand. I can find somewhere else to eat this barely appetizing meal in peace.

Amayah slides in across from us, and Simone scoffs.

"Warm welcome," Amayah says.

"We're having a conversation," Simone replies.

"Conversation implies that there's a back-and-forth, and... it seems like you're talking to yourself," Amayah says. "Ida, have you seen?"

Before I can answer, Simone leans forward, blocking Amayah from my sight line.

"I get that you enjoy being edgy or whatever, but those posters are sick. And now we're going to have to have another BSU meeting to listen to JJ illuminate how disgusting you are," Simone says.

The posters are a little intense, but nothing *that* out there. This reaction is way out of pocket.

Amayah stands, the left corner of her mouth curling up. Her lip gloss today is a deep burgundy, and I find myself staring a beat too long. She's an avowed pacifist, but Simone recoils as if Amayah is going to hit her.

"What about me is so disgusting to you and JJ?" Amayah asks. "I can guess, but you probably don't want me to." She cocks her head to the side.

My eyes widen, but I try to keep my cool.

Simone's jaw drops. "Are you implying that I'm"—she lowers her voice—"homophobic?"

"You said it, not me," Amayah replies.

Simone begs me to defend her with her eyes. I want to, but something stops me. Her desire for me to keep my sexuality hidden or private is like a scab I can't stop picking at with my mind.

"You saw the mock-ups in the Google doc last night; what's so different about the finished product?" I ask.

Simone looks at me as if I've completely lost my mind. In our thirteen years of friendship, I've never felt as out of step with her as I have in the last twenty-four hours. It's unsettling.

"The mock-ups didn't have *blood* on them," she replies. She turns to Amayah. "Sicko."

"What the hell are you talking about?" Amayah asks. "Neither do the posters we put up. Ask JJ. He saw us hanging them."

Simone lets out a noise, like she's going to be sick. "Um, then you need to go out into the hall."

Amayah and I exchange a glance. Is Simone losing it?

"I'm not kidding. You need to *go*," Simone repeats. She looks scared enough that I start to feel guilty

Amayah bolts out into the hallway, drawing stares from several other tables.

I follow her, and Simone is close behind us, still shaken up. Granted, she's been shaken up since we started this campaign.

The three of us end up standing outside the principal's office, where Amayah and I hung one of the largest posters. It was the riskiest location we chose, but luckily, no one was there when we arrived. Sure, we were definitely caught on the security camera, but technically it's not a school rule violation. After all, the wall *is* a giant bulletin board.

Amayah turns to Simone, incredulous. "So you tore down the poster and are making up shit?"

Not only are we not seeing blood or paint, our poster is gone.

"I'm not lying. If it wasn't you guys, then someone put blood all over your poster and then took it down," Simone replies.

It's a bit of a fantastical story, but Simone isn't a liar. If she says she saw blood, then I believe she thinks that's what it was, even if she's wrong. Clearly *something* has happened to the poster.

"How do you know it wasn't paint?" Amayah asks.

"I could tell," Simone replies.

And I can tell that Amayah is rapidly losing whatever patience she had left. The tension between them couldn't be cut with a machete, let alone a knife.

"Well, how much was there?" I ask.

Amayah scoffs. "Don't tell me you're entertaining this. I know she's your best friend—"

The principal's secretary, Deborah, walks out of the office, her red hair pulled back into a particularly severe bun today. She's in her late sixties and was a ballerina in a former life. She approaches us like she's walking on air, her peasant skirt billowing around her.

"What's going on out here?" Deborah asks, her eyes narrowed in suspicion.

All three of us stiffen. I've never had a bad experience with Deborah, but she's always activated my this-person-is-potentially-racist radar. There's something in the way she looks at us whenever we have to ask her for anything or try to schedule a meeting with the administration about BSU. The sudden terse smile and forced-relaxed posture Amayah displays shows me she's had the same feeling.

"Ms. Deborah, we hate to bother you, but there was a poster here earlier. Did you see who took it down?" I ask.

She shakes her head. "It's been a zoo." Her desk has a direct view of the entire hallway, but I keep my mouth shut.

Her *zoo* comment turns out to be more literal than I expect when the boys' wrestling team walks by in a pack, taking up an entire cross section of the hallway. It would be easy for a group to block Deborah's view.

"Did you see anyone throw paint on the poster?" Amayah asks.

Deborah's eyebrows knit together. "No, I haven't seen anyone defacing school property. Except for hanging unauthorized materials," she replies. "Students can get in trouble for that." She gives us a pointed expression.

Ugh. Radar beeping again.

Simone throws her head back, and I can see her biting back a groan. If Deborah gets us in trouble, Simone will be vindicated for her concerns, just not in the way she thought.

"And who gets in trouble for widespread sexism?" Amayah asks.

Deborah purses her lips. "We'll find out."

That's the best answer we'll get about whether the administration is going to address the list. It's been over twenty-four hours. The next scandal, or, hell, basketball game, will capture everyone's interest, and the list will become one of those things that happened one time and everyone moved on. It'll be a funny anecdote at our ten-year high school reunion, as if the standards these boys abide by aren't an albatross around all of our necks.

At the very least, I hope the girls whose boyfriends were

involved push back. There ought to be a number of breakups in the coming days, though I'm not actually that hopeful. Aren't we all a little guilty of giving boys too much lenience when they hurt us? If JJ had written any of those things about me, I'd—well, who knows what I'd do, honestly. I'm still sort of pining for him, or what I thought we could have had, and I would argue that maybe outing me is worse than insulting my facial features.

Deborah goes back into the office and dials her desk phone, watching us. Is she calling an administrator or her favorite civics teacher, who always gets the rest of the staff talking? I suppose we'll find out if and when there's a school-wide email about vandalism or sexist lists.

Amayah rolls her eyes and takes out her cell phone, while Simone still looks stricken.

She must be telling the truth, but it's odd. If someone put actual blood on the poster, which is the longest of long shots, it's gross but not endangering, unless she's suddenly concerned about hepatitis transmission.

A group of JV basketball players walk by, looking every inch the barely pubescent freshmen that they are. They whistle at us, and one has the gall to wink at Simone, who I swear might blush.

Amayah theatrically gags after them.

I take out my phone to glance at the time. Lunch is basically over, and I've barely eaten. And I didn't get to chill before physics. This has all been a colossal waste of my time.

Someone requests to AirDrop a photo to my phone. It looks like our poster; maybe someone overheard us talking? Or it's someone from BSU whose number I don't have. Regardless, my curiosity is piqued.

I accept the photo. In it, our poster is torn up on the ground. Where, I can't tell. It's stupid and childish, but whatever. That's not going to scare me.

The corner of the photo catches my eye, and I nearly drop the phone. It's there plain as day.

Someone has painted a bloodred noose over part of the poster.

CHAPTER 6

I COULD BE DOING CALCULUS HOMEWORK. STUDYING for my AP history exam. Getting an extra dose of the Gardasil vaccine. Listening to my parents give the sex ed talk again. Cliff diving into a bed of rocks.

Any of those things would be preferable to sitting in an extra BSU meeting while JJ rags on my decision to go to the administration about the AirDropped photo. At this point, it's a monologue, and the only person who really cares is JJ himself. Even Paul, who usually takes precise notes, has barely made a single click or clack of his computer keys.

Simone had an out, since girls' basketball called an emergency practice. She hasn't said anything to me since she saw the photo, except to beg me not to run. Again.

What makes this meeting even worse is that BSU has a new member. Sort of. She's "auditing," as she put it, to see if she actually wants to join. Sitting rapt, as close to JJ as possible, is Ashley Beckett in a maroon sweater dress.

The irony of her being here for his tirade about my actions after all the think pieces I've heard about her from JJ is not lost on me. If I were a pettier person, I'd grab her after the meeting and get into the weeds. But I'll take the high road. Depending on how long JJ continues his soliloquy.

Amayah is pissed enough, at me, or JJ, or maybe Simone, to be silent through the whole thing. I don't need her to stand up for me, but it is always welcome. I'm tired. All I did was suggest a run for prom queen, and twenty-four hours in, I'm fighting with JJ, Simone, and Amayah, and there's been a racial incident.

I think someone was just being an asshole. But the racial connotations necessitated an email to the entire student body and all the parents. Mom and Dad, who normally respect that school is supposed to be, at best, phone-lite, have each called me three separate times to make sure I'm okay.

Dad insisted on leaving work early to pick me up, and I think he's currently idling in the parking lot. Mom was in the principal's office within thirty minutes of the email going out to parents, and she's still there, along with a growing contingent of upset adults.

"Do you really not have anything to say for yourself?" JJ asks, finally taking a breath.

Ashley hands him a Gatorade, like he needs an electrolyte infusion to recover from his own diatribe. My desire to venture down the low road shoots into the stratosphere.

"Why should I? You've made up your mind. You've expressed

your very strong opinions for an absurd amount of time, per usual. We'll see how long those feelings last, given your recent proclivity for walking back your commitments," I reply.

I'm at least nice enough to not look at Ashley, even if everyone knows she's part of my reference.

"Don't try to turn this on me. You took a BSU issue and brought it to the administration, who you know has never supported us. Now we've lost control of the situation," he says.

"When our fellow students are drawing nooses on our materials, we've already lost control of the situation. At this point, especially given the lack of response to the list, *still,* adults should handle this."

"We're the adults in a couple of months," he says, as if that's the gotcha.

"But we're not the ones with power right now, and you know that. This is bigger than BSU," I tell him.

Ashley's head whips back and forth between the two of us like she's watching Wimbledon. I almost want her to say something, intervene on JJ's behalf just so I can bite her head off.

No, I chide myself. You're *not mad at her*. There's no need for me to misplace my anger. That would give JJ a pass he doesn't deserve.

"So we take the power back," JJ says.

"Are you purposefully thickheaded or truly clueless?" I ask.

Amayah snorts so loudly that everyone turns to her.

"That's out of line," JJ says.

"So is taking up everyone's time with a one-man show of how mad you are at your ex-girlfriend," I snap.

"We never put a label on our relationship!"

"Oh my *God*. That is so not the point!" I throw my hands into the air.

I need to leave, because JJ won't, and if I stay, I'm going to actually throttle him.

"Ash, you still into this dude?" Amayah asks.

"I'm here to listen and learn," Ashley says.

Fuckkkkkk. I've got to go. I can't. I absolutely cannot stay here. At what point is this a parody instead of my actual life?

You still here? I text Dad. **I can be out in two minutes.**

He responds with a thumbs-up.

"I'm out. See you at the next meeting, everyone, and if you're not JJ, feel free to reach out with any ideas about how we move forward after the poster incident," I say.

"Running away is the coward's way out," JJ says.

"Well, you'd know since that's how you ended our not-relationship," I reply.

Someone—probably Amayah, knowing her—whistles loudly.

JJ, for once, is stunned into silence. I've been iffy on religious beliefs, but in that, maybe there is a God.

CHAPTER 7

DINNER IS ETHIOPIAN TAKEOUT, AND A QUIET AFFAIR. Mom and Dad both keep staring at me, but neither of them actually says anything. I'm still annoyed from BSU and don't really want to talk anyway.

The email that went out to parents was about as sanitized as a hate crime alert can be.

> Banneker Community,
>
> We have unfortunately been made aware of a racial image targeted at our Black student community defacing a poster on school premises. We strongly condemn all hate, and there will be consequences. The matter is being thoroughly investigated, and updates will be given when prudent.

My favorite part of the message was the "unfortunately made aware" portion. It leaves a lot open for interpretation. Is it unfortunate that the hate occurred or unfortunate that the administration was made aware of it? I'd be willing to place a bet on the latter.

They still haven't addressed the list, as if BSU put up that poster for the hell of it. I certainly haven't told my parents, and it seems like no one else has told theirs either. The fact that the PTA, which was once fully activated over the definition of *gifted* as used by the school, isn't all over this indicates that, at least parent-wise, the adults don't know. But teachers do. Administrators do. There are plenty of people who could address the list but won't. At least not until someone makes them.

I rip off a piece of injera. Our protest has gotten attention, not necessarily for the reason we wanted, but we can make it work. The same issues are still there, and now there are eyes on us. How do we capitalize on this?

"So, you're done with this prom queen thing, right," Dad says. It's not a question; he's telling me, but at least cursorily pretending that I have some say in it.

"Not necessarily," I reply.

Dad's fork clatters against his plate. "You were threatened with a noose."

"Someone scribbled one on a poster; it wasn't a direct threat."

"It was AirDropped to *your* phone," he says.

Mom scoops up a forkful of vegetables and chews them as slowly as humanly possible. She never misses a chance to give her opinion…

Damn. She and Dad have already talked about this, and she doesn't agree with him. She's trying to avoid fighting in front of me, and I'm not having it. Dad doesn't get to unilaterally decide, and apparently, it's two against one.

"Mom, what do you think?" I ask.

Mom sighs for a solid five seconds.

"Nelle…" Dad says.

"I don't know that dropping out is the answer," she replies.

Technically, I haven't entered yet since nominations haven't opened, but I don't share that.

"It would be letting them win," I say.

"So let them win. Let someone else take the heat," Dad replies.

"That'd be immoral," I counter.

Dad groans, but I'm right. If it was dangerous to run for prom queen, how could I send someone else into the line of fire when I wasn't willing to do so myself?

"There's safety in numbers, right?" Mom asks.

"I guess," Dad replies.

"Hence the PTA has offered a ten-thousand-dollar scholarship to whoever wins prom queen to encourage a real competition," Mom says.

Mic drop. Ten thousand dollars? Holy shit.

It's brilliant. More people across social groups—and presumably races—will run. More than one person from BSU should *want* to enter now that there's an incentive.

"How did you finagle that?" Dad asks.

Mom shrugs. "White guilt?"

She's the only Black parent in the PTA and has never been voted PTA president despite three attempted campaigns. But she stays on their necks, and nobody has pushed through more initiatives than her. The actual PTA president, Grayson Davis's mom, is one of those crunchy Moms for Liberty types who rails against DEI and "wokeness." Framing the scholarship as a way to increase general competition is the only way Mom would have been able to move the needle.

"When is the announcement going out?" I ask.

"First thing in the morning, once we gauge general community sentiment after the admin's email," she replies. "Our president was unhappy that they made it about race."

The president was unhappy that someone made a noose directed at BSU about race? Cool. No issues there.

"Excellent," I say. "So I'm definitely running."

I'll be enthusiastic about it too. Saying *screw you* to a bunch of guys *and* the PTA? Plus, ten thousand dollars is nothing to sniff at. All I have to do is win a popularity contest? Good thing I have the best campaign manager. It's an uphill battle, but I'll take that incline.

Mom cocks her head to the side. Uh-oh. That look... What's she about to pull?

"When were you going to tell us about this list situation?" she asks.

God, she really does find out *everything*. I should have known, honestly. She's been dropping hints all afternoon, asking me about my self-esteem like we're in a weird mother-daughter therapy session.

"Is the PTA addressing that?" I ask.

"The PTA doesn't know. The principal let it slip in our meeting about the poster."

"I figured you wouldn't be interested in high school drama. It's not like the list involves me in any way," I reply.

"For now."

Such a mom answer. Like I get it, you think I'm the most perfect beautiful girl in the world. It doesn't mean the male athletes of Banneker would agree. In fact, I'd bet the full ten thousand dollars they wouldn't.

"Not worried about that," I say.

Dad clears his throat. "Well, this isn't the first time there's been a list."

Excuse me, sir? A few years back, there was literally a local news story on the sexism girls have faced at Banneker. He certainly didn't mention knowing about any hot/not list then. He didn't think to mention it when he was consulting with the school on how to improve the experience of Black students either.

I close my eyes for a few moments. "When you were a student..."

Dad nods and looks down at his plate. He was a champion power forward on the basketball team. So it stands to reason that if there was a list, he was aware of it for one very big reason. He helped write it. Or, at the very least, spread it around.

"What did you write?" I ask. "Who did you write about?"

"Nothing. No one. But I did help hand it out. I was young and more focused on fitting in with my peers than the consequences of participating."

"Did you try to intimidate anyone who spoke up?" I ask.

"No one spoke up," he says.

Not much has changed, and can't he see how that's a problem? Just because his activism was willing to overlook gender doesn't mean mine is.

"You're demonstrating her exact reasoning for the campaign," Mom says. "And now the PTA is giving students an incentive to enter. No one will be focused on Ida, or BSU for that matter. Capitalism wins."

She's right. The money will take over everything. Sure, people might get nasty in the pursuit of the winner's check, but there's no reason for the male athletes to lash out. And if they do, I can handle it. It's paper and ink. Who cares? Those aren't the people I'm trying to impress.

"You need to be careful," Dad says.

"You want me to carry pepper spray? The list is stupid, and it says a lot about where we are as a society, but those guys aren't going to bother me."

"That's not necessarily true," he replies.

"Why?" I ask.

"Because when we did the list, the then newly formed Black Student Union also accused us of racism."

They were right to do so. Is he about to dispute that? Unless he's going to label it misogynoir, I'm not about to agree with objectifying girls.

"Okay...and that has to do with me because..."

"Because in response they named a Black girl to the top of the list," he replies.

Oh. Shit. That would be interesting. Who would the athletes name at the top of their list? And what would that mean for us girls going forward? For the prom queen campaign?

I guess I'll have to wait and see how it plays out. Until then, I still have a prom campaign to wage. Nominations open tomorrow, and the competition is sure to be fierce with ten thousand reasons to run.

Let's see how this goes.

CHAPTER 8

THE NEXT MORNING, BANNEKER HALLS ARE BUZZING with the news of the PTA's scholarship. All of a sudden, the list, and even the poster, are out of everyone's minds. Nominations for prom court open today too, and a line forms that spans two corridors. The prom committee can barely keep up with the self-nominations.

Safety in numbers, Mom said, and it looks like she's right. Who's going to focus on me when there are twenty-five other girls running?

I spot Simone a few people ahead of me, shifting from side to side. Several girls from the list appear to be walking to their lockers, having already signed up or been nominated by others. Ever since we were in middle school, Simone's wanted to be prom queen. Not necessarily for the title, but because it represents the masses seeing her as beautiful and cool, which she is. She always has been. She's just overlooked.

There's a tap on my shoulder, and I turn to find Ashley behind me. Her gleaming fluorescent-white smile makes me nauseous. She looks airbrushed. In any just world she'd be prom queen, top of the list, and probably a budding supermodel. I can see why someone would be attracted to her, on the surface.

"So you're really doing this," she says. I don't think she means to sound condescending, but she does.

"You are too," I reply.

"So you know, it was my idea to run, not his," she says.

"Same here."

She tucks a strand of hair behind her ear and purses her lips together. Truly, she should start a TikTok of her beauty routine. It'd go viral for sure. I'd probably copy it, to be honest.

The line inches forward slower than a snail's pace. I can feel Ashley's presence behind me, not least of all because she's the only high school senior who wears Le Labo perfume.

"He respects you a lot," she says suddenly. "I know things are complicated between you two, but he does."

I turn to face her. "There are a lot of things you probably don't know that show how little he respects me," I reply. *And you.*

"I think you'll run a great campaign. Make BSU proud," she says.

"And you? Are you planning to run as part of BSU?" I ask.

"JJ asked me to, so yes."

My face burns. It's not new information, but it confirms JJ's stance. Anyone but me, truly, is worthy of the crown.

We're almost at the front of the line. Simone walks past us, her head ducked. Running against my best friend, my ex's girlfriend, and the most popular girls in school. Why am I doing this again?

We have BSU representation now. I could step out of this line and let someone else be the face of our prom bid. Behind-the-scenes work is what I do best anyway.

Amayah appears at my side. She hasn't spoken to me since yesterday, and she doesn't look like she's about to start. She snaps a picture, then appears to be taking a video.

"Banneker Black Student Union VP Ida Carter in line to start her bid for prom queen. Ida, can we get a statement?" she asks.

I blink for what I know is way too long while I try to get my thoughts together. Are we live? Is this going to be edited? Could she have warned me to come up with a freaking sound bite?

"Um, I'm excited and hopeful that we can make some change in who is considered prom queen material," I say.

Amayah lowers her phone. "We'll refine that."

"I'm running on behalf of BSU too; do you want my statement?" Ashley asks.

"No," Amayah replies.

I snort, despite myself. It's not Ashley's fault that JJ is using her as a pawn between us. She probably doesn't even realize that she's being used. Plus, she'd run anyway, I'm sure. BSU simply offers a convenient support system in addition to the tennis team.

"Why now?" I ask Ashley. "Why are you interested in BSU now?"

"Why am I interested in BSU, or why am I interested in JJ?"

"It's not about JJ," I say.

"Isn't it? You two broke up, he's moved on, and you're having a hard time. It makes sense." She's twisting the knife at this point.

Amayah is still at my right, watching. Thank God she stopped recording. All I need is a video going around that makes me look like a jealous ex. That wouldn't hurt my credibility *at all* after yesterday's meeting.

"You have been very vocal about being a citizen of the world and not identifying with our mission," I say. "Like for years."

"I was born in Belize, and I'm an army brat. I am quite literally a citizen of the world," she explains. "I never had a problem with BSU's mission; I had a problem with the way it was run." And there goes that knife again.

With only two people ahead of me at the sign-up, I bite my tongue.

She'll learn JJ isn't the be-all and end-all of being a Black kid at Banneker. And how someone treats the girl before her is probably how he'll treat her. Here's hoping Ashley never deviates from her perfect feminine image, for her own sake.

Amayah starts taping again as I write my name on a nomination form. She motions for me to hold up the form, and she snaps another picture.

"Good luck," Ashley says. "It's an uphill battle."

It's not clear if she means for me specifically, or as a Black girl in general.

"You too. You're going to need it," I reply.

It's not clear if I mean in her prom queen bid or with JJ. Honestly, I might mean both. Though she'd be a perfect prom queen. She's a perfect everything.

Amayah starts down the hall, and I jog to keep up with her.

"Are we going to talk about any of this?" I ask.

"About any of what?"

"Come on," I say. "The bench, the meeting yesterday, these videos you're taking? We have a lot to cover."

"I'm running your prom campaign. We'll have a lot of discussion." Her tone is clipped so I understand she doesn't want to keep talking.

So I'm left in the hall alone in some sort of existential, if not actual, sense. There are plenty of people around, but the people I hang out with, the people I thought were or would always be on my side are keeping their distance. And to be honest, I'm not even sure what I've done, besides somehow not live up to my friends' expectations.

I have to focus. The PTA scholarship would be immensely helpful for next year. Plus, it gives everyone an agenda for running, beyond the usual attractiveness contest. Though it'll still be a tough battle since this is basically a popularity contest. Being Black popular isn't going to win me this. I somehow have to coalesce several other groups that may already have their own candidates and a notable financial investment.

I give her a wave and head toward my first class. Once again, the thought creeps in that I'm not the right person to win prom queen. Someone like Simone could get the athlete votes along with BSU votes. Ashley could get athletes, BSU, and several of the generally popular white kids she hangs out with. I'm working with BSU and Spanish club, which, not to knock them, don't give me a sizable voting bloc. Plus, at this point, I don't have the BSU vote. JJ runs the group, and JJ will throw his support behind Ashley. It'll be me and Amayah against the world, which is not a terrible thought, but also not going to secure me the position.

My phone buzzes with a text.

Apparently Amayah and I are in sync after all. She wants a full inventory of all the clubs I've ever been a part of at Banneker.

Welcome to the campaign, I guess.

CHAPTER 9

BY THE END OF THE DAY, THIRTY GIRLS ARE RUNNING for prom queen, which is almost a quarter of the entire senior class. Given it's unlikely everyone will rally around one specific candidate, the administration has announced that there will be a preliminary round of voting first thing next week to establish a short list.

Cue the freakouts.

A good prom campaign, at least in the past, has taken a solid three weeks. *At least*. It's basically a pageant. The girls running have theme days, sell baked goods, make physical and digital posters. It's a whole side hustle that is now being whittled down into two school days.

If early voting doesn't create a clear consensus with favored candidates, the administration plans to impose new requirements, like a prerequisite GPA or certain behavioral standards.

Behavioral standards that were apparently set by the PTA. Or, at least, its president. Glancing over the list of prom queen candidates that's been posted on the school intranet site, I don't think an academic requirement would take the list below twenty. We're an impressive group of girls. The behavioral standards were weird. Basically, if you've done something against the school honor code, you can't run? But the school honor code basically prohibits plagiarism and hooking up in the teachers' lounge so...I don't know who that's hurting.

Amayah has already taken stock of my GPA (should be good enough to stay in the race, no matter what) and is basically ignoring the morality thing on principle. God, she's cool.

Lauren Buckley is already handing out cupcakes, sourced from a local bakery, at lunchtime. Cassidy Burke baked cookies decorated like soccer balls and has been leaving little gift bags of them along with Starbucks gift cards around the school.

Morality clause?? Simone texts. It's her first time reaching out since the poster incident. Not that she has anything to worry about there. Simone has barely dated, and she certainly hasn't done anything inappropriate in the school building. She hasn't had the chance. If she wasn't Black, the PTA president would probably have her on a pedestal.

I glance around the hallway to make sure she's not within view before putting my phone in my pocket and ignoring her text. I *have* violated the morality clause, more than once. It's just been a minute.

Ashley breezes by me, her weave flowing from the propulsion generated by her kitten heels. She holds a small stack of papers, which she begins handing out to any senior who passes. Everyone who gets one titters.

I make a point to walk toward her and see what all the fuss is about.

She holds the papers close to her chest when she notices me. Then, after taking a deep breath, she forces a smile and hands me one.

Ashley Beckett: Leader On and Off the Court. Make History with Her As Your Prom Queen.

"What kind of history?" I ask, as if I don't already know.

Her smile doesn't falter. "That's open to interpretation."

I'm about to come out with some snarky retort when I see JJ handing out the same fliers.

Rage boils inside me. Even if she's his girlfriend, which, rich, given how reluctant he was to define *our* relationship, I'm his VP. This is supposed to be BSU business, and she joined BSU five minutes ago. It's bad form, and it makes it look like BSU is fractured. Which, it is, but isn't he supposed to care about optics? Especially if the optics of my bisexuality were too much for his faux-feminist neoliberal sensibilities to bear.

I've done a really good job of not confronting him, at least not until that last BSU meeting. But this? This might be the last straw for me.

I power walk toward him, and I don't know if the figurative smoke is coming off my heels or out of my flared nostrils. The last time I was this livid, I was being called out as disloyal via text by my not-boyfriend.

JJ spots me, his eyes widening.

As I get within three feet of him, someone's arm loops through mine, spinning me in the opposite direction.

Before I can speak, Amayah says, "Not worth it; don't cause a scene."

"But—"

"Take it out in the campaign; we have fliers too." She hands me a thick stack of papers with my face on them. I don't know where she found this photo. Has she been stalking my Instagram?

A sunset photo of me looking breezily unbothered is framed with my accomplishments in beautiful calligraphy. *Honor Society, Black Student Union Vice President, Spanish Club Member, Incoming Howard Freshman*. Underneath she has written, *Beauty is in the eye of the beholder; history is in the hands of all of us.*

"It's stunning," I say.

She shrugs. "It's what I could come up with on short notice."

"Thank you. Truly. For all of it. If I win…I know it's a long shot, but I want to split the scholarship with you, fifty-fifty."

"That's not—"

I hold up my hand to stop her. However far I get will be to her credit. It's the least I can do. Mom and Dad would totally agree.

"We're in this together, remember? A team. Partners," I say. "Plus, you can then say you've run a campaign that raised ten thousand dollars, while still in high school."

"Be careful," she says sarcastically. "Would being partners violate the morality clause?"

"Only if we get caught." I wink at her.

"Good thing I know places," she says.

I flush, my cheeks burning. What I wouldn't give to know those places too. JJ kissed me on school grounds only once. Which makes me wonder... Who has Amayah been exploring secret places with? And can we trade places?

Amayah and I stare at each other for what feels like minutes. Someone slamming their locker shut jolts me back to attention, I catch JJ watching us.

Even from this distance, I can see his mouth twitch, and I feel petty satisfaction. He's jealous. I'm glad he knows how that feels.

Amayah notices where my gaze has gone, and her face falls.

"I'm working on it," I say. I know it's not the reassurance she wants, but it's all I can give right now.

"What?" she asks.

"Getting over him. I just want you to know. For reasons."

Simone comes barreling down the hall from JJ's direction. For a star basketball player, she's never been particularly light-footed. She glares at him and Ashley as she passes.

Having her on Find My Friends was a total mistake. I really need to remove her now that we're in a fight.

She stops in between me and Amayah. "It's fucked up that he's flaunting her in front of you."

Of course it is, but I don't need her to point that out. He wouldn't have anything to flaunt if it wasn't for the prom situation.

"Well, maybe if you hadn't backed down on your own prom idea, I wouldn't have to see it," I reply.

"Ida, it's more complicated than that," she says.

"Why?"

I can tell she doesn't want to answer me, which makes me even angrier. She's supposed to be my best friend, and she's been keeping something from me for days. *And* she wants to pretend that nothing happened between us. That's not what friends do. I'd never keep something serious from her.

"Can you just trust me?" she asks.

"No."

"Come on," she says.

"No. Tell me, or I need a break from this friendship."

Ultimatums have never been my thing, but this one slips out. I'm frustrated, and I can't keep sitting in this limbo with her. I need her to be honest. I can't keep this up.

"You don't mean that," she says.

"I actually do. Amayah and I have prom business, so we're going to go." I throw Amayah a look, hoping she'll play along.

Simone sucks in her cheeks. "Fine. Remember that you asked for this." She pulls her phone from her pocket and hands it to me with her texts open. She clicks JJ's name and scrolls up a few messages.

He's sent her a series of screenshots of texts between the two of us from when we were together.

Texts that are decidedly not safe for work, school, or public consumption. Why the fuck would he send these to her? And how dare she not tell me that he betrayed my confidence like that?

This is a horrific invasion of my privacy, and I am completely sick to my stomach.

Before I can respond, Simone says, "Keep reading."

What the fuck? How dare you share these? What is wrong with you? she said.

They're online, he replied.

What do you mean?

They're online, he repeated.

My vision goes blurry. Online where? And how? The only way they'd be online is if he shared them with someone. Someone who wasn't Simone. Someone who then posted them.

Amayah, who has been reading over my shoulder, starts typing on her own phone. I don't know who she texts, but her eyes go wide, just like Simone's did in the meeting.

"Um…someone made an online group where they're posting explicit messages and photos that girls at Banneker have sent them. Originally, it seemed to be focused on girls on the list… but it's expanded," Amayah says.

"Expanded how?"

"To any girl in the school," she says. "It looks like every male student has been invited."

Oh my God.

A group of boys whizzes by, dropping several fliers at our feet.

I bend down to pick one up, but it falls from my hands.

Number two on the list has been named. Lauren Buckley, swim captain and editor of the literary magazine.

This time, there's no list of her pros and cons. Instead, the flier has a selfie of her in the girls' locker room with her swimsuit partially pulled down, revealing her cleavage. Anything too scandalous is covered by giant number twos.

The loudspeaker crackles, and Deborah's voice echoes through the hall. "Lauren Buckley, if you are still in the building, please make your way to the principal's office. Lauren Buckley."

Of course Lauren is called to the office, and not whoever is disseminating the fliers.

Now I guess we'll find out if the administration and PTA really intend to enforce that morality clause.

CHAPTER 10

BY THE NEXT DAY, LAUREN BUCKLEY'S NAME HAS QUI-etly disappeared from the school's list of prospective prom queens, and in its place is a reminder about the behavioral expectations for the scholarship. It's fucked up. The photo was released without her consent, and she's the one being blamed.

According to the administration, it's Lauren's fault for taking the photo in the first place, and not the boys who are distributing it. The prom king rolls remain untouched, of course. Bullshit.

Lauren isn't in school today either, but she's the only person anyone is talking about. Number two on the list, shamed. It's pretty brutal. The other girls on the list are reveling in her ouster, now that it means the path to prom queen is clearer for them. Taking particular joy is Cassidy Burke, who has been sending everyone in her phone contacts a picture of herself with threes over her soccer jersey and the slogan: **Captain=Example. Follow mine and vote Cassidy.**

Being number one looks like even more of a curse now, if this is how they release the runner-up. At this point, who would want to be perceived as the hottest?

Simone had the good sense to give me space after yesterday; however, she must have alerted JJ that she showed me their texts. He has never had good sense, and I have thirteen texts from him that I haven't responded to.

I want to believe that he couldn't have shared our texts, that someone hacked his phone. That maybe Ashley saw them and submitted them out of spite. But he's a high school guy. I know that he either submitted them himself or sent them to another guy at some point who did. He's not *that* evolved, despite what he proclaims.

I'm not ashamed of sending a few scandalous texts to my then-not-boyfriend. Sure, those texts being seen by people other than said not-boyfriend is more than a little embarrassing, but the real issue is that I didn't give permission for them to be shared. And now they could be used against me. And JJ knew that. He knew that before the PTA even started talking about morality...

How long has this group been active? And how many girls' texts are on there?

Simone hovers next to my locker, anxiously spinning one of her braids with her finger.

I roll my eyes. "I thought you got the memo that I am uninterested in talking."

Simone hands me a piece of paper. Her photo from the athletic website is printed out and slashed through with black Sharpie. Someone drew Xs over her eyes in red, and the message *DROP OUT* drips down in what appears to be fresh paint.

"Someone is just trying to scare you," I say.

"And it's working."

"Don't give them the satisfaction. That's what you would tell me, right?"

"I don't know anymore," she replies.

I take the paper from her and rip it down the middle. In doing so, my fingers brush against the paint.

Except…

I'm no artist, but I've never felt paint this consistency. There's a stickiness, a warmth…

Oh my God. I retch onto the floor and drop the paper. The way it's drying. Are those clots?

"It's blood," I gasp. Another retch overtakes me.

Several students gather around the two of us. I feel a hand on my back as I start to get tunnel vision.

I need to get to a bathroom. A water fountain. Anywhere I can get this off me. I stumble forward into someone.

Something cold and wet hits me in the face, and I flinch, my eyes closed as it drips down my cheek.

Ashley Beckett stands in front of me holding her Stanley cup, which, now that I'm coming back into my body, I realize must be full of lemon water. She squints down at me, close enough that I can see mascara flecks on her lashes.

When I fully open my eyes, they sting. Literal lemon water, not lemon-flavored. Thanks, girl. Were those even mascara flecks, or am I losing my vision?

"What the hell?" I ask.

"You're welcome?" Ashley says. "You were having a panic attack."

"And you thought your water bottle was the cure because…"

"Saw it on TV. Seems like it works." She grins.

I blink a few more times and groan. JJ comes up behind Ashley, his arm outstretched. I wince, thinking he's going to reach out to me.

No, it's almost worse. He slings his arm over Ashley's shoulders. He presses a kiss into her cheek. As if he wasn't all up in my messages yesterday.

I open my mouth to say something, but instead smack my lips closed. I don't need to stoop to his level. She'll find out what he's like soon enough. Hopefully it's before she sends him anything flirty.

"Can we test it?" Simone asks.

"Microscopes in the science lab," Ashley suggests.

"That's a bit dramatic," JJ says.

Simone, Ashley, and I all glare at him. Wasn't this his big concern in the first place? Now it's coming true. Plus, he should realize that if this is happening with Simone, his much more popular new girlfriend is probably next. It's not like Simone even has time to date, so the morality clause can't knock her out. Someone's resorting to intimidation.

Teachers and administrators have started to mill about the hallway. They glance at the paper, at the red on my hands, but no one says anything. It's almost dystopian, like this is normal. They're not even reacting.

The assistant principal starts ushering students down the hall. For a second, I think he's about to ask Simone and me to come with him and tell him what's happened. Except he walks away with the crowd, saying something that gets muddled on his walkie talkie.

So they're enforcing the rules selectively, per usual. Fan-fucking-tastic. Who's going to stand up for *us*?

Amayah appears with her phone out. She's narrating the sequence of events and even captures the AP retreating.

As always, her timing is impeccable. Knowing her, this is going to be on social media within the hour. Then, the administration will be forced to act.

Amayah turns the camera back to me. "Ida, do you have a message you want to send in the wake of these recent developments?"

This time I'm ready for her. "The adults who are supposed to protect and guide us are allowing sexism, harassment, and racism to go completely unchecked. As girls, it is not our fault that *some people* want to reduce us to our looks. And it's not our fault if we take or send pictures or private messages that are shared without our permission. Treating us like we are to blame demonstrates the ingrained sexism at this school. Lauren Buckley should be allowed to run for prom queen. Anyone who wants should be able to run without intimidation. That's the Ida Carter platform."

Amayah stops the video and smiles at me. "There's my girl."

I bite my bottom lip. The words *my girl* have never sounded so good, and after today, I don't think I ever want to hear anyone else say them.

Amayah's smile transforms into a smirk, like she knows exactly what she's doing to me.

"Oh, don't look so satisfied," I say.

"Don't be jealous. I'd be happy to make sure you feel the same way," she replies.

A zap of heat radiates from my chest to my toes. Forget making out with JJ; I *really* want to be satisfied by Amayah in any way she's willing. But right now we have to focus. If I've learned anything in the last few months, it's that I need to be careful starting romances in my extracurriculars.

"I've got calc," I say.

"Sorry, that sounds awful. Is that some kind of condition?" she asks playfully.

"Yeah, it means I should stop flirting with my campaign manager and go to class."

"Buzzkill."

I agree. I hate calc, and I'd much rather stay in the hallway with Amayah. I also know if I don't start walking now, I'll never make it to class, and I will torpedo this campaign in an empty broom closet.

"We'll hang out later? For the campaign," I say.

"Yeah. For the campaign," she replies.

"I'll text you." I hold up my phone, as if she needed the visual.

She snorts.

I open my texts, trying to figure out what to say as she heads down the opposite hall.

Another AirDrop request comes through. After last time, I know I should decline it. But curiosity gets the best of me.

This time I actually drop my phone. The screen cracks on the floor, obscuring the photo.

I'm shaking as I pick the phone off the floor.

It's a screenshot of a Notes app message that simply says: **It was blood.**

A text from JJ comes through, and I wish the phone had shattered. I plan to ignore it, per usual. Another text from him flashes across the screen. Then another. And another. Jesus. It must be something for BSU. He certainly didn't double, let alone triple or quadruple text when we were dating.

IDA.

YOU NEED TO SEE THIS.

SAFETY=COMPROMISED.

DON'T IGNORE.

JJ has screenshotted a photo from a social media group. He's blurred the group name, which makes me side-eye him even more. For someone who claims to be an outsider in the good ol' boys club, he sure has found a way to fit in online. I'm guessing this is the not-so-secret all-boys group where Lauren's pictures recently circulated. I open the picture and gasp.

It's another photo of Lauren in the locker room, except this time, she's holding her hands out like she's trying to stop an attacker. And her hands are covered in blood.

They're saying it was taken today, JJ's final text reads.

She's not in school, I respond.

I'm just reporting what I've heard.

Fuck. I've got to get to the locker room. But I also need to get to class. I've literally never skipped. And this is not the time to get caught ditching class.

Ugh.

I don't want to do this but...I text Simone.

Hey. I know you have a free period right now, and I need you to go to the girls' locker room and see if a. Lauren is there, and b. if you notice anything weird. I send her the photo JJ sent me.

Her reply comes in right away.

What the f?? Who sent you this?

Simone, PLEASE. If this is really dangerous, we need to know.

Fine.

This is about to be the longest class period of my entire life.

CHAPTER 11

I SPEND THE FIRST FEW MINUTES OF MY LUNCH PERIOD pacing back and forth in front of my usual cafeteria table. Simone hasn't come in yet; usually she's one of the first people to arrive, hunting down the turkey wraps and protein bars. Part of me worries she's going to avoid me. That maybe she didn't go to the locker room in the first place. The last few days have been the weirdest time in our friendship, so there's nothing I would put past her.

Amayah is spending the lunch period in the computer lab, working on campaign materials. She's taking this so seriously that it makes me wonder if she's trying to use it to get a summer job on a local campaign.

JJ walks in, with Ashley beside him. She's wearing a pencil skirt that matches his dashiki.

Stabbing my own eyes out would be preferable to witnessing this. JJ wouldn't even hold my hand in public, lest we display too much PDA. We skipped every homecoming dance, pep rally, anything he considered too ritualistic.

And yet…

I know she's nationally ranked in tennis. Is he going to be courtside at her next tournament? Or is the United States Tennis Association too much of an institution? Tennis is a predominantly white sport. Maybe going to a match would be subversive, standing up to the majority.

"She'll be over him by the end of next week, don't worry," Simone says, sliding in beside me.

She's not holding a lunch. This is another new development in our friendship. As the most active person I know, she's eternally hungry. I've never seen her skip a meal.

"I wasn't worried. At least not about that."

"There's nothing there," she says. "No Lauren, no blood."

I throw my head back. It's all a fucking trick. Probably AI-generated or something, and like an idiot, I fell for it. Lauren Buckley is fine. She might even be in on it all. It doesn't explain why I'm being targeted. My prom candidacy was never a forgone conclusion. There are other people they could mess with, if this was truly about prom or even the list.

"And your flier?" I ask.

"Paint. The art teacher confirmed," she replies. "Sorry."

"No need to apologize for not actually being threatened," I say.

"The threats are what made me mess with our friendship, so…yeah. I need to apologize."

Well, that's fair. She does need to apologize, but this was never about the fake blood threats. This was about JJ and the threat of my messages or my sexuality making their way into the halls for public consumption.

"Those messages were personal, but not the worst thing that could have come out. Not like Lauren's pictures being leaked. So why were you so shook about them?" I ask.

Simone shifts in her seat and looks away.

"I assumed that JJ was giving me a precursor, and other, worse messages were out there," she replies.

What would be worse to her? More explicit? Pictures? I'm honestly too afraid to ask.

"And what do you know about the guys' group the messages were posted in?" I ask.

"Just that it seems like every guy is in it, and the pictures are mostly of girls on the list."

That's nothing new.

"So why are my messages posted?" I ask. "I'm not on the list."

"How am I supposed to know? It's not like I'm involved in things like that."

"Since you and JJ are so chummy now," I reply.

She puts her head in her hands and scratches her forehead. *She's* exasperated? None of this was my idea. And "*things like that*"? Is she shaming me for those photos too?

"He won't tell me," she says. "All he'll say is that he's worried it can get worse for you."

I rack my brain. I can't remember every potentially charged conversation we had. I know that whatever pictures I sent were relatively innocent. I figured that messages were fine; who'd care about my bad metaphors, especially if I could counter with JJ's poetry? But pictures were pretty unimpeachable, and too easy to find. Better to keep it in person.

I just don't understand how JJ could be connected to the list makers. Sure, they're all guys, but JJ hasn't really associated with athletes since freshman year, when he was a backup quarterback on the football team. He left the team after he kneeled during the national anthem and no one joined him. He didn't get in trouble, but he also didn't get solidarity—even from the few other Black kids on the team. So he quit, despite the promise he'd end up in the starting lineup by junior year.

The coaches have tried to woo him back ever since, but the players have held a grudge. I get it. Being abandoned by JJ sucks.

I guess that grudge doesn't extend to their fucked-up little gossip channel. For someone who emphasized consent in all our interactions, he sure did throw that out the window to brag to his not-even friends.

If JJ was a true ally, he'd be our inside man on the forum, instead of trying to score points using the girl he tossed aside.

"Well, if things get worse for me, I'll make sure they get even worse for him. You can let him know, if you're going to be his mouthpiece," I say.

"You're both putting me in a really shitty position," she replies.

"You're the one who put me in the line of fire suggesting this prom thing, then turning your back on me. What kind of friendship is that?" I ask.

Her mouth purses as though I've slapped her in the face. We've never had a fight like this before. To be fair, she's never chosen someone else's side over mine, and I've never thrown jabs at her.

One of the other basketball players walks by our table. She motions for Simone to join the rest of the team. For the first time in our entire high school careers, Simone does.

CHAPTER 12

AMAYAH SITS CROSS-LEGGED ON MY BEDROOM FLOOR after school. I'm vibrating that she's here, alone with me, in my *bedroom,* even though Mom insisted we keep the door open. She walked by once, and otherwise, I can hear her on a call downstairs. A lot can happen before that call ends.

Amayah taps on her computer keys. Looks like her head is somehow still in the game. Meanwhile mine is swimming in the smell of her hand lotion and the image of her hands all over me. "Polling indicates that you're down 27 percent with the girls' basketball team."

"Okay, AP statistics," I say. That makes sense, given what happened earlier in the cafeteria.

"When are you going to make up with her?" she asks.

I shrug. "Who knows if I will?"

Not me, that's for sure. I miss her, of course; Simone's my

best friend. But she kept something huge from me, only telling me when I gave an ultimatum. She threw me into this position by nominating me with BSU, then pulling back when JJ said *jump*. She voted for Ashley in the meeting, instead of abstaining like she should have.

Amayah sighs. "Of course you will," she replies. "You're kind."

"What would you do?" I ask.

She sucks her teeth as she plugs something else into her statistics program. "I'm less forgiving."

She once told Simone and me about cutting off some old friends for saying homophobic things behind her back. She always manages to stand on business, making it look easy.

"Maybe I should be more like you."

"Nah. I don't want to date myself," Amayah replies.

There go those butterflies again. They've been fluttering around since she got here, but now they're in full force.

"But you want to date me?" I ask.

She cocks her head to the side, but she's smiling. "Let's see how the campaign goes. I'm only into winners."

"Well, then I guess I'd better get that crown."

She groans, and the butterflies freeze. Was she not flirting? How badly did I mess up?

"How is there no polling available for girls' swim? Are they boycotting?" she asks.

It'd be an impressive show of solidarity for the sport at Banneker known for having the most infighting. Their lineups are the most malleable, based on who's performing which stroke best, and there are rumors that the locker room fights have sometimes gotten physical.

Maybe that means Lauren…

"Could that photo have been real but from another time? Maybe the guys were referencing one of the swim team fights. Sorry, *alleged* fights," I say.

"Possibly. Not our issue though," Amayah replies.

She turns her computer around to show me that I'm up with the girls' tennis team. Take that, Ashley.

A throat clears, and I look up to see Mom in the doorway. She's smiling and holding a plate of cookies. Not that she's baked, because I've seen her burn butter and mismeasure a cup of sugar. She has arranged Entenmann's cookies in the shape of a sun on one of our cheese platters.

"Oh, Mom, you really did not have to do"—I gesture to the platter—"this."

She scoffs. "Excuse you, I'm always whipping up fun little snacks for you and your…*friends*."

Putting Totino's Pizza Rolls in the oven when JJ came over to do algebra freshman year simply does not count, but I won't point that out.

"You know Amayah," I reply.

"I know Amayah in the context of you, Amayah, and Simone. Not just you two." She looks between us.

Great. I have that much of a hopeless-infatuation vibe that my mom has picked up on it? I'm never going to hear the end of this.

"Well, now you really know Amayah," I say.

"Thank you for the snacks, Mrs. Carter. Sorry, Dr. Carter? You have a PhD, right?" Amayah says.

"Call me Nelle," Mom says, a statement she has literally never made to any of my friends before.

Amayah swallows loudly. Every bit of her home training must be telling her not to give in to Mom. No Black kid has ever been able to call a friend's Black parent by their first name. Ever. And I don't need statistical software to tell me that.

"My mother would kill me," Amayah replies.

Mom winks at her theatrically. "You passed the test."

"Mom!" I exclaim as Amayah breathes, "Thank goodness."

Is there a level beyond humiliated? Because I'm going to be there if Mom stays in the doorway another minute.

"Do you ladies know Lauren Buckley?" Mom asks.

Oh my God, I *do not* want to talk about the perils of sexting with my mother. She already suspects that JJ and I have rounded more bases than I even want to acknowledge exist. I can't get into what may or may not have been shared.

"Yeah, we do," Amayah replies. "Not well."

"Apparently she's threatening to sue the school and the PTA for discrimination," Mom says.

"Are you supposed to be telling us this?" I ask.

Mom scoffs. "We're not in the FBI, and word will get around the school tomorrow when she's back in the prom queen race. I just wanted to give you a heads-up. She's pretty popular, right?"

Damn. I suppose that's one way to stick it to the man. Should

I abandon my run and see if Mom and Dad want to sue the school for racism? Would it work?

"I'm glad she's able to run. She's incredibly popular. The whole morality thing was stupid anyway. We can let democracy run its course," I say.

"Agreed," Mom replies.

"So are you all nixing the morality clause?" Amayah asks.

"No. But we're trying to make sure all of our members understand that leaking photos, no matter the nature, without someone's consent, is not a moral failure on the part of the victim," Mom replies.

She's giving me a pointed look. She can't know about the boys' group; if she did, I'd be receiving a talking-to and a trip to the OB, depending on which messages had been posted. And she'd be covering for Dad, who would be on his way to casually threaten JJ with a speech she was the one to write.

"Is that everything?" I ask.

"No," she replies. "In an effort to *really* encourage many people to run, the PTA is discussing adding another smaller merit scholarship for those who may have been underrepresented on prom court. They don't have to win, just run."

"Ah, a loophole," Amayah says. "For when the same kind of girl who always wins wins again."

Mom nods. "But we can't say it's for any specific underrepresented group. Anyone who can demonstrate exclusion is under consideration."

Amayah snorts. "So because the last four queens were blond, a brunette could claim underrepresentation."

"Bingo," Mom replies.

Affirmative action for brunettes on prom court. Perfection. Why am I even trying at this point? There's no chance I'll get either scholarship. All I'm doing is wasting my time.

But if I'm going to waste time, there are worse ways to spend it than with Amayah.

"Thank you," Amayah says. "That is very helpful for the campaign." She's already typing.

Mom grins. "I'm excited to see what you two come up with. You'd have my vote." She does a little shoulder shimmy, and I try not to let my face go visibly red. Melanin makes it hard, but not impossible, and Mom is really giving it her best effort.

Thankfully, she leaves the cookies and heads back downstairs.

Amayah flips her computer around again. She's taken her original poster and added: *Historic Diversity Pick: Brunette!*

Oh, now this is getting fun.

"Let's hang them tomorrow," I say, unable to hold back my smile.

CHAPTER 13

AS I'M HANGING OUR NEW CAMPAIGN POSTERS THE next morning, I feel someone's breath on my neck. At first, I assume it's one of the athletes, looking to throw in a little extra intimidation for fun. Then the breath tickles my nose, and it smells like oranges and iced coffee.

Internally, I invent three new swear words, swallow all my annoyance, and try to give myself a pep talk. Externally, I turn around slowly, so I seem chill.

Ashley is close enough to kiss me or kill me, and with her plastered-on fake smile I can't tell which is more likely. Her earrings dangle so low that they almost touch my shoulders, and her eyes, despite being heavily coated with green eyeliner, somehow look wide and wild.

She's holding her own laminated stack of fliers, as well as a small container of locker magnets with her face on them.

"Thanks, but I think I'll pass," I say, gesturing to her magnets.

Ashley runs her tongue over her teeth. Her mom is a cosmetic dentist, and Ashley's mouth is impeccable advertising.

"What exactly do you think you're doing?" she asks.

I blink at her. She was literally at the meeting where we talked about my prom bid. Same one where her boyfriend took a giant shit on my life choices in front of an audience. If this is the intimidation campaign, I'm not exactly quivering, just confused.

"The same thing you are. Trying to get a crown and scholarship," I reply.

She snatches one of my fliers off the wall and shoves it in my face. "You stole my idea. Making history?" she says.

I take a deep breath. Do I really want to quibble over whether or not she came up with the idea of making history? Is that how I want to expend my energy at eight a.m. on a Friday?

"I guarantee we aren't going to be the only two people using that line," I say. "There are a lot of ways that someone could make history this prom season."

"Yeah, but you know what you're doing. You had all those questions about my fliers yesterday," she replies.

Okay...so we're doing this. She keeps getting closer to my face, and she's started waving her index finger *way* too close to my eyelids. We're going to fight over this. We're going to fight about putting a totally innocuous, commonplace slogan on our prom campaign posters.

Amayah is going to be livid, either that I'm engaging at all or that she didn't get it on camera so she could label it BSU VP DESTROYS ANTI-BSU MEMBER and post it on YouTube.

"I asked you what kind of history you'd be making, and you were cagey. I've been very clear with what history I'm planning to make, and these posters, the brunette ones, are a joke. Learn to take one," I say.

"You want to make everything about race when this is about how I have what you want," she replies.

I laugh incredulously. "JJ? You think I want JJ? Are you kidding? I'm the one who dumped him."

Her face twists cruelly, and she barks out the most unladylike laugh possible. Thank goodness her *boyfriend* isn't here to see it.

"No. He broke up with you," she says.

Oh my God, I'm going to kill him. It wasn't enough to out me, berate me, and be ashamed of me in front of BSU. Now he's lying to his new girlfriend too. Just perfect.

"He caused our breakup by being an asshole to me, but no, I'm the one who actually ended the relationship. And you aren't superior because you're with him," I say.

"Just like you're not superior to me because you're willing to make everything about race," she replies.

"If that's your perspective, then I absolutely wish you luck with JJ. While you're at it, why don't you ask him what he's said about you? I think you'll find it very illuminating to your colorblindness."

I stalk down the next hallway, trying to find anywhere

else to hang posters. If race isn't the reason she's making history with her campaign, what is? Is she the first prom queen to have a fifteen-inch sew-in? The first prom queen who trained to become a dental hygienist? Truly, what the fuck is she talking about?

I hate that she's using BSU and our mission to elevate her own platform, without actually being a part of the group. She gets to benefit by association, despite the fact that she has done everything to distance herself from our work. I would rather see the racial implications of everything, even if they're not there, than be willfully blind to my own position. Ashley was literally called the N-word during a playoffs match by one of the parents. It was a huge deal at the time, covered by the local newspaper and everything. We reached out to her as BSU to offer support, and she never responded. In the paper all she said was, "I'm sorry they felt that way. I'm just trying to play."

She had the chance to make a statement, make a difference. And she just . . . didn't. That, I don't understand.

I see her looking around the hall, presumably for me, and duck into the nearest classroom. There's still a half hour until the first bell, so I'm only in danger of being stuck in here with a teacher and maybe two overachievers trying to cram before a test.

I lean against the nearest wall and sigh. Having to deal with Ashley is a side effect of this prom campaign that I would love to eliminate.

"Hiding isn't exactly the best way to win prom queen," a voice says.

I jump. They're not wrong, but they're also not the one trying to escape their ex's new girlfriend and a public spat.

Lauren Buckley sits at a desk in the front of the room, looking amused. She's wearing a baggy sweater and seems ready to curl into herself.

"I hear that goes both ways," I reply. "Aren't you still in the running?"

She shrugs. "I guess. Still deciding."

Interesting. She'd be a formidable competitor. Number Two on the list and all. But if I were her, I also wouldn't want the attention right now. Someone wrote *slut* in Sharpie on her locker, and there have been rumors she's about to be pulled from the swim lineup over the photo.

"Can I ask you something?" I ask.

"Sure."

"Someone sent me this picture of you—"

"Yeah, feel free to not ask me about my sexts," she interrupts.

"Not that photo."

She raises her eyebrows. "Okay."

Hopefully I've caught her in a mood for honesty, even though we barely know each other. That picture was fucked up, and I want to know where it came from.

"You were in the locker room and had blood on your hands," I say. "It looked like you were being attacked, maybe?"

She glances down at her desk for a moment before making defiant eye contact. "Yes, it would look like that."

"But it's not? Like that?" I say.

She nods toward the window next to her.

I cautiously take a few steps toward her. Something about this makes the hairs on the back of my neck stand up. I look out to see Jason Miller, presumed list architect, surrounded by a group of other athletes. I scan the crowd and spot the captains of every single boys' sports team. And…

Fucking JJ.

"The disrespect, right?" Lauren says.

I look back to her, and she shakes her head at me. But the way she does it makes me feel like she's implicating me in some way.

"So the picture," I say.

"The guys have their Discord channel. They've been posting the photos and messages they've received from us girls. We've tried reporting the group to the company, but it always gets reinstated after a few days. And, to boot, they've started making new photos."

"Photos that look like you've been attacked?" I ask.

"Artificial intelligence. They're making violent or sexual AI photos of us and sharing them. We kept thinking they'd stop, or someone would stop them, but…nope."

If it's a private Discord channel, that means the guys are the ones moderating it. Unless the pictures end up outside the group, who is going to stop them? It would require the people in it to take a stand and report it to the company, the police, or some adult, which doesn't seem likely.

"You really think someone's going to whistle-blow in that group? Clearly, they don't care what damage they're doing," I say. "Especially if there are no stakes."

"It's an out-of-school group, and you see how the administration reacted to my photo being leaked. They're not going to do anything, so it's up to us," she says.

"How is it up to us? What are we supposed to do?" I ask.

"The list is based on the messages and photos. To make the list, a guy has to have a less-than-appropriate photo of you. Then, they vote hotness based on that. I'm trying to get the photos deleted from the group, and make sure no more are posted?"

The logical fallacy here is that the photos will never really be deleted. If they're out there, then they're out there for good. Who knows which guys have saved the photos. Whatever promises they make don't matter in the end.

"Wouldn't it be better to get the group deleted?" I ask. "And how do you even know about it?"

"Deleted by appealing to the founder," she replies. "I know because I dated one of the guys who created the list."

So appeal to him. What do I have to do with this?

"How are you going to do that?" I ask.

"With your help."

With my...? I look back to the courtyard.

JJ is gesticulating wildly, per usual. However, none of them are guys he usually talks to. God. How many betrayals does he plan to rack up?

"JJ started this?" I ask.

"From what I know, he started it a while ago with a couple guys. Just a few messages. From you. One of the members started adding other guys, and it exploded."

Fuck JJ. I'm done with him. All of this—the pictures, the messages, the list—they're all because of him. He is singlehandedly the impetus for the destruction of several girls' lives and relationships. He's the reason for the list, and that's why he decided I shouldn't run for prom queen? Complete horseshit.

"And where do I come in?" I ask. "Besides being the first, apparently."

"Get him to delete the channel."

I snort. "You're vastly overestimating my influence."

Lauren's gaze turns intense again. "Do it, and I'll make sure that you win prom queen. I will vote for you, and I'll get the other girls on the list and their friends to as well."

At this point, who cares about being prom queen? It's meaningless. I'm not going to disrupt anything on behalf of BSU when the literal president of BSU is the reason this mess is happening.

"There's no reason to keep running. And if he hasn't deleted the group already, nothing I do is going to change that," I say.

"You can still make history at Banneker. And you can use the platform and the scholarship to change things before you leave. At least make it easier for the next girl. And help current students by getting that group deleted. The guys have something on him. He doesn't really participate, but whatever they have keeps him from deleting it."

"I don't exactly have influence anymore. You might want to check with Ashley Beckett. JJ's girlfriend."

"She turned me down," Lauren replies.

Ah, so I'm not even the first choice. Par for the course. But that doesn't matter, does it? Getting the group deleted is a net good, especially if the guys are starting to generate their own disgusting content.

"What about one of the other girls? Jason Miller made the list, right? Can't Cassidy help?" I ask.

Lauren snorts. "Apparently the photos are my fault. They're worse than hers, so." Her eyes start to well up.

I feel terrible for her. All the photos and messages should have stayed private, but hers seem to be getting the most backlash. Some of that, actually a fair amount of it, is because of the PTA. Apparently Grayson Davis's mom really, really hates the idea of consensual sexting, but specifically, the kind that girls send.

I overheard Mom on the phone with her, and the things she was saying about Lauren and girls who would send "those kinds of messages" was brutal.

"I'm sorry," I say. "It's really fucked up. I'll try to get the group taken down. No prom support needed."

"You do that, and any votes I can swing are yours. Think of it as reparations for girls like me winning all these years," she says wryly.

Well, when she puts it that way...

CHAPTER 14

I DON'T KNOW WHAT TO TELL AMAYAH. WE COULD REALLY win this thing, but it involves me getting JJ to do something I want. I couldn't get him to go apple picking (Was the farm formerly a plantation? He won't be picking produce like our ancestors for free); how am I going to make him delete his creepy sext group?

Plus, maybe he's being blackmailed too? What could those guys have on him? Sure, he can be absolutely insufferable, but minus posting my messages, he hasn't really done anything that amoral. He doesn't drink, he won't touch a banned substance, and his romantic life has typically been kept under wraps.

At this point, he's also barely involved in school activities, minus BSU. So it's not like whatever dirt they have could get him in real trouble. If they try to discipline him for starting the group, they also have to address the guys who are keeping it going with revenge porn.

And if those guys are essentially forcing him to keep the group up, why is he out there kiki-ing with them? It's all so weird.

There are some holes in the story; I just don't know which side they're coming from.

Unfortunately, this means I need to do the thing I'd prefer to avoid. I have to have a private conversation with JJ. Which means I need to find a way to get him alone without his seemingly attached girlfriend and away from BSU.

We don't have another BSU meeting for a couple of days, and who knows if Ashley will be at that one. Actually, now that I've told her I'm the one who broke up with JJ, I'm willing to bet she will be front and center at any future meetings. She might even skim *The Autobiography of Malcolm X*. If she's feeling spicy, maybe she'll point out all the lessons JJ seems to ignore, including Malcolm's later evolution on protest methods and the role of women in the movement.

I tried, but JJ had a hard time giving up his role as the center of attention, and I never really wanted the title. Sometimes I wonder if all of this is my fault a little bit. If I had tried to rein him in more or been more willing to be a leader, would things be different? Maybe that's the real reason he lost his attraction to me. I was too passive. He stopped thinking of me as a partner because I deferred to him too much.

Lauren, who I've had maybe two conversations with before today, seems to stare me down every time I pass her in the hallway. Our lockers are very close together, but I swear I've never seen her as much as I have this morning. How fast does she think I can operate?

In contrast, despite having three classes with JJ, I haven't been able to exchange a word with him.

If I text him, I'm worried Ashley will see. If she's already unwilling to help, seeing me advocate for the group being taken down might make it worse. Then, she'd know that I sent him pictures. Even some after our breakup, which I'm still horrified about. She wouldn't be the first girl to feel compelled to go through JJ's phone, and I wouldn't blame her. How could I, when I made practically a weekly habit of it toward the end?

I could ask Simone to arrange something, but that would also require having a conversation with Simone. If she knew JJ was the one to start the group in the first place, she'd fall into the "safety" argument about running for prom queen even more. Especially if she knew guys AI-ing pictures we never sent.

God, it's all so disgusting and invasive. I can't believe that the guy I invested all that time and those feelings into would be a part of something like that.

What does that say about me and my judgment?

My lunch period arrives, and I barely care about eating. Now that I've hyped it in my head, the idea of talking to JJ makes me feel sick. I'm nervous, and I hate that he has that kind of power over me.

I grab a sandwich from the cafeteria and take a lap around the room.

Simone sits with the girls' basketball team, and I notice her watching me. She cocks her head toward the table, and I pretend not to see.

Then, I find the person I was looking for. Ashley is sitting with the girls' tennis team, picking at a salad. JJ is nowhere to be found, which must mean he's eating in study hall.

I pretend I'm still looking for someone, in case anyone is watching. Then I hurry out of one of the side doors to the cafeteria.

How exactly am I going to play this?

I stand outside the study hall for what feels like five minutes. When I finally resolve to push open the door, JJ is already looking at me through the glass window above the knob.

I walk inside. There's no one else here. We are truly alone for the first time in a while.

"Hey," I say.

"Hey..." he replies cautiously. "I'm not sure—"

"Don't think I'd be here if I didn't need to be," I say.

He slams the textbook in front of him closed and stands up to face me. Well, caution's gone, I guess.

It's absolutely wild that he thinks he has the right to be mad here. Why did I like him again? Physical attraction is a hell of a drug, and it has worn the hell off.

"You're acting like I'm the devil, when *you're* the one who broke up with me! We'd still be... Things would be..." He doesn't seem to know how to finish that sentence given the current state of things.

"You *outed* me!" I reply. "How else am I supposed to think of you?"

"Well, it wasn't on purpose."

"Impact over intent, Jesus, JJ. How many times have you preached that?"

Yeah, this is one of several reasons we broke up. We fought like this constantly, and even though the makeups were A-plus, they didn't fix the underlying problem. I started to realize that I wasn't sure JJ actually liked me anymore, which really, really sucked.

"Why are you here? Besides to yell at me. First Ashley, now—"

"Oh, come off your high horse. Ashley confronted me. I'd love to not have to interact with her, but alas, that doesn't seem possible. And I'm here because apparently you have even more problems with women than I thought," I reply.

Okay, not exactly the chill, no-frills approach I'd planned. This isn't going well. It's not even going a direction that could be considered positive. I'm totally not going to get him to take down the group, but this will release some of my personal frustrations.

"Go away," he says. "I'm over this. I'm over you."

I scoff. "I'm over you too. But unfortunately, it looks like there's another way I can advocate for girls at Banneker, and it's by asking you to do the right thing for once."

He glares at me. "What are you talking about?"

"You made a group for guys to show their girlfriends' sexts. For them to AI new violent or sexual photos. And you won't take it down." He opens his mouth to respond, and I can't resist the opportunity to take another shot. "Sorry, their situationships' sexts. I wouldn't want you to think I was ever under the impression that I was your girlfriend. Who knows if you'd share the messages of someone you were actually committed to."

His eyes go wide. Did he really think Simone wouldn't tell me? Well, it wasn't clear. Hence our current situation.

"It's not what you think," he says.

"Then what is it? Because it seems pretty obvious and pretty fucked up. And the fact that you won't delete it is very telling."

"I've tried," he says. "I can't."

"Why not?"

He throws his head into his hands. He can pretend to cry all he wants, or whatever this is. The performance could be better. Razzie Award incoming.

"I can't tell—"

"You'd fucking better, or I'm telling your parents, my parents, the administration, Ashley, whoever I have to," I reply.

"You're bluffing," he says, but he doesn't sound sure.

"Try me."

He takes a few steps toward me. What's his move here? Is he going to try a little seduction? Or whisper some vague, secretive warning?

"Ida, *please.*"

"Your mom still has her girls' happy hour at Caribbean Jerk's on Fridays, right? I've been craving their plantains. Maybe I'll need to make a stop after school," I say.

He lets out a loud groan, and I smirk. He's already pissed, and I'm determined to do anything I can to make it worse, so he'll blurt out some kind of truth. Finally, he sits back down, pushing his lunch away.

"Remember when I was on the football team freshman year?" he asks.

How could I forget? He very publicly quit because they didn't kneel in solidarity with him during the national anthem, which was how he got on the then–BSU president's radar and was taken under his wing. JJ has been riding on that for his entire high school career. There were even articles about it in the local papers.

"Of course. You made the friends that help keep the group running," I reply.

"They're not my friends!" He slams his hands on the table.

"Okay! Jesus. No need to be so dramatic."

"The texts I shared were from freshman year. I made the group with two guys who were on the team with me. It was mostly unused after that, until the beginning of this school year, when one of them started adding other athletes and photos of their girlfriends."

In texts I wrote freshman year, I waxed poetic about all the ways I wanted our first kiss to go. It was a little pathetic, but nothing like the texts he had sent Simone.

"The texts you sent Simone were from six months ago," I say.

He swallows. "Yeah. I knew the actual posted ones wouldn't freak her out, so I picked some of the more...explicit ones so she'd encourage you to drop out."

"Fuck you. But please, none of that is why you can't delete the group."

"The guys on the team said they'd kneel with me. They didn't, and I quit. Official story," he says. When I glare at him for telling me what I already know, he continues.

"Unofficial story, the guys didn't kneel, so after the game I came back and destroyed the locker room. I burned the playbooks.

Two of the guys, including one in the original group, caught me. They had—have—pictures. They were willing to keep it to themselves, and we blamed the team we'd beaten, saying they did it out of racism. Now, they'll release the photos if I don't keep the group running. The statute of limitations on vandalism, and technically, arson, isn't up. And the pictures in the group are technically also a crime. So. Who'd take the fall?"

My jaw drops. I remember when the locker room was trashed. It was a big deal at the time. The other team's coach issued an apology, even though none of the players admitted to the destruction. They'd made enough racist statements about JJ kneeling that everyone believed they'd done it.

And if those photos got out now, along with the group, JJ could be facing expulsion or, honestly, jail time. He was a minor then, but he turned eighteen last month. The photos in the group probably feature girls who aren't legal yet. And he's the one running it.

Shit...

"Why didn't you tell me?" I ask. "I could have—"

"What would you have done, Ida? You were so impressed when I kneeled. That was the night you kissed me for the first time, remember? I was afraid you'd think less of me. Then, it became easier to keep up the lie. Especially when everyone thought I was a brave kid willing to stand on principles."

JJ can't delete the group without getting his life, his future, ruined. Mutual assured destruction, except he's the one who'd be destroyed.

"Okay. So I'll figure out another way—"

"Why does this matter to you anyway? Don't try to sell me on the feminism angle. You wouldn't be here unless you had some direct benefit. Otherwise, you'd handle this at a meeting."

"One of the girls whose pictures were uploaded has offered to rally support behind me for prom queen."

He scoffs. "This is about *prom*? Are you serious?"

"Of course it is! You didn't want me to run in the first place because of the group, so how would it not be?"

He throws his hands into the air. Yeah, this is about how conversations went in the last month or so of our relationship. Theatrics from JJ included.

"I didn't want you to run because those guys will never vote for a Black girl, and second of all, they're posting pictures of any girl in the running. They'd find something. Or they'd make it. I'm protecting you."

"They'd find nothing, unless it was from you, which you know. Don't pretend this was about protecting me. You just don't want anyone else to find me attractive," I say. "Plus, you're willing to let your actual girlfriend run, knowing they're inventing shit."

He opens his mouth to retort, but the door swings open. Ashley stands there holding a lemon water. She looks back and forth between the two of us.

I rush out past her before she can say anything. This isn't my fight, and I'm done dealing with her if I don't have to. And I'm really, *really* determined to make sure I don't have to.

CHAPTER 15

AMAYAH AND I MEET UP AT A LOCAL COFFEE SHOP Saturday afternoon to continue to strategize. I'm polling up in almost every group, with the notable exception of the girls' tennis team. But there are still twenty other girls in the race, and at least eight of the ten girls are on the list. Lauren has yet to reenter the race, true to her word. We'll see how long that lasts if I can't get JJ to take the group down.

New photos of her and other girls in the race keep popping up. As do the requisite messages calling them sluts. Now, even among the girls running, there are feuds. Sure, Girl A's photos are also posted, but they're not nearly as revealing as Girl B's.

If we thought the boys were bad, the girls are quickly making a play to be a close second.

I'm trying to come up with what turn out to be increasingly improbable ways of explaining the sudden bump in my candidacy.

The campaign materials have gotten compliments, at least in the hallway, but they can't explain why I'm now actually in contention. And I'm really wondering why I even want to run, when it seems like everyone is fighting. Do I want to represent the girls calling each other whores instead of standing together? We aren't the problem! At least, we're not supposed to be. Ugh.

Amayah is a never-ending well of ideas. Magnets that say *Brunettes make history,* cookies in the shape of a black power fist, a library demonstration of the history of Black students at Banneker. When she decides to get into actual politics, she'll be a killer campaign manager.

She turns her computer to show me something, and out of the corner of my eye, I notice we're being watched. Jason Miller, of the list, sits with the captain of the wrestling team, Grayson Davis, a few tables away from us. Grayson has tight curls that he almost always shaves off, and we've almost never seen him without a bucket hat in the summer months, like he's afraid if he tans his PTA president mom will disown him.

Simone and I have always had a conspiracy theory that Grayson is secretly liberal and pretending he agrees with his mom's weird conservative agenda. Somehow, the books she very publicly removed from our school library while live streaming on Instagram ended up right back in the library the next week. That week was also the only time Grayson was spotted in the library. He and JJ used to be friends, back when they were both on the football team. Like really, really good friends. Which means…

Is Grayson the one who added people to the group? Before

I can contemplate that, Amayah's phone starts ringing. The call pops up on her computer too.

JJ's number.

She declines the call, looking at me sheepishly. There's no reason for her to be embarrassed. It's not like she's obligated to block his number on my behalf. It's just strange that he's calling her in the first place.

He calls again, and she declines. The third time his number pops up, I accept the call for her.

"Hello?" Amayah says, leaning in close to me so I can hear.

"Are you with Ida?" JJ asks. Damn, not even a hello for Amayah? Rude.

"Hello to you too, JJ."

"We don't have time for this; *are you with Ida?*" he asks.

Amayah looks to me, her eyes questioning. Normally, I'd tell her to say no, but there's something in JJ's voice. Not the usual anger or annoyance. He sounds scared, like he really needs to find me.

"I'm here," I say into the phone.

"Thank..." he says, before interrupting himself. "*Where* are you? Who's around?"

"Feel free to explain why you're calling Amayah and demanding to know where I am before I give you any information."

There's a loud crash, and Jason bolts out of the door. Grayson is still at their table, staring at his phone as if he's in a daze.

Amayah and I exchange a glance. Um...what the hell is going on?

"Someone posted a photo in the Discord group, I don't know who, of Cassidy Burke unconscious," he says.

"Okay... You do realize that the guys are AI generating content too, right? Why are you freaking out?" I reply.

"How do you know that?" Amayah asks.

Ugh. I never told her about the conversation with Lauren, and I certainly didn't mention anything having to do with JJ. There's not a great way to get around that now and, more importantly, no reason to cause panic if it's not needed.

"Because I think the photo is real," he says.

Jason, Cassidy's boyfriend, just ran out of the coffee shop. We know he's in the group. Grayson, also presumably in the group, still looks like he's stunned.

But that could have nothing to do with the picture.

It doesn't make the picture real.

My phone buzzes with a notification and my stomach drops. Whenever anything big happens at Banneker, like a crisis, a message is sent out to families. But those take time, as the school figures out what information to give. Time is not afforded to students though. Social media gives us the real-time updates.

I open my Instagram, where I have a DM from an account I don't follow: thelaurenbuckley.

I open the message. She's sent three messages.

I don't know how else to contact you.

I'm out rn, and someone is following me.

Two of my friends who are running said someone has been watching them at night.

What? Watching them from where? And is this connected to the photo of Cassidy?

?? Call the police? I respond. Not my usual MO, but what exactly am I supposed to do about several girls I barely know maybe being stalked? That is well above my pay grade.

Cassidy is one of the girls. Now there's this photo, and no one has seen her since a party last night, Lauren sends. She attaches the photo, which, to be fair, does look real. But isn't that the whole point of artificial intelligence?

Just because it *looks* real, doesn't make it real.

Then why does it feel like there's a boulder in my gut? I'd like to think of myself as digitally savvy. There is some part of me screaming that the picture is authentic.

"Ida? Are you still there? Are you okay?"

Shit. We're still on the phone with JJ, who now sounds fully panicked, and Amayah looks completely befuddled.

"I'm fine, just trying to figure out what's going on. Lauren DMed me and said no one has seen Cassidy since last night," I say.

"Lauren Buckley DMed you? About Cassidy Burke? Why? What is happening?" Amayah asks.

All of a sudden, a voice cuts across the shop.

Grayson is standing, his phone pressed against his ear.

"Jason, *stop screaming*," he says, loudly enough that it honestly sounds like he's the one yelling. "What are you saying?" He pauses, while Jason presumably explains. He blanches. "Fuck fuck fuck. I'm on my way." He takes off running outside.

"Was that Grayson?" JJ asks. "Why are you with Grayson?"

"Is that what matters right now? We're at a coffee shop. Grayson and Jason were here, leering, but they both flipped out and left," I reply.

"Hold on..." JJ's computer, which he always keeps at full volume for some reason, starts going insane with notifications.

Amayah holds the phone away from our ears. I'm going to have so much explaining to do, and I have no idea how to do it.

A minute passes without JJ saying anything.

Then, deadpan, he says, "Sorry you won't be winning prom queen."

"Screw you," Amayah says at the same time I say, "What are you talking about?"

"I can't delete the group. I'll probably never be able to," JJ says.

"Why?" I ask.

"Because it's officially evidence in a crime. The photo is real. Cassidy was found dead this morning."

He ends the call.

"What the hell is he talking about? He controls the group? Cassidy is dead? What's going on?" Amayah asks.

I wave my hand. I can't find the words right now. How am I supposed to explain something I barely understand myself?

My phone starts ringing. It's Mom.

Now I *really* have some explaining to do.

CHAPTER 16

MOM, DAD, MR. AND MRS. BROWN, AND SIMONE ARE IN our living room when Amayah drops me off at home. Amayah's parents called her too, which is how I know this is extra serious. Her parents are hippies who, now that she's almost eighteen, have given her a wide berth and no curfew. If they're demanding she comes home, then something bad is happening.

As much as I don't want to be around Simone right now, I understand why they're all here.

Mom paces back and forth in front of the couch.

"If this is about our classmate, I already know," I say. "But I get why you wanted to tell us this way."

"You already know what? And how?" Mom's voice is steady, but there's freneticism that betrays her anger.

"People are posting on Instagram," I say. "She died. After a party last night?" Technically, I did hear from Instagram. Just not *first*.

"Are people posting on *Instagram* that she was killed? Because the school administration is dealing with their communication plan." She says *Instagram* like it's a swear word.

Wait—killed? Like alcohol poisoning? A traffic accident? Or murder?

"Girls are reporting being followed, and now one of the girls running for prom queen is *dead*," Mom says.

Still nothing about the list? And nothing about how the photo is circulating. This isn't about prom; this is about the misogyny of the list. And how that misogyny may have led to a girl being killed.

Obviously, Jason should be suspect number one, both as the creator of the list and as her boyfriend. It's always the boyfriend. And he's creepy anyway. His reaction in the coffee shop might have been him finding out that someone knew what he did.

My mind starts spinning through theories like a white woman on a true crime podcast. I have the insane and somewhat insensitive inclination to start sleuthing on social media. I want to message people. Who? No clue. I want to build a case and find a way to get Jason Miller in trouble. Maybe then the group can be shut down too. Just because JJ started the group doesn't mean he's implicated in what happened to Cassidy.

Speaking of…

"Do we know how it happened?" I don't realize I've said it out loud until Mom laughs incredulously.

"*That's* your question? What is going on with you?" Dad asks.

I shake my head. "No. Sorry. I was just I saw.... Nothing."

"I'm going to drop out," Simone says, finally speaking. "I

don't really have time for the campaigning anyway, and clearly, it's not safe."

I give her a long, hard look. "Simone, you know this isn't about prom. This is about...*you know*. And you know who's involved. And you know whose idea this was."

There's no reason to drop out. If anything, this is a greater incentive to stay in the race. It's not only a disruption of what Banneker defines as beautiful. It's a platform to address the way boys treat us. I can make this a referendum.

"Simone, what is she talking about?" Mrs. Brown asks.

"Is this about JJ?" Dad asks.

Neither Simone nor I answer. I'm not going to sell out JJ. I believe that he didn't intend for things in the group to go this far. He'd never hurt anyone, at least not physically. And the messages he shared from me, while invasive, happened three years ago. The messages he shared with Simone were obviously much more recent. But hers is the bigger betrayal to me. She never would have told me about those messages if I hadn't forced the issue. I wouldn't have known about the group until Lauren told me.

"We're not going to tell either of you whether or not to run," Mom says. "But we are concerned. Something is going on with the girls at your school, and it's not clear where the threat is coming from. Prom is a big event, and it could end up being a flash point."

She's right. Even if none of this is connected to prom, prom is an inevitability; the dance itself could become significant.

"So what are you going to do? Is the PTA planning anything?" I ask.

Mom purses her lips. I know she's not technically supposed to talk about PTA business, but these are extraordinary circumstances, so she does.

"Potentially, private security for school events. Some want it every day in the building as well. We'll see what happens with the police investigation," Mom says.

Dad is visibly seething. Removing police presence in schools has been a big project of his, and Banneker has a not-so-great history with its former school resource officer. Private security, presumably paid for by the white wealthy parents that make up most of the PTA, would be beholden to that contingent. It could exacerbate the already deep racial divisions at the school.

JJ is going to have a field day. This is exactly the kind of thing that he loves to rail against, and he's damn good at it. But...

He can't do that if he's somehow implicated in whatever happened to Cassidy. Which means that I have two options here, and both are way out of my comfort zone. I either have to figure out how to get the group taken down while keeping JJ out of the line of fire and also becoming a front-runner in the prom race, or let the chips fall where they may and possibly become the face of BSU when all of this comes out against JJ.

Somehow, the former seems less scary to me.

"Are there really concerns that school isn't safe?" Simone asks. She chews at the edge of one of her cuticles.

Mrs. Brown rubs Simone's back. "We don't know, baby."

"The picture of Cassidy circulating is a concern," Mom says. "It's not clear how any of the students would have gotten that. And there are multiple photos going around, some real, some apparently AI generated? People are sick."

She doesn't even know how sick.

"Are they looking at her boyfriend?" Simone says. "He's—There are a lot of rumors about what he puts out about Cassidy."

Thank God she didn't mention the Discord. Our parents really don't need to know about that, especially since then I'd have to tell them who started it, and that screenshots of my private texts are on it. I've received enough parental lectures about texting and sharing photos, and how things I don't intend to spread can end up on the internet. They always emphasized consent and that my body is mine to make decisions for, especially at this point in my life. But they've always said that sending out certain pictures could be detrimental to my future, and technically a crime since I'm still seventeen.

That entire Discord is a crime, considering the ages of the girls involved.

"I would assume so, but we don't have details. Right now, the PTA is focused on supporting her family and figuring out if this is connected to the school, so we know how to move forward," Mom says.

Simone raises her eyebrows at me, and I finally, after the events of the past week, feel like we're back on the same page.

Jason Miller has to be involved, and Cassidy's death definitely has something to do with the list.

We just have to figure out how.

CHAPTER 17

THE HALLS MONDAY MORNING ARE A PECULIAR MIX OF grief, tears, gossip, and tension. The district has sent in their crisis response team of mental health professionals, who are milling about, offering their services to anyone with a twitchy eye or a soccer jersey. The principal has made at least four announcements about where we can go for support.

The local police are also here, conducting interviews in the teachers' lounge. From what I can tell, no one has seen Jason Miller yet today. Emotionally, it would make sense that he's not here—the death of your girlfriend is hugely traumatic—but socially, students are finding it suspicious.

The PTA also went through with their private security idea, which has created an uproar I haven't seen since the list. Some students are expressing relief and a sense of safety, while others, especially the Black and Hispanic students, are pissed.

I've been fielding texts from the rest of BSU all morning. They want a meeting; they want action. But JJ has gone radio silent, both via message and on social media. As someone who, at a minimum, reposts Malcolm X and Fred Hampton quotes daily, his lack of engagement is alarming, at least to me. I've considered reaching out to Ashley, to get a pulse on how he's doing, but given the absolutely lethal look she gave me when she passed my locker earlier, I've reconsidered.

I guess she's still unhappy about me being alone with him last week at lunch. Especially since I'm sure he didn't tell her why I came to talk to him.

The most visible tension, however, has been between the private security and the police. The security officers came in all big and bad, weapons in tow and highly conspicuous. Rumor has it they've also been trying to pull students to talk, which the police officers *do not* appreciate. This only adds to the uneasy sense that something even worse is about to happen.

Simone slides up beside me at my locker, holding a textbook with shaking hands. We've come to a tentative truce after Saturday's family ambush and have been texting nonstop about what we're seeing on social media about Cassidy.

"I was in the weight room this morning, and several members of the girls' soccer team were there too. It seems like, after the list came out, Cassidy did dump Jason. *And* Friday, they were both at the same party, and he tried to confront her. She dumped a drink over his head," Simone says.

Shit. So there's his motive, and a party is a hell of an

opportunity. I've never been to one of the athlete parties, but according to Simone, they get pretty rowdy. It'd be easy to arrange some kind of negative outcome in the margins of someone's six-thousand-square-foot mansion.

"Any word on the Discord group and what's being posted there?" I ask.

Simone shakes her head. "The guys are apparently keeping it pretty locked down, ironically. Only way we're going to find out what's going on is to talk to one of the guys in it and hope he's forthcoming."

I groan. The only guy I could even conceive of talking to would be JJ, and there's no way he's going to help now. I'm almost certain he's been avoiding me today, and I don't know if it's because of what I know about the Discord or because his girlfriend hates me.

"So who should we target?" I ask.

Simone shrugs. "I'm friendly with a bunch of the guys on the basketball team, but not enough that they'd trust me like that."

BSU has, since JJ quit football, not exactly been swimming in athlete members. On one hand, they tend to be pretty busy during their seasons, and BSU meetings overlap with practices. On the other hand, JJ, minus the Discord involvement, is pretty universally unpopular with a lot of the athletes given the fact that he quit in the middle of the playoffs, so...motivation is low.

The closest we have to a sports star is Paul, secretary extraordinaire, who is one of the equipment managers for football in the fall and wrestling in winter, in addition to his girls' tennis team duties. Paul is also very openly gay, so there's no reason for him to be in the Discord. Our only hope is that he's nosy enough to listen to locker room talk. Which, knowing him, he is.

I text him, inviting him to eat with me and Simone at lunch. Right now, he's the best shot, and he might know more than we anticipate.

I text JJ too, asking if we should schedule a BSU meeting for later. To my surprise, he responds immediately. Also, to my surprise, he says, **It's your call.**

This is the first time he's ever deferred to me without a fight. I should be thrilled, but instead I'm worried. This is out of character.

We have to address the security situation, right? I respond. **I know you have thoughts.**

Whatever you want, I'm good with, he replies.

Oh my God, has he been body snatched? I show Simone the texts, and she looks as shocked as I feel.

"Um...do we need a wellness check? Or do you think homegirl got his phone?" Simone says.

A fair question. Could Ashley be the one on the other end?

I text, **I have no mercy or compassion in me for a society that will crush people,** the first half of one of his favorite Malcolm X quotes.

He responds instantly: **and then penalize them for not being able to stand up under the weight.** Then he adds, **It's me. I'm deferring to you. Isn't that what you've wanted?**

Of course it's what I've wanted, but I wanted it in better

circumstances, not because JJ is too afraid to speak up. It doesn't really count if he feels forced into it.

Today after school. You'll be there?

His three dots pop up, then vanish. This happens another two times before the text appears. **We'll see.**

JJ has literally never missed a BSU meeting. Ever. When he's sick, he still calls in. He even FaceTimed into a meeting from his grandfather's funeral. He takes BSU, and his role, incredibly seriously.

I'm officially worried. But what can I do, besides hold the flame? I highly doubt Ashley wants to or needs to hear from me about this. JJ's not himself, which is obvious enough for anyone to see.

I send a message to the rest of the BSU members scheduling a meeting for after school. Then I cross my fingers that the day passes quickly. AP lit just doesn't feel important right now.

CHAPTER 18

PAUL SITS ACROSS FROM SIMONE AT OUR USUAL TABLE, smiling as I approach. There's a little sparkle in his eye. He for sure knows something and is bursting to tell us.

I sit down next to Simone, and we all take a couple of cursory bites of our food, as if that's why we're here.

"So, what do you want to know?" Paul asks, putting down his fork.

"We can't want to have lunch with a friend and fellow BSU member?" Simone asks.

Paul smirks. "You can...but I know better. And I know a fair amount about various things. Things that could help a burgeoning prom campaign?"

Hmm. Now I want to know what he's talking about, but I know he'll play coy. We have to get into specifics, even though I'm sure Paul could give us the rundown on a whole lot of topics and people. Having a photographic memory and access to the boys' locker room, a notorious hotbed of gossip, has its perks if you're inquisitive.

"We were wondering if you know about the Discord group that the athletes are in. Especially if there's been posting in there as of late," I say.

Paul whistles. "You mean the group JJ started?"

Well. Damn. Is that public knowledge or just Paul knowledge? He and JJ were close friends for part of our freshman year. Maybe he was a member of the original group, if he isn't still there now.

"The Discord group with all the athletes," I say carefully, on the off chance that he's guessing at the founder. No need for me to be the one to provide confirmation. "What has the vibe been since this weekend?"

Paul sighs. "There's been nothing."

What does he mean, *nothing*?

"But the photo of Cassidy..." Simone starts.

"That was the last thing posted," Paul replies.

"And who posted it?" I ask.

He shrugs. "No clue. It was an anonymous account."

"Well, can you pull it up?" I ask.

"On school property? Hell no," he replies.

So that was it? The very real photo of Cassidy, and the whole group goes silent? Does this mean it's over? Something doesn't seem right. As if the guys suddenly got a conscience? Or they're taking a break to mourn? No way.

"Has there been any news on the list? Who they plan to name as number one?" I ask.

Paul takes a long sip of his lemon Snapple. He smacks his lips as he finishes. "I have heard some rumblings."

Oh God. It's juicy, at least to Paul, which makes me think that Dad was right. They're naming a Black girl to the top of the list. But who? There aren't that many of us in the first place, and even fewer who would be considered traditionally "hot" by a bunch of Neanderthal white boys. I know who I would personally pick as number one, and she's definitely not who Jason Miller would be into.

"And?" Simone asks, leaning forward.

Paul gives me a sheepish look before focusing on Simone. It clicks before he even decides to say it. It's fun gossip, but that's not why Paul is playing coy. He knows who this affects.

"Ashley Beckett," Paul says. "But they're holding off out of respect to Cassidy."

It takes everything in me not to snort. There's no respect for Cassidy in any of this. There never has been. Her own boyfriend insulted her face to the entire school for clout. Continuing to ponder which girl is the hottest would be par for the course even after her death.

"Does she know?" Simone asks. "That would explain why she's suddenly being especially...extra."

Paul shakes his head.

"What are they saying about her?" I ask.

"That she's hot for a Black chick," Simone replies. "Right?"

"That they're not usually into Black girls, but she's the exception?" I add.

We could riff back and forth about this all day. The weird supposed-to-be compliments that are actually racist and insulting. It's not flattering for someone to tell you that they're not attracted to your entire race of people, which spans countries, complexions, and cultures, but that you're the one they can imagine seeing as a person worthy of being interested in.

Paul grimaces. "The streets are saying that she's down for anything," he replies. "And that there's proof."

"Oh no way," Simone says. "I've never heard a bad word about her."

Paul raises his eyebrows. "She's a killer on the court and a fashion icon in the halls, but she's also a well-known bitch in the locker room."

"What proof do they think they have? Or are they generating it?" I ask.

Paul shrugs.

Something clicks for me. Whether or not it's true, Ashley might be named number one on the list. The guys think that they have *some* kind of evidence that justifies her position, which, according to Lauren, requires that a certain type of photo be sent to the list architects.

I'm willing to bet that, sure, the original group has been quiet since Cassidy. Especially if the guys were figuring out when to release their number one. They couldn't do that in a group where her boyfriend, who has, let's say, *strong* feelings on his female companion's conduct, was the creator.

There's another group. There has to be. They can't post photos or messages from Ashley without invoking JJ's wrath.

That also leads me to another conclusion. If the guys have migrated, JJ could probably move to delete the original group. That would get rid of a bunch of the messages and photos, and it would satisfy Lauren's condition. I could nab votes, and I hate myself for thinking about that.

"Have you told JJ?" I ask.

Paul blinks once very slowly before cocking his head to the side and looking at me. "Of course I haven't."

Paul and JJ had some kind of falling out sophomore year, which neither of them have been particularly open about. It happened around the time Paul publicly came out, which led several other members of BSU to assume that's why it happened. But Paul has typically been outspoken about homophobia, particularly in the Black community. I can't imagine that he'd let JJ slide or that he'd stay in BSU under JJ's leadership. Then again, who knows? JJ has surprised me lately, and not for the better.

"Do you think you can find out what they have on her?" I ask.

I may not like Ashley, but she doesn't deserve what's about to happen to her. None of us do. If she sent messages or pictures, those are her business. JJ doesn't need to know, and neither does the entire school. Someone has to warn her. I just don't know that I'm the right person to do it. What I can do, however, is try to keep them from being released.

How? I'm not sure.

"They don't talk to me," Paul says. "I'm basically a nonentity. I overhear things, but I'm not in the discussion."

Simone clears her throat. "What if...?" She shakes her head as though even she can't believe what she's about to say. "What if some of the photos, not just the violent ones, aren't real? They could name Ashley as number one and AI generate pictures of her to show she's down for anything even if it's not true. And no one will believe her when she says they're faked."

She's right. There are barely laws on revenge porn. Actual images from the girls are illegal, but AI? Still a gray area. Especially in a new group, if the content is AI, they might not get in trouble. But JJ would still be on the hook for the photos in the original Discord.

No wonder he's not talking about the new security presence. He's probably going to be quiet until this all blows over.

If it ever does.

The doors to the cafeteria crash open, knocking against the walls and echoing throughout the room.

Everyone turns to look.

Bridget Lewis, number ten on the list, has burst into the room, blood pouring out of her forehead.

A pall of silence overtakes the room for several seemingly infinite seconds. Someone, presumably upon seeing the blood, vomits loudly. Another person faints.

Then the screaming starts.

CHAPTER 19

SCHOOL IS CANCELED FOR THE NEXT TWO DAYS WHILE the police and private security investigate what's happening to the hottest girls in the senior class.

They've kept information pretty locked down, but from what I can gather based on social media and the little my mom will tell me, Bridget doesn't know who attacked her. She was in the locker room, grabbing something from her gym locker, when someone hit her from behind. She slammed her head against the corner of her open locker door, and the cut, though surface level, bled a ton; she needed eight stitches.

Other female athletes have talked about feeling watched in the locker room or at practice. No one can identify exactly who would be doing the watching. Right now, it seems localized to athletes, which also heavily overlaps, but not perfectly, with who's on the list.

My phone buzzes. Amayah hasn't talked to me much since

the whole coffee shop incident. She won't tell me exactly what she's thinking, but I suspect she knows I'm hiding something. Something that could be related to the violence happening. Now she's texting me about prom polling.

It seems unimportant. It *is* unimportant. One girl is dead, another attacked. Others are maybe being stalked. Who cares about a crown?

Still, I check. Out of…hope? For good news? Just to hear from her? I don't know what I want, except for us to be good. This prom campaign was supposed to bring us closer together. Maybe her text means that it still can.

Hey.

I set up an alert for the polls. You've cracked the top five. Congrats.

What? How? Nothing has changed, beyond one of the competitors having died. This is weird.

I pull up Instagram, where I have a smattering of DMs. As always, there are memes and gossip from Simone. Apparently, several of the basketball girls have been Instagram-Storying what they say is a shadow following them.

The videos aren't particularly clear, but the sense of danger remains pervasive. There is *someone* menacing the girls of the school; it's just not clear who. Cassidy may have been an isolated incident, even if, according to the ever-active rumor mill, Jason Miller has barely been questioned, let alone arrested.

Bridget, however, is a real question. Some people are saying that she tripped into the locker and is capitalizing on the uncertainty around Cassidy's death.

There's a sense of active hysteria that Simone is very much keeping me informed of.

Another DM surprises me. It's Lauren again. This time she's sent a thumbs-up emoji along with the message: **Thank you. Should see the results soon.**

Thank me for what? I haven't done anything. We never ended up having that BSU meeting, given what happened with Bridget, and JJ still hasn't spoken out. I can't imagine Lauren would be expressing gratitude for the one thing I have done: I posted a Notes app memorandum last night on the perpetuation of violence by school-based security.

It didn't feel right to me to be silent, even though, with actual violent incidents happening, people want more security. But half a day in, those private contractors had been harassing the Black kids. It was only a matter of time before something erupted there. Just because they give the illusion of safety doesn't mean they actually make us safer. I got some likes from the other BSU members, JJ excluded, and a couple of comments about how I'm being insensitive from two of the JV boys' basketball players who are obsessed with Simone.

Interestingly, Grayson Davis liked the post too. He's another person I've barely talked to, and, as a Jason acolyte, I wouldn't expect him to have particularly progressive views. He even DMed me saying he appreciated my speaking out.

Of course, given his social status, he didn't comment on the post for others to see. It's nice for people to care about my opinions on racial justice, but when it's only done behind the scenes, it doesn't really move the needle forward. Getting a public cosigning from a popular athlete could truly start a conversation.

Grayson has sent another DM. A crown emoji.

Our posters must really be working, I text Amayah.

Days later when no one is in school? Did you sell your soul or something? she responds.

Who is ahead of me? I ask.

She starts sending names. Number four on the list, Hannah Gregg, a blond soccer player is polling first, closely followed by number eight Jackie Johnston, a redhead on the girls' swim team, then Cassidy, as a posthumous honor.

She pauses before sending me the person polling right above me. I shouldn't be surprised. If anything, I'm surprised she isn't polling higher.

Ashley Beckett and I are neck and neck in the results.

If the administration starts slimming down the number of girls running, we could end up being the only two non-white competitors. We'd split the vote. If I want to win, I really have to find a way to make sure that BSU and any other cultural organizations are behind me.

Me suddenly having all this support still doesn't make sense. What's changed?

I flash back to Lauren's message. *Oh shit.*

You took it down, I text JJ.

He doesn't respond, but he flips on his read receipts so I can see that he's seen the text.

Petty.

But why? He was adamant that the other guys would blow up his locker room secret. Could Bridget's attack have changed that?

It just lends support to my theory that there's a new group. And that means…

They're gearing up to name Ashley as the hottest girl in school.

And if someone is targeting girls on the list, she's about to become public enemy number one.

CHAPTER 20

WE NEED TO MEET UP. MY TEXT TO JJ SITS, READ, FOR three hours. I cycle through a series of emotions, anxiety—*Will he respond?*—then, annoyance—*Will he* ever *respond?*—then, anger—*How dare he* not *respond.*

School reopens tomorrow, so I could try to ambush him in the hall, but then I run the risk of running headfirst into Ashley, who has been the first view on my Instagram Stories with alarming regularity since our last conversation.

Now, it was rather bold of me to assume my parents would be cool with me leaving the house, but they're both at work, and I have Find My Friends activated, so they can't object that much.

I contemplate texting Amayah and seeing if she wants to come over to strategize, since we'll be back in the building. I hesitate though. I don't know where we stand, and I'm kind of afraid to find out since I know where *I* want to be with her.

I'm outside. JJ has finally responded.

Outside...my house? I peek out of my bedroom window, and he is, indeed, standing in the driveway. He looks up and waves at me. Even from here, his facial expression looks grim. To be fair, the last time he was at my house, I did dump him, but whose fault is that, really?

I take the steps downstairs two at a time, but not quickly enough that he thinks I'm rushing to let him in. Playing it cooler than cool...totally.

When I hold the door open, he hesitates. It takes everything in me to not roll my eyes. His "traditional" masculinity makes it nearly a crime for him to allow a girl to hold a door for him.

"I don't have all day," I say, even though I do, in fact, have all day. JJ might not, though, because if Mom comes home and sees him, she might take his head off. She doesn't know what happened, but she doesn't need to. She knows that I was hurt by him, which makes him her nemesis.

He grunts, and his internal battle flashes across his face. "Fine." He looks around outside for a few seconds before stepping inside.

"Worried you're being followed?" I ask.

He glares at me. "And who are you implying would follow me?"

Okay, I probably shouldn't have taken that shot, given why I've called him here. He just brings out the pettiest version of me. I spent years trying to be his perfect girl, his exemplar of feminine partnership. And he still abandoned everything we built, then made it official with the one person he'd held up as "not the right kind of Black girl."

"I didn't ask to meet up so we could keep fighting," I say.

"So stop picking a fight with me," he replies.

"Stop making it so easy."

He sighs and gives me a single nod. A pause in our back-and-forth. It's necessary, and it feels like a slight relief. We need to work together.

"You summoned me? Why?" he asks.

He lingers on the indoor welcome mat. When I invited him in, I guess he took that to mean that he could only take two steps inside the door.

"We have a lot to talk about," I say.

I'm, once again, keeping it very chill.

He folds his arms across his chest. "We have a lot we *could* talk about; that doesn't necessarily mean we should."

"So you'd rather let everything fester? That'll make it better," I say.

"I can go."

"Don't," I say. "I reached out for a reason."

He taps his foot on the floor. How much longer can I get away with having him wait? I need to come out with it.

"Well, I think we should talk about the BSU response to the private security company at Banneker," I say.

"Your response was sufficient. Well said," he replies.

A compliment? I find myself blushing with pride, then chiding myself. Who cares what he thinks? (Obviously, I do.)

"Thank you. But we still need you," I say. "I also wanted to talk to you about Ashley."

"Not interested. I don't need to justify my choice in romantic partner to you," he says.

"I'm not saying you do. I wanted to talk to you about the group and the list."

He grits his jaw. I'm losing him, fast. Why does he make me so tongue-tied, unless I'm, like, insulting his entire existence?

"I don't need your opinion on Ashley. I'm confident in my choice."

"I've heard that she's going to be named hottest girl in school. And if you shut down the group, I'm pretty sure the only reason you're not getting backlash is because they either have, or are making, photos of Ashley and posting them in another group without you," I say.

"What?"

"It's just a theory, but I feel pretty certain. And based on what's been happening, that would mean Ashley could be in danger. I wanted you to know," I say.

For the first time in this entire exchange, I can tell that he's panicked. I reach out to comfort him, before withdrawing my hand. It doesn't feel like my place anymore.

"How do you know about the list?" he asks. "And that the group has been deleted?"

"A reputable source, for the list. I was asked to get the group deleted, and I received a thank-you message. So I put two and two together."

He nods. "Okay. Thanks. For telling me. Ashley has mentioned someone's been watching her when she's practicing serves after school. But she gets stared at a lot, obviously."

Obviously. Because she's so hot. *Rub it in, why don't you, as if I don't know what she looks like.*

I force myself to smile, and I can only hope it doesn't make me look as deranged as I feel.

"I'm also not going to ask you to choose, but I want you to know that right now, Ashley and I are neck and neck in the prom polls. I know that BSU will have to make an endorsement. I'm not going to ask you to vote against your girlfriend—"

"We can take a vote for BSU. I imagine that they'll vote for you, which I don't have an issue with. I'll individually support my girlfriend," he replies.

"Thanks."

"Is that it?" he asks. "I should get going. I have plans with… you know."

I know. I do want to talk more, but I know that he's not mine to keep anymore. If he ever was.

"Yeah. But I can text you if I hear anything else. If that's okay."

"That'd be okay," he says. "Now that you've unblocked me." He smirks.

Well, at least he noticed. There are small victories in that, maybe.

Not for the first time in the last six months, I watch JJ leave my house with his head hanging.

And not for the first time, I don't call after him, even though I want to.

Maybe that's why we couldn't make it work.

CHAPTER 21

FOR ONCE, JJ SEEMS TO TAKE ME SERIOUSLY, AND ON our first day back, he posts handwritten statements on several bulletin boards of the school, denouncing the private security. Obviously, said private security tears down the statements, leaving them crumpled and ripped on the floor like some kind of litter response.

He's also almost immediately called to the principal's office and given, I assume, a warning, since he walks into our Spanish class on time and looking stoic as ever. He gives me a single nod, which is basically the equivalent of a presidential pardon.

From the back of the room, I can see Amayah watching the two of us. We've exchanged a handful of texts over the last few days, but it's clear there's tension.

I don't know how to explain any of this to her, so I've avoided the opportunity. Which also means I've sort of been avoiding her.

In reality, I'm self-aware enough to know that I'm embarrassed. Having to tell the girl I've had an irrevocable crush on, who has taken so much time to help me run a prom campaign, that I'm rising in the polls because my ex-not-boyfriend shut down a Discord group he made that was disseminating inappropriate photos of the other front-runners without consent feels like too much. I'm complicit, because I didn't report it, and that goes against so much that I've said I stand for.

By lunch, everything that's been causing commotion over the last few days seems to have died down. There's still an investigation into what happened to Cassidy, but the prevailing theory is that she died of alcohol poisoning after a succession of parties Friday night. No foul play suspected. As for Bridget, the private security guards claim they have proof she was never pushed; she tripped, and in the fog of pain, her mind invented an attack.

It's almost better than the theory I thought they'd advance, that some unseen, dangerous person made their way into the locker room to attack a defenseless girl and only they can protect us.

Bridget hasn't been back in school, and from the Instagram posts I've seen from other members of the field hockey team, she isn't backing down on her original story. #IStandWithBridget has become a rallying cry among the girls of the school.

Amayah slides in across from me in the cafeteria. We eat in silence for several minutes before she sighs.

"I don't want it to seem like I don't believe in you, because of course I do. But there's no way you shot up in the polls just because of my incredible posters," she says.

I almost laugh. Is the reason she's barely been speaking to me because she doesn't want me to think she believes in me less?

"You're right. Even though, yes, your posters are fabulous. I had a boost because of unrelated factors." I pick at my square of lethally greasy cafeteria pizza.

"Those factors being...?" she asks. "I know it has something to do with JJ; I just don't know what. You two aren't... You're not... Are you back together?"

This time, I do laugh. "Oh God, no. He's very confident in his choice, and it's not me," I reply.

"Idiot," she says. "And what does he have to do with the list?"

I take a deep breath. Then, I tell her everything, from the initial encounters with Ashley that led to my moment with Lauren, and eventually the Discord group and list. I even tell her about my conversation with JJ at my house.

"So do you still want to be with me?" I ask. At the quirk of her eyebrows I add, "As my campaign manager."

"Of course. I respect what you tried to do with the Discord. Lauren didn't have to do anything to help you, and she chose to. Now we just have to figure out how to maximize that help," she says, before adding wryly, "as your campaign manager."

Jason Miller, wearing all black like he's in mourning, speeds past our table. He whispers, "Congratulations," to either me or Amayah. Neither of us can tell who he was talking to, but both of us know that whoever it was directed toward, it was likely a threat.

Amayah lowers her voice. "I think he did something to

Cassidy, and I wouldn't be surprised if he hurt Bridget too. His reputation precedes him in the worst way."

"Can we prove it?" I ask.

"Of course not," she replies. "But, in the era of social media clout, do we need proof? We can plant seeds."

Why though? Sure, I'd believe that he did something. Hell, we know he's broken the law with the Discord. But murder? Assault?

"What would planting seeds get us?" I ask.

"A surefire way to get any Discord shut down, protecting the girls of the school and drumming up the last of the support you'd need to win. Duh."

She makes it sound so simple. There's no guarantee that if we nailed Jason on the Discord, or even the attacks, that we'd be able to rally additional support. This is still a popularity contest, and, in that way, the crowd has never been on my side.

Before I can respond, Simone drops into the seat next to me, slamming her hip into mine.

"Ow? What was that?" I ask.

Is she *sweating*? She looks like she ran a half-marathon to get here. She hands me two pieces of paper.

It seems the Discord boys have decided that the time for bereavement is over. Number one is officially listed, and as predicted, it's Ashley Beckett.

Pros: her legs (which she always shows off in skirts), her ass (which she has despite a lack of belly or hip fat), and her full lips (which look perfect for something unrepeatable). Cons: uppity, prudish, and dark.

They don't specify what exactly they mean by *dark*, but the three of us are willing to venture a guess. *Prudish* gives me the slightest bit of hope for her that there's nothing they can post to violate her privacy, even though I know they could AI generate whatever they want. *Uppity* gives me something to bring to BSU. Even if Ashley doesn't really want to stand with us, she can't be okay with these white guys harkening back to masters' descriptions of runaway slaves to describe her.

"I'm calling a BSU meeting," I say, taking out my phone.

Simone puts her hand on mine. "Look at the next page."

Amayah beats me to the punch, pulling Ashley's picture away to reveal the second flier. It's my campaign photo alongside a block of text that makes me sick.

Honorable Mention/New #10: Ida Carter. Apparently, since Cassidy's death, they've decided to bump everyone below her up a spot, leaving an empty space at number ten. An empty space for me to fill.

My cons are listed first. Shockingly, I don't also get uppity. I'm a social justice warrior, which is, I guess, bad. I don't date white guys, which is hilariously presumptuous, given that I've only ever dated one guy, who happened to be Black. My hair is the third. The white athletes of the school really feel I should keep it looking a little more kempt.

Now can I call that meeting?

My pros? Also my ass or, rather, my entire lower body, which is "stacked." My boobs, which I apparently should be showing off more. And...fucking hell.

My biggest pro is that I'm down for threesomes.

Is this because I'm bisexual? Did I just get outed to the entire school by a fucking hot or not list? Monogamy is so clearly my jam. I was with the same guy for years, even if he wasn't really with me.

The same guy who created the original Discord.

The same guy who was one of the very few people who know about my bisexuality.

I stand up fast enough that it rattles the table. It's then that I notice a lot of people have started staring at me. I flush, unsure if it's because of the noise, or because others have seen the list.

"Where are you going?" Simone asks.

"To find that asshole and rip the dashiki off him. Hopefully along with a layer or two of skin," I reply.

"Do *not* give him the satisfaction," Simone says. "Play it cool. It'll blow over."

Amayah sets her jaw before turning her attention to Simone. "How did you get this?" she asks. "I'm not seeing anyone else with it."

"Paul," Simone replies. "He found it in the locker room. I think it's getting dropped later today, maybe tomorrow."

So this is why Jason said congratulations.

Amayah lets out a wry bark of a chuckle. "Well, it looks like you've disrupted the beauty standard. You're hot."

This is not exactly how I wanted her to call me hot for the first time, but I suppose I'll take it.

"What do we do?" I ask. "BSU-wise, I've got to address *uppity* and perceptions of our hair."

But do I address making the list? Especially as an afterthought, basically because a girl *died*? And how do I address anything without bringing in the JJ of it all? Will he even let me? Damn it. He can't *let* me do anything. He isn't in charge of me. And he has decided that popularity with a bunch of assholes is worth selling me out and betraying my trust *again*.

"We win. And we use your prom speech to tear down the entire institution. We address the macro- and microaggressions, call out the administration for their lack of action, and donate the PTA's scholarship to a local mutual aid organization," Amayah says. "After everything that's happened lately, it will get covered in the local news, and the attention might lead to some changes, not only for Black students but for the girls here who have been victimized."

Okay. That I can get behind. It still means we've gone from entering the prom contest as a disruption to having to win to affect change. It's a tall order. But now I really want to win. None of this—the lists, the photos, the shaming, the insults—should happen to any other girl at Banneker. Whatever I can do to be a part of ending that, I know I have to do it.

But to do that, I still have to beat the nine girls hotter than me—and those who are ahead of me in the prom polls.

And fend off whatever has been posted about me on the new Discord, given that I've made the list.

I text Paul. **Hey. Thank you for the heads-up. Do you know what they have on me?**

He texts back. **What are you talking about?**

I look over at Simone, who looks excited, like she's discovered something substantial.

What now?

CHAPTER 22

I'VE NEVER MOVED FASTER IN THE HALLS THAN I DO between last period and the start of the BSU meeting I've called for after school. Still, I'm not the first to arrive. There's a verifiable crowd, and they stare at me.

Paul is at his perch, his hands already trained over his keyboard. He smiles at me knowingly. But *what* does he know?

"Hey," I say, sidling over to him. "Any news?"

He shakes his head. "I think they're naming Ashley soon, like this week. They're being extra secretive. Something about amendments to the list, but I don't know what."

I swallow. Confirmed, Simone lied to me again. He doesn't know. She didn't find out from Paul. And now, I have a choice to make. Do I address what I know, despite the fact that it's not public knowledge? What if it gets back to the guys, and they change it up on us? Will I look stupid?

Simone walks in, and her eyes widen when she sees me sitting with Paul. She settles in across the room from us and doesn't make eye contact with me.

Amayah seems to clock this right away, and her fingers are flying. I feel my pocket buzz with a text message. If anyone tries to come after me, she's the one I want on my side. Nothing seems to escape her notice.

JJ stomps in, the clomp of his boots echoing. He's holding Ashley's hand, but she walks a step behind him, her soft-soled ballet flats making no noise whatsoever. His gaze meets mine, but he doesn't give me any acknowledgment. Ashley glares at me.

This is going to be *oh so* fun.

The last couple of people trickle in, and I recognize that everyone is waiting for me to start. I'm the one who called the meeting, and JJ, for the first time maybe ever, is sitting in the back of the room. He makes no move to speak.

I walk to the front of the room, trying not to dig my nails into the palm of my hand. I hate public speaking. I hate having everyone look at me.

I start in. "Thank you all for making time to come to this meeting. I know it was last-minute, but I think I speak on behalf of all BSU leadership when I say that we're appreciative."

Simone claps. It's tepid, but still. I don't know if it's an attempt at an olive branch, but I am confident that I'm not sending her one.

"Anyway, I've called this meeting due to new developments in the ongoing situation of the list." I avoid looking at Ashley. "Number one is likely going to be released any day now. I have it on good authority that she will be a Black student." Now several people are looking at Ashley, who doesn't seem surprised.

I envy her confidence.

"There may be other modifications made to the list as well. However, in any case, there are sure to be some very harmful and negative stereotypes used. I think—"

"We all know that this is about me, so why don't you let me handle it? I didn't ask you to appoint yourself to speak for me," Ashley says.

JJ tries to whisper to her, and she summarily and very visibly shoots him down.

"I'm not trying to speak for you. You're more than welcome to offer your perspective. Some of the things that have been said—"

Ashley stands and strides up the aisle. She positions herself right in front of me. Of course she does.

"People," she says, glancing back at me, "have been trying to insinuate that the only way to make the list is to have incriminating, *inappropriate* material shared about you. To have sent *photos* of your most intimate parts, or texts of your most private thoughts. I'm proof that isn't the case. As someone darker than a paper bag"—she glances back at me again—"I am also challenging the perception that lighter is better." She looks at JJ for several seconds until he starts a slow clap.

"You don't have all of the information yet," I say.

She motions toward JJ, her nails clicking against each other. How does she play tennis with those?

He's holding so much tension in his jaw that I'm convinced

it might crack. He gets up and hands her a piece of paper that has been folded into a small triangle, then sits down so fast that it's almost as if he never moved.

Simone immediately looks to the floor, as JJ spares a glance in her direction. Ashley unfolds the paper carefully, like ripping it would be some kind of faux pas. She holds it up for everyone to see.

"*Number one, Ashley Beckett,*" she begins to read. It's like she has to enunciate every word while also speaking at half speed. She pauses after every third word of her pros, looking up like she's giving a class presentation.

JJ is clearly about to explode. What would be a point of pride for other guys, their girlfriend being named the hottest girl in school, is embarrassing for him. That's not the kind of attention he wants.

Bookending the list with his current girlfriend and his ex… It's almost like the guys want to piss him off for claiming to be so liberal. But why? Not a playoff grudge from three years ago. The main guys who created the list aren't even football players.

When Ashley emphasizes the word *lack* to describe the belly fat she doesn't have, I lose it.

"They said your Blackness, how dark you are, is a detriment to your beauty *and* called you uppity. Who gives a fuck about your abs?" I say.

"Are you jealous because you're only number ten by default?" she asks.

JJ's jaw drops. His face is turning from embarrassed to angry. At whom remains to be seen. If anyone should be angry, it's me for catching strays from Ashley about a list I didn't even want to be on.

Paul types faster than I've ever seen anyone's fingers move before. We really don't need a transcript of this. He's just being messy.

"No, I'm upset that they reached back in the annals of racism to describe you in slave terms, and I'm offended that they placed my complexion in higher regards than yours because it's lighter. Also, they insulted my natural hair. Not great either," I reply.

"I think we can reclaim *up*—"

"Girl, no. Do not even start," I interrupt.

"JJ, are you going to let her talk to me like this?" Ashley asks.

Simone winces, and I hear Amayah's sharp intake of breath.

"Were you actually going to say that we can reclaim *uppity*?" I ask, turning to her.

JJ's not getting her out of this one. He should want to hear her answer, given where he stands on the word.

"Why not? We've reclaimed the N-word," she replies.

"Yeah, but not when white people call us that. Are you purposely obtuse, or are you dumb?" I say.

I halfway regret the words as they leave my mouth. I don't need to dunk on her in front of this group.

JJ stands but doesn't say anything. *Oof.* As bad as I feel for what I've said, it can't be worse than her own boyfriend not speaking out in her defense, especially to his ex.

"I'm not dumb, and you're not better than me because you raise a Black power fist and post inspirational James Baldwin quotes on Instagram. I've been in the trenches here making a name for myself, becoming a leader, being respected and admired. No guy here has made me feel beautiful until JJ, but that list means that maybe, *maybe* someone else can acknowledge that I don't have to look like, well, *you* to be considered attractive," she replies.

There's nothing I can really counter there. I am lighter-skinned than her, which affords me a degree of privilege. I know that, intellectually. But I look at a girl like her, someone who embraces what I see as the worst parts of traditional femininity, and it makes me. . .it makes me feel uncomfortable and insecure.

"I'm sorry," I say. "I didn't mean—it wasn't about. . ." What can I even say to her?

"If me being someone who doesn't fit into the boxes others try to put her in, who fights against the status quo makes me uppity, then call me uppity. I don't care. Me being in the space is a revolution. Like you think being named prom queen would be. You don't like the way I do it, which is fine. And you don't like that my boyfriend likes someone you see as different from you," she says. "But I know who I am and what I want. Maybe you should figure yourself out."

She walks back and sits down next to JJ, but when he tries to take her hand, she holds her arm against her chest.

This has gone off the rails so spectacularly that I feel humiliated, even though I know that I did it to myself.

Ashley is right. I don't like how she presents herself. I have a problem with it because I see it as regressive. But to her, it's not. And clearly to JJ, it's admirable.

We've had a lot of fun at Ashley's expense as BSU members, and I'm starting to see how wrong that was.

I don't have to agree with her. But I also don't have to treat her as my opposition. I look at Amayah, hoping she can telepathically tell me how to handle this.

"Um. Wow. So yeah. Ashley isn't wrong," I say. "I apologize again, sincerely. We all have different perspectives. However, the list has caused a lot of harm to the girls of our school. So I hope that we can use this, and whatever platforms we have, to make change. A girl like Ashley, who has accomplished so much on and off the court, and is, objectively, gorgeous, should be considered beautiful without caveats, and without race being brought in."

It's a good message, I think, but it's not landing. At this point, I don't know what would, after everything that has happened.

I open my mouth to keep talking, but the door slams shut. JJ has walked out of the meeting. Ashley is still sitting there, giving me a warranted dirty look, but JJ is gone.

It has become very evident to me how badly I've messed up today, and I don't know how I can come back from this.

CHAPTER 23

WHEN AMAYAH AND I MEET UP IN THE SCHOOL LIBRARY the next morning before school, she shows me that, while I'm still in fifth place in the prom rankings, I've dropped in BSU rankings. Ashley has overtaken me in my own organization.

"Yesterday was bad," Amayah says. "I didn't think you had that in you."

I put my forehead in my hands. "I know. I wish I could take it back."

"We can figure out next steps. You apologized, took accountability. People will move on, especially once the list additions become public."

I can only hope. The one group I thought I had in the bag has turned against me.

Amayah begins showing me mock-ups of other campaign materials. Buttons, posters, even an Instagram page.

She could have a career in social media marketing in addition to campaign management. I'm lucky to get in on the ground floor before she's in demand.

Out of the corner of my eye, I see something move in the bookshelves behind us. Whatever, it's probably the heat ducts blowing air into the books, or a freshman trying to cram before a test.

Amayah pulls up a supercut video of me announcing my candidacy, stitched with several of my Instagram quote posts.

Something thumps on the floor behind us.

I turn. Nothing.

I'm just being jumpy.

I try to focus on the video, but there's still that rustling, on and off. Something darts across my line of vision again.

"Do you hear that?" I ask.

"Yeah, it's just the clock. Ticktock, whatever."

"Ticktock? That's not—"

There's a loud crash, and before I can turn to see what it is, something smacks me in the back of the head.

Amayah screams and yanks me by the arm.

What hit me was a falling book. The shelf three feet behind us has fallen to the ground, and the books have gone flying.

"There's no reason that should have fallen," she says. "Someone pushed it."

"Oh, come on," I say. "I'm sure it was an accident."

She points at one of the books, presumably the one that hit me.

When I pick it up, I almost laugh.

It's a copy of *The Other Black Girl.* I hand it to Amayah, like, *Girl, can you believe this?*

She shakes the book, and a piece of paper falls out.

I lean down. It's one of my old campaign posters, except someone has x-ed out my face. Across it, they've written THERE CAN ONLY BE ONE.

Clearly, someone wants us to think this is Ashley's doing, but there's no way. Maybe someone looking to help her, but it's not her.

"I don't like this at all," she says. "There's something really freaking weird going on here."

She's not wrong, but in this case, I think it's a stupid prank. Ashley and I are pitted against each other in many ways, mostly by our own making. But here, in a race for prom queen that no Black girl has ever won, there can only be one, even in the race. Right.

I highly doubt any Black person did this. It's too on the nose, yet completely out of touch.

Amayah snaps a photo of the defaced campaign poster and the book.

Unfortunately for us, the librarian chooses this exact moment to walk in. She shrieks when she sees us.

Never a good sign.

Amayah seems frozen. So much for her being the one to think fast in this situation.

"Thank goodness you're here!" I exclaim. "We were working, and someone knocked over the shelf. They threw a book at me too. We didn't get a good look; I think they were hiding in the stacks. We can help you clean up."

She's on her walkie before I can protest, calling for admin. The way she's looking at us, it's clear she doesn't believe me.

This is how Amayah and I end up spending the period in the principal's office.

The principal has called in reinforcements in the form of the AP and one of the counselors. At first, I think they're checking in on us, offering mental health support given everything going on. That was obviously naive of me. They're running a threat assessment. Of *us.*

They separate the two of us. I'm sent in after Amayah, who takes my place waiting in the front office, a few feet from Deborah's desk. That chair sits in front of floor-to-ceiling windows. No one pulls the blinds, so we're on display.

Another humiliation.

The principal's office is the size of the faculty lounge and has two couches, as well as an oval meeting table and chairs. The counselor, who isn't even *my* counselor, sits across from me. She leans onto the table with her elbows.

"Aida," she says in a soft, breathy tone. "Do you know why we want to talk to you today?"

She pronounces *Aida* like *Aye-eee-dah,* which isn't technically incorrect, but just *so* exaggerated. Also, not my name.

"I, *Ida,* think I know why you want to talk to me," I reply.

She nods. "And why is that?"

"Because someone knocked over a shelf while Amayah and I

were working in the library." *And you want to do a thorough investigation, right?* I know better than to actually say that.

She types for a few seconds on her laptop. "I'm just going to take a few notes."

For the investigation. To get all the information? I think.

"Of course," I say.

"And what were you doing?" she asks.

I blink a couple of times. How is that not clear from my previous answer?

"Um...I was working with Amayah on prom materials. We heard some rustling a couple of times but didn't think much of it. Then the shelf fell," I say.

"The shelf fell," the counselor repeats. "And what were you doing?"

I look over to the administrators, as if they're going to help me. How many times can she ask the same question?

"I was sitting in the library, working with Amayah on prom materials. I've said that at least three times," I reply.

"There's no need to be defensive, Ms. Carter," the principal says.

"I'm not. I'm confused. I've been very clear about where I was and what happened."

"And how do you think Ms. Lake, the librarian, feels about what happened?" the counselor asks.

She's looking at her computer, not me. Clearly, the questions are prescribed, but they're still annoying. She's treating me like a suspect.

"Probably upset, like we were. Alarmed. Annoyed at having to reorganize the books."

"And what was the reason behind your actions?" the counselor asks.

"Working on prom materials? Because it's campaign season," I reply.

"Don't be snarky," the principal says.

I'm *not*. Nothing I do will make me look *not* guilty to them.

"I want to call my parents," I reply. I am aware of my limits here, and Mom is a member of the PTA. Plus, both of my parents are uniquely adept at dealing with administrators. If admin can have backup, so can I.

"You're not in trouble. We're simply trying to learn what happened so that everyone can feel safe," the counselor says.

"Well, I don't feel safe right now. Someone targeted me for whatever reason, and now I feel like you're trying to blame me or Amayah. Neither of us have a history of anything like this. This happened *to* us, not because of us. And if you all don't want to listen to us, I'd like to have my parents here."

The counselor sighs and looks over at the assistant principal.

"If you aren't honest with us, we have to consider this as an ongoing threat. That would involve the resource officer and potentially other security measures," the assistant principal says.

"Either you can call my parents, or I will," I say. "Because this is very quickly infringing on my rights. And by not looking into who pushed that shelf over, you're compromising my safety. My parents need to know so they can figure out next steps, for both our family and within the PTA."

I fold my arms across my chest and wait. The counselor seems to be looking at additional questions that she doesn't know if she should ask. The principal and AP have started whispering to each other, just out of my earshot.

A knock on the door silences them. Deborah cracks the door open.

"Mrs. Carter is here," she says.

All three of my interrogators turn to look at me.

I shrug. Maybe Mom is psychic, I don't know. When would I have had time to call her?

The principal walks out of the room, and I can hear Mom excoriating him before the door even closes.

My phone buzzes, and I pull it out of my pocket to look at underneath the table. Amayah has sent a smiley face in a group chat. Simone has responded with a thumbs-up.

I'm back in class for next period, with unenthusiastic apologies from the two administrators.

Moms get it done every time. Especially mine.

CHAPTER 24

I'M SITTING IN STUDY HALL, REREADING THE SAME PAGE of *The Great Gatsby* over and over. My mind is still in the library, trapped between fallen bookcases. That's why I don't notice that someone is sitting across from me until she clears her throat loudly enough to earn a shush from our academic adviser.

I look up to see Lauren holding a stack of papers against her chest, watching me expectantly.

"Hey," she whispers.

"Hey. Sorry, I didn't realize..." I don't know what I didn't realize. That she was here? That she would want to talk? That there's something in her eyes that makes her look absolutely terrified?

"It's okay. I've learned to be stealthy these days," she replies.

The bags under her eyes are still visible even with whatever high-coverage concealer she has on. One of her pros on the belated pros and cons list that came out about her was her "perfect creamy skin," making it unclear whether the list architects wanted her to reveal her routine or eat her face. Right now, it looks like she's breaking out. Hopefully we don't get an amendment about how she needs to get back to her hyaluronic acid.

"What's up?" I ask, glancing over to make sure the adviser isn't watching us too closely. We're supposed to be quiet in study hall, meaning nothing over a whisper and a real effort to avoid unnecessary conversations.

Time will tell how necessary this talk is.

"Congrats on being a list alternate and top five prom contender." It's not entirely clear to me that she's being sarcastic. Her voice tends toward monotone in usual times, with only the slightest lilts to give away her true feelings. I kind of wish I had that quality. Another pro of hers: She's *mysterious*.

"Thanks, I think? Congrats on being basically the hottest girl in school," I reply.

She wags her finger. "Ah, but I'm not. Ashley Beckett takes the crown. But hopefully not the prom one."

"Why? Because she beat you?" I ask.

I need to invest in a filter between my thoughts and my words. Over the last few days, mine seems to have evaporated.

Lauren laughs, earning a look from the adviser. She mouths *Sorry* and pretends that we're sharing my copy of *Gatsby*.

"No. I fully appreciate that she's hotter than me. She certainly works harder at appearances. She's just not a girl's girl, you know? Yeah, *you know*. There's a reason that the tennis team is divided on voting for her," Lauren says.

I have to keep myself from asking what that reason is. I don't need to be concerned with Ashley, especially not after yesterday. Minding my business is my goal for the next several months.

"I assume you didn't come talk to me to throw a little shade Ashley's way," I reply.

"True. But it's always a bonus," Lauren says. "I heard about the library, and I wanted to check on you."

That's sweet, but I'm fine. There's something she's not saying. I can tell.

"Oh, um, thanks. I'm okay. It was a prank, I assume," I say.

"What if it wasn't? I mean, yeah, someone wants to mess with you, but what if it's more than just a prank?" she asks.

"In what way...?"

I think I know what way she means, but I'd rather not. I can't mind my own business if there's actually someone targeting the girls in the school.

"Cassidy and I were friendly acquaintances, in the same circles. I was at the party last weekend." She sighs.

"A lot of people were, right? What does that have to do with me?"

She gives me a curious sort of look, and I realize how terrible that sounds. *Hey, you're telling me something important about a girl who just died, and I'm only worried about what that means for* me.

"She was on antibiotics for chlamydia, thanks to Jason and his whorish tendencies. She told *everybody*," Lauren says.

Okay, still gossip. But antibiotics... I think I get what she's trying to tell me. If Cassidy was on antibiotics and telling everyone about it, then she probably wasn't drinking. That could throw a wrench in the whole she-died-of-alcohol-poisoning narrative we've been given.

"You think that someone attacked her. That it wasn't an accident," I reply.

Lauren nods. "The same person who went after Bridget in the locker room. The same person who has been watching Ashley at practice. The same person who pushed the shelf over on you."

"But why? What would be the point?"

She shrugs. "I don't know. But everyone is running scared. I have talked to every other girl on the list, and no one is willing to investigate. They want to accept the official story."

I would also like to accept the official story, but if that story is wrong, then several other girls and I are beyond screwed and maybe in danger.

"How would we investigate?" I ask. *And why should we not just focus on saving our own skin?* I think.

It's a silly thought, to be honest. I know who I am, and I've never been able to overlook what I think is injustice. If there's anything I can do to help these girls, in addition to myself, I will. It's who I was raised to be.

"Keep tabs on the girls on the list and who's hanging around them? We can meet up every couple days and trade insights? And, in exchange, I can help with your campaign. Though you have an excellent manager."

I smile at that. I really do, and I wonder how Amayah will feel about all of this. Will she go along with it? Will she think more of me if I somehow save some lives?

Fingers and toes crossed.

"Sure."

We exchange numbers and make a plan to meet up after school on Friday, before Lauren starts swim practice.

We divide and conquer: four girls to monitor for her, three for me, and ourselves of course.

I get the dubious honor to try to keep tabs on Ashley. It makes sense, since we have some social overlap, especially now that she's sort of in BSU. But it's going to suck. And it will be a pretty big challenge considering her deep-seated hatred for me.

That doesn't even take into account how JJ will react to me hanging around.

But if it keeps Ashley safe, he'll have to come around, and so will I.

CHAPTER 25

AMAYAH LOOKS AT ME LIKE I'M INSANE, WHICH, TO BE fair, I might be. We're sitting next to each other on a bench outside the school gym, arguably *our* bench, while I wait for my ride home.

She called me unhinged.

Okay, not me, exactly, but this idea. And she's seriously side-eyeing Lauren as an ally.

"No offense, but what is her interest in you anyway?" Amayah asks.

Okay...she could have put that literally any other way. Lauren's not *interested* in me; she just needs an ally.

"Offense taken. I'm the only one who was willing to address the danger in what's happening," I reply.

"I didn't mean it like that. Of course I understand why someone would be interested in you, but it's..." She sighs. "Do you really think this is a good idea? If there is someone going after girls on the list, or prom queen candidates, you could be putting a target on your back."

"Think about the library; there already *is* a target on my back. And I can't sit back while other girls are victimized. I've got to do something."

"That's part of why I like you so much," she says.

Fireworks shoot from my stomach to my throat. I think that I'm literally seeing stars. "I like you too. So much," I reply.

"I just worry about you," she says.

"Eh, I can handle myself. You haven't seen my moves," I say.

She smiles halfheartedly. It's almost as if she knows I've never actually been in a fight and would not be able to hold my own unless I cheated.

I open my mouth to add another joke, to try to lighten the mood.

Amayah leans in, almost like she wants to hear me better. She watches my lips like I'm about to make some sort of life-changing announcement.

I hold my breath as I nod.

Her lips close the space between us. Kissing Amayah is different than kissing JJ, but not in the ways I expect. Her lips are fuller and softer, yes, but she also kisses me with a tenderness that JJ never had. Mixed in is a hunger, like she's been wanting this as long as I have.

I could kiss her for hours. I *want* to kiss her for hours. I want to throw away the prom campaign, my next three AP exams,

BSU meetings for the rest of the year, everything to just keep kissing her.

She breaks the seal first, and I feel like I could cry. This doesn't have to end, right? Please.

"I should probably go," she says.

But what if you didn't? I can't be that desperate. Amayah has that effortlessly cool girl vibe that wouldn't respond well to instant clinginess. I can't act like she's my first kiss. She's not my first kiss with a girl, but she's my first kiss with this much buildup. My first long-term crush that took months to lead to this.

Years, if you count the whole time I was in denial about my attraction to her.

How do you match the coolest girl in chillness? Can I even be quippy? I've got to have a quip.

"Ah. Scared that if you don't walk away now, you'll spend the rest of the night kissing me?" I ask.

Oh my God, that was way too bold. *Why* did I say that? I swear she's smirking at me, and I don't know that it's in a good way.

"I wouldn't call that a *fear,* more like a best-case scenario. But I have a calc test tomorrow, and something tells me that your lips, no matter how nicely shaped they are, aren't going to help me with theoretical equations."

She fixes me with a gaze that nearly makes my knees fall out from under me, even though I'm still sitting.

"Should I take that as a rain check?" I ask.

"For kissing all night? Why not?"

"Would you like to be my prom date?" I blurt.

She blinks several times in quick succession. "What?"

So much for playing it cool. I haven't really considered the possibility of a prom date. Originally, I thought I'd convince JJ to go. Even starting the campaign, the idea of going to the dance didn't really resonate, let alone finding a date.

But who better to come with me than my crush, who is also the only reason I'm even in the prom queen discussion at all? There's no one else I'd rather have by my side on the off chance that I win that crown.

"Would you like to be my prom date?" I repeat.

Should I have made a poster or some other grand gesture? Amayah seems like someone who'd hate a promposal, but maybe I'm wrong.

She groans, and my stomach drops through the bench. This is quite possibly going to be the most embarrassing moment of my life, and I have literally been outed *and* gotten into a fight with my ex's girlfriend all within the last three days.

"I had a plan," Amayah says. "Okay, more like an idea. I wanted to redecorate some of your prom posters asking you to be my date, but I have been chickening out. And now you've stolen my thunder with a simple question on our bench. Rude!"

Oh, thank God. I didn't completely misread this situation. Wait—she was going to *what*?

"You were going to ask me? Me?" I ask.

"Of course I was going to ask you. I have had ulterior motives this entire time. I wanted to see the hottest girl in school win prom queen, and I wanted to be by her side when it happened."

I feel myself flush, and I take the opportunity to kiss her again.

We melt into each other, and part of me thinks that, somehow, we'll always be intertwined like this. She feels like more than high school. She feels like the first time I sat in a BSU meeting, the only time other than church where I had been around so many other Black people at once. She feels like the first time I posted a call to action on social media for a protest I'd organized. She feels like coming out and not being ashamed or scared of it.

Kissing someone who actually accepts all of me, even the parts that don't fit the pretty picture I've tried to present, feels different. It feels better.

Kissing Amayah reminds me that I deserve someone who actually likes me.

It's sad that I ever forgot that.

CHAPTER 26

TRYING TO FIGURE OUT HOW TO DISCREETLY KEEP TABS on the other girls running for prom queen is a taller order than I anticipated. I don't really know them, and given everything going on, if I start hanging around too much, it'll only draw suspicion to me. That's all I need. To become a suspect in a nonexistent murder investigation.

Whichever authorities are involved don't seem to want to admit that someone could be targeting the girls of Banneker High. That makes me even more suspicious, like who are they connected to? Is their lack of investigation a clue?

Amayah doesn't think so. She thinks it's par for the course—wanting this to all be random—instead of a targeted campaign. Admitting it's anything more means the powers that be would have to address the culture here that allows that kind of thing to proliferate.

Still, she comes up with a school-sanctioned and sort of brilliant way to infiltrate the groups we're not a part of.

The two of us want to partner with a local martial arts school, to teach a self-defense class.

In proposing the idea to the assistant principal, we frame it as a prom campaign activity. Other girls have done similar things, usually Pilates or barre. Mom even throws in a plug with the PTA, and they endorse the activity.

The school may want to deny there's something deeper going on with the girls here, but the PTA isn't as sure.

The day of our session, Amayah and I nervously affix one of my campaign posters to the wall of the classroom we've emptied. We made sure to advertise in the girls' locker room, the cafeteria, and anywhere else where we knew we'd get eyes.

We even tried to replicate some of the postings of the list to really catch the girls' attention.

I'm not sure if the plan will succeed. At least, until the first girl walks in, ten minutes early. It's Bridget Lewis, who has just returned to school after her attack.

Amayah sees her first and nudges me. It takes a gentle elbow to the ribs for me to approach Bridget.

I wave. "Hey. Thank you for coming. Um…how are you feeling?"

She runs her hand over the still-puckered scar on her forehead. "Pissed," she says. Her eyes meet mine, and there's an almost telepathic connection.

The people who are supposed to protect us here don't want to believe that she was attacked in the school, most likely by another student. Bridget has been vocal, both in school and on social media, and still, she's not being taken seriously.

"Hopefully today can help get some of that frustration out," I say. "I don't know if we've formally met, but I'm Ida."

"I know," she replies. "You dated JJ."

"You know JJ?" I ask.

She snorts. "Everyone knows JJ."

I don't have much time to consider what she means, as another two girls walk in. I recognize them from my AP history class. Neither of them are on the list.

Simone walks in next. She does a little shimmy as approaches us.

Things are still weird, but she's in my corner, and I can't really afford to lose allies. I haven't told her about Amayah, but the way she's been staring at the two of us during our lunch period makes me think she knows.

To be fair, we're pretty obvious.

I check my phone. I included my number on the fliers advertising the event, in case anyone had questions.

It was supposed to make me "accessible," but instead it's led to me getting random spam texts from, I assume, various male athletes.

There's a text from Lauren. It's a screenshot of a virtual event flier, featuring Ashley and her seventy-four upper abdominal muscles in a perfect-fitting Lululemon workout set. The caption is simple: "Learn self-defense with black belt and history maker Ashley Beckett."

The date and time are now.

She somehow booked the school gym. *And* she's having it catered by a local pizza parlor?

It's so petty, I have to respect how she's moving. She's committed to hating me, and after that BSU meeting, I don't know that I can blame her.

I tilt the phone to show Amayah, who mutters a curse under her breath.

"What do we do?" Part of me wants to storm the gym and call her out. Or, even better, attend her demonstration and be better than she is at all the moves.

I haven't played a sport outside of gym class since eighth grade. There's no way I'd be better than Ashley, an actual black belt and tennis star.

Hey, a girl can dream.

"We do our class and pretend she doesn't exist," Amayah replies. "Focus on who's here." She nods toward Bridget.

Our instructor comes in, and after an introduction to the principles of self-defense, she takes us through several steps.

There are only seven of us here, and the only girl from the list, besides me I guess, is Bridget. But Bridget is also the only person alive who has had a confrontation with whoever is after us.

We can make this work.

After forty minutes, the instructor takes questions from a couple of the other girls.

Bridget silently comes across the room and sits down next to me.

"They came after you in the library?" she asks quietly.

"Yeah. Knocked over a shelf and tried to frame someone else."

"Mine left a note telling me to stay away from Jason Miller. It looked like Cassidy's handwriting, except..." She lets the statement stand on its own. Cassidy was already dead at that point.

So, whoever is coming after us is trying to frame the other girls. It's a good idea, admittedly, but who'd have the motivation?

"Did you see anything? In the locker room?" I ask.

She reaches up and runs her fingers over the scar on her forehead, as if by reflex. "No. I heard footsteps, but I assumed it was one of the other girls or a coach. The shoes squeaked though. I remember thinking it was weird."

"Weird, why?" I ask.

"It's winter. The only girls' sports right now are indoor track and swimming. The shoes they wear when they're going to practice are typically quieter."

Random, but sure. It makes sense. The swim girls would have soft-soled shoes to wear by the pool, and the track girls' shoes should fit tightly enough and have enough traction to not be as loud.

"So you're thinking whoever it was doesn't play a winter sport?" I ask.

She shrugs. "That's my suspicion. They were superstrong too. They didn't *have* to swing as hard as they did, since they caught me from behind before I could react. It felt personal."

"Is there anyone—" I stop myself. What could she have ever done to make someone want to hurt her like that?

She snorts lightly. "You're more sensitive than the police. They wanted to know if I'd slept with someone's crush or cheated on my boyfriend. Apparently, the only motivation here can be sex."

I wouldn't be surprised if sex had *something* to do with all of this, given the nature of the list and the Discord group. But to assume that the only reason someone would go after Bridget is because she slept with someone is deeply sexist and reductive. She's also a star athlete, who I'm sure has made more than a few enemies on the field during the playoffs. She's on the honor roll too, which can only accommodate so many students. Some colleges only want the top 10 percent of the class; that's a motive right there. I guess prom could be a motive too, but who takes a plastic crown that seriously? Though the ten thousand dollars is another story.

"What do *you* think the motivation is?" I ask.

"Jealousy? I think someone didn't make the list, and they're going to pick us off until they do."

That seems far-fetched. Like, beauty is currency, especially in high school, but do girls really care about who made a stupid list? The guys who put it together are hardly the cream of the crop. Maybe they wanted their preferred guy to put them on the list.

So not about the list, but the guy.

That feels reductive too. But it's a start.

I need to figure out exactly who made the list, and who the girls on the list are linked to.

It might not be an exact science, but it's a step forward.

As the instructors pack up their mats to head out, Bridget writes down the girls on the list and their connections to the guys we think were involved.

She connects herself to some guy on the soccer team and Grayson Davis. Then, there's my name. Even though I know it's coming, I still hate seeing it connected to both JJ and Ashley.

Bridget draws another line. This one takes my breath away. I play it cool in the moment, but it changes everything.

Jason Miller is connected to Cassidy, obviously. There are also lines to him and three other girls on the list. Not surprising, given his rumored penchant for cheating. But as far as I knew, Cassidy had only ever dated him.

Apparently, that's not true.

She's connected to one other name.

It's JJ.

CHAPTER 27

I TELL AMAYAH RIGHT AWAY. PART OF ME WANTS TO keep it a secret, like I'm ashamed. I sort of am. Not because of Cassidy—I have nothing against her—but because until Ashley, I thought I was the only one he had dated. Sure, he flirted with other girls, went out on dates, but he wasn't *dating*.

Plus, I knew who he went on dates with. They were almost never girls from school, and if they were, they were never in our grade.

And they were never white.

Not that I would have had any more of an issue with JJ's actions back then if the girl was white. It's just that JJ has had *so* much to say about interracial relationships in the past. It would compromise his Blackness; it would make him less dedicated to the cause; it would undermine his activism. All sorts of notions that, while not unheard of, I completely disagree with. Him dating

Cassidy would fly in the face of all of that. And it would give him a really, *really* good motive to want her out of the picture.

It's possible that he dated her early freshman year, before he and I got together. Except he was starting on the football team at the time. People would have paid attention to his dating life. I don't know how to find out. Who would know? Her friends probably wouldn't tell me, and JJ isn't exactly chomping at the bit to talk either.

"I have an idea, but you're not going to like it." Amayah leans her elbows against the table of the diner we're hanging out in after the self-defense class.

She slides the plate of fries we're sharing closer to me.

I take one and pop it into my mouth. "Go ahead," I say with my mouth full.

She simulates horror at my lack of etiquette. "A prom queen must only chew with her mouth closed," she says in a fake British accent.

"Don't deflect. What idea am I going to hate?" I ask.

"He's not going to talk to you. So you have to bring it to the attention of someone with an incentive to get it out in the open."

I groan. I don't simply hate that idea; I think it's completely improbable. Ashley is even less likely to talk to me. Shit, Ashley wouldn't believe any of this if it came from me.

"What am I supposed to do? Dress up as the ghost of Althea Gibson and hope she listens to me?" I ask.

Amayah rolls her eyes, but in a *you're-so-silly* way, with full exaggeration. "That's an idea. I was thinking more planting the seeds on social media, or with one of the girls on the tennis team, hoping it gets back to her."

Ah. Indirect warfare. I can only think of three thousand ways this can go incredibly wrong.

"And what then? You think she'd want to help us?" I ask.

"Of course not," Amayah says. "But she still deserves to know. Plus, it gives her a motive."

That thought has occurred to me too, even though I know that logistically this new development points more to JJ than to Ashley. But I can't imagine JJ physically hurting a girl.

"Bridget did say that the person was strong and probably doesn't play a winter sport," I say.

"Which fits Ashley. Who better to take a swing than the star of the tennis team?" Amayah asks.

"I just don't think it's JJ," I say.

"Or you don't *want* to think it's JJ because that would say something about your judgment?" she asks.

Well, damn. Okay, girl. I spent so long making myself smaller, quieter to appease the person I was into, that it never occurred to me you could want to be with someone romantically and so easily call them out. Though it does give me the nagging feeling that maybe Amayah thinks my intuition is questionable and judges me for my past with JJ.

That hurts.

What defense do I have here? He has the strength and the social connections from his football days to have attacked both Cassidy and Bridget. The question with JJ is whether his social standing among the Black students at the school, particularly the BSU sect, matters enough to kill.

I grab another fry to avoid responding.

Amayah sucks in her cheeks. "Sorry. That sounded harsh."

Just a *bit?*

"It's okay," I reply.

Still placating. But at least now I'm self-aware, right?

"Is it?" Amayah asks. "It doesn't have to be."

She's giving me an opening to let down the walls, for the facade to fade. She's literally looking at me with shining eyes, and I can sense her silent encouragement.

It isn't enough.

"You're totally right though," I reply. "JJ is looking really sus." My voice has gone up half an octave, and it takes active effort to prevent it from going up even further.

It's obvious I'm lying.

Amayah pauses for a few moments, like she's considering acknowledging that she knows what I'm doing. She doesn't though. And I'm not sure how that makes me feel.

I look at the rest of Bridget's relationship connections with the list. JJ, with three of us, has the second most after Jason Miller, who is connected to a whopping six girls on the list. He's not even cute. Like truly a mediocre dude inside and out. I didn't realize that constantly negging people could land you girlfriends.

"Jason looks way worse, clearly. But is he too obvious? Like he's so connected with ex-girlfriends on the list that it would be silly for it to be him, right?" Amayah says.

"Yeah, but isn't it sometimes the most obvious person?"

"True. The latest list developments are just weird though. Of course *I* think you're the hottest. But it's pretty random that all of a sudden, after news of the Discord leaks, JJ's current girlfriend and ex-girlfriend are both named to the list. Maybe someone's trying to fuck with him?"

Great. Now I'm a pawn in someone's game to mess with JJ? Can I ever get out from under his shadow? This gets more and more humiliating by the second.

Sally Dickenson, number five on the list, breezes by our table, holding two sodas. Sally has long red hair that she keeps braided behind her head. One of her pros was that she works for the local diner, which has an old-timey, admittedly sort of short uniform for the servers to wear.

I watch as an old man reaches out and tries to touch her as she passes. She takes the smoothest slide to the side, as if by coincidence. The old man doesn't seem to pick up on it, but I see the slightest grimace cross her face.

She must have to deal with that a lot.

On Bridget's list, Sally's linked to one of the guys in the theater department. They've been together since freshman year and are basically a Banneker institution at this point.

I'm shocked she even made the list. No one else has ever had a chance with her.

Then I remember that to make the list, it's not about being an eligible bachelorette. Someone had to send inappropriate photos to the Discord.

That means her boyfriend of four years, who just asked her to prom by decorating her locker in roses, shared her private photos with countless other guys.

I feel betrayed on her behalf and confused. Does she know about the Discord group? Why would you stay with someone who did that? Though I guess I did the same thing. At least her guy was willing to define their relationship.

Well, JJ did define ours. Just not in the way I wanted.

"It's hard to end things," Amayah says, almost like she can read my mind.

Sometimes it shouldn't be. But as much as I felt mistreated by JJ, he also made me feel beautiful in a way I hadn't felt before. The only person who has made me feel like that since is sitting across from me, and even she doesn't fully get me yet.

The diner door swings open, and a group of guys walk in. I almost gag at the sight of Jason Miller, who looks completely relaxed with a broad and casual smile etched across his face. He's trailed by Grayson Davis, per usual, along with several other athletes.

Holding up the rear, making my jaw drop, is JJ.

Why the fuck is JJ here with *them*? At some point, the claim that they're blackmailing him strains credibility. He wants to hang out with these guys. These guys who willfully humiliate us.

He's one of them.

Amayah reaches out to take my hand on top of the table, and I feel myself tense.

As the group passes us, JJ makes hesitant eye contact with me.

His gaze flicks to Amayah's hand on mine, and his jaw tightens. As if he has any right to be offended.

I glare at him until the group sits down at the counter.

"Do you think Jason knows? About JJ and Cassidy?" Amayah asks.

Jason rather notoriously got into a fistfight at a lacrosse game because a guy on the opposing team was Cassidy's first kiss at sleepaway camp in eighth grade. I highly doubt he knows about her and JJ, unless this is all a setup for revenge.

"Doubt it. Should we go tell him?" I regret that last bit after I say it. Not because I don't want to absolutely obliterate JJ's bubble, but because I don't want Amayah to think I still care.

I really hate that I still care.

And I hate that I can tell by JJ's body language, the stick-straight spine, the clenched fists, that he's incredibly uncomfortable being squeezed up against the counter with this group of guys.

I especially hate that I want to invite him to eat with us to ease his discomfort. The last several years have been an exercise in trying to make JJ feel strong, feel cared for, feel contented at my own expense.

For my own sake, I have to be done with that.

Out of the corner of my eye, a sudden motion catches my attention. Then there's a crash of dishes breaking and silverware clattering to the floor. It's not unheard of, obviously, since this *is* a diner, but my head still whips around on reflex.

Sally stumbles back from the counter, her eyes wide. She holds her stomach like she's about to throw up.

JJ, who is seated closest to her, leaps up from his stool with a yelp.

"You sound like a chick," Jason says. A laugh starts to bubble out of him, but it quickly fades as he looks at Sally.

Blood seeps through her fingers, steadily dripping onto the floor. Above her hand is the handle of a knife, stuck inside her. She looks at JJ in horror as she starts to crumble.

JJ runs toward her, catching her before she collapses onto the floor.

The other guys are frozen; no one even moves to call 911.

One of the other servers starts to scream.

The other patrons start to spring into action. Several people are calling 911. A nurse is applying pressure, and a school counselor leads Sally through breathing exercises.

The whole time JJ holds on to her, looking more terrified than I've ever seen him. I wonder why for a few moments before the police show up.

Of course, JJ is the first person they want to take for questioning.

CHAPTER 28

AS NEWS OF SALLY'S STABBING SPREADS THROUGHOUT the school the next morning, I learn that not only was JJ the first person pulled for questioning; he was the only one.

The police waited until everyone had been cleared from the diner before they led him to the car. Still, even though he wasn't handcuffed, there's video of him looking like he's being perp-walked.

He wasn't arrested or formally named as a suspect, but that video links him to a crime. I can't help but think of his college admissions, and how now, if someone googles his name, those videos will come up. It's not fair.

I don't believe JJ has anything to do with this. There's no way he'd be stupid enough to stab someone in a crowded restaurant during the predinner rush. Maybe he is being set up, but why?

Sally is okay; she's in the hospital recovering. She posted an

Instagram Story thanking everyone for their support. In it she mentioned JJ as her white knight, the first person to help her.

I know that, if he was on social media right now, being called a *white* knight would have stoked his ire, because he's ridiculous. In this case, it lends further support to my belief that he had nothing to do with this.

"So you were *there*?" Simone asks as I stuff my bag into my locker.

"Yep," I reply. "It was pretty crazy."

"And JJ was with Jason and Grayson?"

"Yep."

I swear this is like the fourth time she's asked me about it. I get morbid curiosity, but it feels a bit much. Clearly, something is going on, and the girls of Banneker are in danger. It's not just gossip.

"Oh my God," Simone says.

I'm about to chide her, thinking she's being flippant about the whole thing, until I see what she's reacting to.

Ashley is walking down the hall, her fist in the air, dressed in a white *#BLM* T-shirt and a floor-length black tulle skirt. Her hair is pinned up in a tight bun, and she has a lace veil covering her forehead. She's also wearing a button that says *make HERstory*. I'd kind of love the camp of this if it were anyone else.

As she passes me, without meeting my eyes, I read the back of her shirt: *Ashley Beckett for Queen*. Underneath, she's added in Sharpie: *Honor Her King*.

Please be kidding.

JJ would be horrified by this entire display. There are more than a few chuckles as she passes our classmates, but it's almost as though she doesn't notice. Or maybe she doesn't care.

It'd be admirable if it weren't so cringe.

I swallow everything I want to say. With my luck, someone, most likely Ashley, would hear me, and then I'd be the asshole again. I can judge her choices all I want internally, but it's not for me to make those statements public.

Ashley pauses in the middle of the hallway, looks around at everyone staring at her. She slowly lowers her fist, and struts back toward where Simone and I are standing.

Until she's barely a foot away, it doesn't occur to me that she could be coming over to speak with us. After that BSU meeting, after *everything*, there's no world where I think Ashley just wants to have a conversation. If anything, I'm half expecting her to come at me with a bucket of pig blood and a withering monologue about how terrible I've been to her.

Simone is practically vibrating with excitement when Ashley stops by us.

"Hey, Ashley," she says, almost stammering.

"Hello." Ashley's eyebrows knit as if she's trying to figure out who Simone is, but she doesn't ask. She turns to me. "Ida."

"Hi," I reply. "How are you?"

Literally, what else can I say? It's the only polite thing that pops into my mind.

Ashley sighs. "Well, I've certainly been better," she says. "To have your partner treated like a criminal is— There aren't words." She puts her hand to her chest.

"I can only imagine," I reply. *Still doesn't explain why you're talking to me.*

"That's why I wanted to speak with you," she says.

Why? To remind me she's JJ's girlfriend and I'm not? Hardly the time to be bragging about that, honestly.

"If JJ needs anything, he's welcome to reach out," I say.

"Oh, he's not allowed to talk to you," she replies.

He's not…*what*? She can't be serious. At this point, she's basically baiting me to respond. He's not allowed to talk to me? That's beyond toxic. And is JJ, in his big manly man era, really going to listen to that?

"Okay," I say.

Amayah would be proud of me, even though, if someone was taping this moment, I'm sure the disgust is written all over my face.

Ashley whacks my arm, not as lightly as if she were being chill about it. "I'm kidding, obviously."

"So did you come over for jokes and games?" I ask.

She folds her hands together. She's wearing lace gloves too. What I wouldn't give to have this level of borderline delusional confidence. Wearing this outfit would give me the kind of agita that makes you think you're having a heart attack.

"Actually, I'm here on BSU business. As the first lady," she says, the whispers of a smirk crawling across her lips.

I feel Simone's fingers digging into my arm. As my best friend, she knows I can only be *so* evolved, and being erased as the longtime actual first lady of BSU in favor of Ashley is way beyond my current growth.

"Hmm," I reply, trying not to look as rattled as I feel.

"Clearly, what happened to JJ yesterday was racially motivated. BSU should release a statement defending him, since he's done so much for you. All. *You* all." Oh, she's fully smirking at me now.

"BSU will, of course, make a statement, but we wanted to make sure we had JJ's consent given that this is *his* trauma," I reply.

"Isn't it all our trauma, as children of Ham?" she asks.

Now we're getting biblical? I'm hanging on by the thinnest of threads, pulled so far back that I'm about to snap.

"Historically, JJ has been very careful with his image, so we defer to him," Simone says, at last trying to help.

"And as first lady, I speak on his behalf," Ashley says.

"You may be *his* first lady, but Ida is the first lady of BSU. Are you even a member?" Simone asks.

"You don't get to gatekeep Blackness," Ashley says, looking at me, even though Simone was the one talking.

"We're not," I reply. "I don't want to take away JJ's agency, given what happened. He was just trying to help Sally, and he was treated like a suspect. It was terrible."

Ashley's smirk fades. "How do you know what he was doing?"

Oh, come on. He didn't tell her that Amayah and I were there? What does she think he was doing at the diner with those guys? And if this is how she reacts to my simply being in the same space as him, how am I supposed to tell her about JJ and Cassidy? She won't believe me.

"Amayah and I were grabbing some food when he came in

with a bunch of the athletes. Don't worry, he didn't say anything to us. He probably didn't even know we were there," I say.

Great, now I'm placating Ashley too. Though this is more out of guilt than obligation. I've been kind of terrible to her, and I don't want to cause more drama. Plus, I sort of have to help protect her from whoever is targeting the girls on the list. Or at least keep an eye on her.

She plasters a fake smile on her face. The consummate potential prom queen. "It doesn't matter, of course. What's important is that BSU is prepared to fall in step behind him. Right?"

She's missed her calling as a mafia boss. Maybe there's still time.

"We'll do whatever JJ thinks is best," I say. *No,* actually. "We'll do whatever we as an organization think is best."

"Mmm. Remember who's the head of said organization," she replies. "*Don't forget.*"

"Got it." I give her a thumbs-up.

Her eyes flick from my face to my thumb, and she looks almost disgusted. This is going so great.

"See you at the next meeting," she replies, turning on her heel to go back down the hall.

As soon as Ashley rounds a corner, Simone snorts.

"What?" I ask.

"She's mounting a coup," she replies.

"How? She's barely a member."

Simone holds her hands up. "Just you wait."

CHAPTER 29

A MEETING INVITATION ARRIVES IN MY SCHOOL EMAIL barely thirty minutes later, requesting a BSU think session after school today. It has to be her. Who else would call it a "think session"? And what are we thinking about? Printing T-shirts with JJ's face on them?

When I walk into the meeting room, everyone turns to look at me expectantly, as if I have any idea what's going on.

Paul has his laptop at the ready, his hands hovering over the keys as I make my way to the closest seat to the front. He slowly lowers them when I don't stand in front of the board.

Amayah watches me more carefully than anyone, looking concerned, but also a little annoyed? I can't read her right now, which is almost scarier than Ashley taking over BSU. But maybe that's my own fault, given she's been pretty straightforward with me this entire time.

I'm reading too much into all of this. Amayah is just waiting for me to start talking, since she probably thinks I called the meeting. And Ashley isn't trying to kick me out of BSU; she's just worried about her boyfriend and trying to make sure to do right by him; that's why she called this meeting.

So then…why did Ashley walk in and sit down toward the back of the room, looking like she's waiting for someone else to get up in front of the group? She makes eye contact with me, despite me assiduously trying to look anywhere else besides her direction, and raises her eyebrows. She nods toward the teacher's desk, where we usually stand when we're leading a meeting.

Is JJ going to pop out of there? What is going on? And who called this meeting, if it wasn't either of us?

Simone jogs in like she's late, but freezes halfway into the room when she sees no one is leading the meeting.

The other members have started exchanging tentative glances.

What am I supposed to do? I guess I could speak up. Does it really matter who called the meeting? Our leader was probably profiled; someone is targeting girls. I have to take my opportunity. We're already ten minutes past the hour, and everyone is clearly getting antsy.

I stand, trying not to feel extremely self-conscious as all eyes land on me.

"Thank you all for coming," I say. "We have a lot to talk about, but in the interest of everything going on, it's important to have the other voice impacted by recent events up here. So, Ashley? Will you join me?"

Paul's eyes are wide, and each keystroke of his minutes-taking sounds like a grenade.

Amayah is not so subtly taping, and I wonder how exactly this will end up in a campaign video.

Ashley folds her arms across her chest and glares at me like she's angry I put her in this position. As if she's not the one who wanted me to make sure BSU did something for JJ!

But if she's not the person who called the meeting, then who did?

"I'm good," she says.

"I just think—"

"No."

Well. Okay. Not off to a great start.

"All right, noted. I'm sure we've all seen the video of JJ at the diner. It's horrifying, and an obvious example of a Black boy being at the wrong place at the wrong time. Here's what I think we should do. First—"

I'm interrupted by a bloodcurdling pterodactyl-sounding scream, so loud that it makes me jump. It takes a few seconds for my brain to settle and realize that the noise came from Ashley.

What looks like blood has pooled underneath her chair, covering her shoes. She jumps up. It's coming out of the vent behind her.

It really doesn't look like paint this time.

Something white slips out into the red.

Ashley has backed away from the vent, leaving a trail of footprints. Amayah, braver than all of us, walks over and plucks the white out of the red. It's a piece of paper.

She unfolds it and holds it out for the group to see.

Someone has written *Not a Girl's Girl* in calligraphy.

"You bitch," Ashley spits out.

It takes me a few seconds to realize she's talking about me.

"I didn't—" Why would I do something like this, especially after asking her to get up here with me? I'm not a sociopath.

"He doesn't want you anymore. Deal with it. Guys think I'm hotter than you. Big whoop. We're running against each other, and you can't handle it. I'm done acting like this is a competition. Leave me *alone*!"

She storms out of the room, leaving a trail of red footprints in her wake and the rest of BSU in a stunned hush.

Simone looks between me and the door. And if I didn't have doubts about the state of our friendship already, I would have been more surprised.

My best friend chooses the door.

CHAPTER 30

AFTER THE DISASTER OF A BSU MEETING AND THE SUB-sequent cleanup so that we aren't somehow blamed, I meet up with Lauren by the pool after her swim practice. She's still toweling off her wet hair, but the bleachers are empty.

"What the fuck?" she says, waving her phone in the air as I approach. I sent her pictures of the floor before we cleaned it up along with my SOS that we needed to talk.

"I don't know," I reply. "But this time there was a note calling her 'not a girl's girl,' so she thinks I'm behind it."

Lauren groans. "Great. Now we're being pitted against each other. Even more than we were before, I guess."

"What about you? Have you seen anything since we talked?" I ask.

Lauren scrolls through some pictures on her phone until she gets to a series from yesterday. She's in the senior parking lot, and just over her shoulder is a person-shaped shadow hovering behind her. The pictures continue over seven minutes, culminating in a short video where each time she moves closer to her car, so does the shadow. Finally, video Lauren lets out an eardrum-shattering shriek that echoes across the pool we're sitting in front of, and the shadow vanishes.

"Swimmer's lung capacity," she says, shrugging.

"Good to have," I reply. "I talked to Bridget. She had some notes on potential connections between the girls on the list and the guys who made it. Allegedly."

Lauren snorts. "We're not in a court of law, so no need to offer them the benefit of the doubt. We know who made the list. Let me see."

I hand her the list with dating connections.

She nods at some and raises her eyebrows at others. When she gets to Cassidy and JJ, her jaw slacks a bit, and she looks at me.

"I didn't know," I say.

"Yeah, I'd think that if you did, that would have come up. It must have been a long time ago, right?" she replies.

"Who knows. We were never super exclusive. At least he wasn't."

She grimaces. Then, she draws a line between her name and Jason Miller. God, he really is everywhere. She draws another line to Grayson Davis.

Well, this is juicy. She's connected to a pair of best friends and the guys who almost definitely made the list? That, coupled with the fact she has the kind of skin that companies brag about being able to give you, explain why she was so high up.

"Jason was a one-time hookup when I had lower self-esteem," she explains, even though I didn't ask her to. He seems to have some magical hold on the white girls of Banneker. "Grayson and I dated for a couple of years."

"*Years?*" I repeat.

They are two of the most popular people in school. How did they fly under the radar like that?

"Like from eighth grade through last year. We broke up over the summer. He wanted to *find himself* before college," she says.

I.e., he wanted to screw around. But with who?

"Do you know if he's seeing anyone?" I ask.

"I'm confident he is, but no, I don't know who. I've even tried flirting a little with Jason to find out, but no dice. And I have to keep what little dignity I have left."

It says a lot if someone like Lauren feels she has to flirt with one of the guys who released her private photos to try to get information on who might be stalking us.

"Bridget thinks the motive might be jealousy. Do you think that Jason or Grayson has anything to do with this? Or maybe someone they've been seeing?" I ask.

She sighs. Apparently, she's been having the same thought. "Jason is so transactional. Anyone who wanted to make the list would if they were willing to hook up with him. Grayson, less so. So maybe someone who's dating him. Especially if they know about our history."

"How many people know about you two?" I ask.

She shrugs. "Our friends. Families. When we were in it, being private felt good, you know? Like we were protecting something special. But now I can't help but feel like he kept me a secret. Like he was always waiting for something—someone—else."

I know the feeling. It's how I felt with JJ. And I wasn't wrong to feel that way, given everything I know now.

I'm sure there's plenty that I still don't know. And that almost hurts more. At any moment, the image I had of who we were together could crumble once again.

"It sucks," I reply.

She seems to think for a second. Then her eyes light up before returning to a vague kind of sadness.

"Grayson has a secret. One that would be a big motive," she says.

"Okay. What is it?"

She rubs her forehead. "I promised I'd never tell anyone."

"Well, if it could help us, I think you have to."

She flips over the list of names and dating connections and motions for me to give her something to write with.

I do and she writes one word.

Liberal.

Oh my God. Simone and I were right! We thought Grayson might be hiding something. It doesn't explain why he'd want that to be a secret; I mean, it is the twenty-first century after all. Our town is pretty progressive, even if his mom is very much not.

But it *is* a hell of a motive. If someone discovered him, he could be trying to keep the information from getting out to his own family.

Cassidy could have known if Jason did, and maybe in the wake of their breakup, she was willing to spill the beans.

Grayson was at the diner when Sally was stabbed. He was at the party with Cassidy. He's an athlete, so being in the locker room with Bridget wouldn't be out of the question.

This is the first real lead we've had, and I have to see it through.

But how?

Damn it.

I need someone who will talk to me. Someone with a foot in both worlds. Someone who has a reason to want this all to end. Someone who would be horrified that someone pretending to support BLM would come after several members of BSU and make themselves part of some sort of misogynistic mission.

I need JJ.

CHAPTER 31

AMAYAH IS SHOWING ME A PINTEREST OF PROM DRESS ideas as we lie on the floor of my bedroom. Her eyes flick through three different shades of red strapless chiffon gowns as she tries to process the information I've given her.

"Passing as a conservative? Is this 1964?" she asks. "And why would that make Grayson want to kill people? It's his own fault there's a list in the first place."

"What other leads do we have? He's keeping a huge secret, has connections to several girls on the list, and has been at several of the attack sites."

"I'm sure that could apply to a few people," she replies.

She's not wrong, but it's more direction than we've had so far. Even if it's not Grayson, the jealousy theory could mean that if we find out who he's been seeing, we might have an idea of who's behind this too.

My phone pings.

Speak of the devil. Lauren has sent me a link to Ashley's campaign Instagram. Obviously, Ashley blocked me on her personal account. But, like all good political campaigns, she's made sure that access to this one is school-wide.

I nudge Amayah and click the video.

Ashley's face fills the screen, and I wonder what ring light she's using. It hits the highlighted contours of her face perfectly. JJ is seriously punching above his weight.

"Being in this race has taught me that people will accuse you of being what they really are," she says. An image of the words *girl's girl* floats behind her. "Jealousy is a hell of a drug." A blurred-out photo resembling the one of Lauren that was released appears, as well as blurred text messages. Like the ones I sent JJ. "Stay stressed. Stay pressed. I'll stay blessed." She smiles into the camera and lifts her hand, with her fingers intertwined in someone else's.

JJ's.

Ughhhhhhhh.

I don't realize I've groaned out loud until Amayah clears her throat.

What the hell did Lauren do to Ashley besides be less hot, according to a bunch of dudes?

Catching strays? I respond to Lauren.

Like she's never sent something inappropriate, Lauren replies.

It *is* giving holier-than-thou. I'd love to respond, go tit for tat in campaign videos, but I know that I need to leave it alone. I've done enough to piss off Ashley, and none of it has made me look good. It hasn't even made me feel better. It certainly won't help me get JJ to divulge whatever information he has on Grayson or any of the other guys.

Amayah clears her throat again. God, I shouldn't be ignoring her over this bullshit.

"Sorry," I say.

"Um. You're going to want to see this," she replies, handing me her phone.

She's on Ashley's personal page, which is filled with glamour shots, professional-looking tennis photos, and sporadic photos over the past few months where she's clearly with someone else, but the person is never shown. She clicks the latest video.

Ashley sits on the floor in front of what looks like a canopy bed. She's wearing her tennis sweatshirt, and her makeup is done in that barely-there dewy style that makes clueless dudes think that girls are barefaced.

"This prom campaign has been a lot, especially since the death of my friend Cassidy Burke," she says, making sure to enunciate each word. She wipes her eye, even though I don't see a tear there. "I want to dedicate my run to her memory. She went through so much in the last weeks of her life. People underestimated her. Insulted her. Humiliated her. And she rose above, like she always did. It took its toll though. All of this does. Especially when the people you think should be on your side, your fellow girls, your fellow queens, want to tarnish your memory. Lies about Cassidy will not be tolerated. That's why I'm speaking out to deny the rumor that one of my competitors is trying to start. My boyfriend had nothing to do with her, ever. Start focusing on what's important, and stop trying to drag us down."

The video ends.

She's got to be kidding me. I haven't said anything. And posting this when she knows I can't follow her because I'm blocked? Coward. Just say it to my face.

How does she even know? Did Bridget tell her? Why would she? None of this makes any sense.

"Whatever this stunt is, it's not winning her any votes," Amayah says, refreshing the campaign polls.

"Who tipped her off?" I ask. "And what are the odds that she's wrong about JJ and Cassidy?"

"I don't know. But I maybe just invited JJ over here to tell us."

I gape at her. "You *what*?"

My parents are downstairs, and they haven't seen JJ since our breakup. How exactly are we supposed to confront him before they do? If he even shows up.

"We need to know the truth, and right now, he's the best source we have. He has no reason to lie to you at this point, and every reason to lie to her. Let's settle this once and for all, and see what he can tell us about Grayson. They used to be friends, right?"

Right. Until they weren't. Which seemed to coincide with JJ quitting the football team. It's compelling, but it all feels too farfetched, and having to rely on JJ to clear things up doesn't exactly appeal to me.

I've always trusted him, even when I clearly shouldn't have. Asking him to explain is basically giving him an invitation to break whatever faith I still have in him.

Well, if I'm already assuming he's going to lie, I don't have that much faith left in him to begin with.

JJ lives up the street, so if he's home, he could be here any minute. When Ashley does a simple location check, she's going to be *pissed*. He'll probably have to move.

The doorbell rings, and I jump up. He couldn't text that he was outside and, like, hide in the bushes or something? Does he *want* to face Mom and Dad? Dad's pretty safe, actually. It's Mom he should be worried about.

"JJ!" Dad booms from downstairs.

I jog out to the hall and lean over the banister to see what's going down.

"Mr. Carter," JJ says, reaching out his hand. He looks up and spots me watching.

Mom walks over, and she clears her throat. "JJ."

"Mrs. Carter," he says. "Good to see you."

"Hmm," she replies, and I hear Amayah snort behind me. "How can we help you?"

Damn. Imagine how much she would hate him if she knew the reason we broke up. She'd probably bury him the backyard.

"I wanted to see Ida," he says.

"I'll grab her," Dad replies.

"Does she want to see you?" Mom asks.

Amayah whistles behind me. Geez, Mom really does not play

about me. I'm grateful and also wondering how far she's going to take this. Is she going to kick him out?

"Yes, ma'am. She and Amayah wanted to talk about BSU and prom," he says.

He sounds downright timid. Maybe I need to start channeling Mom's energy when I deal with him. All that bluster and bravado is gone. He's practically sheepish.

Amayah gives me a little push toward the stairs.

Ugh, fine. I'll interrupt the show. I walk as slowly as possible, knowing JJ can still see me.

"Ah," Mom replies. "Coordination can be good. Though the two of them going to the dance together will be enough of an event."

My jaw drops. She dropped that so casually, knowing it was a barb at JJ.

"Yes, their friendship really has changed the face of prom this season," JJ says, sounding so stilted it's like he's reading the statement from a teleprompter for the first time at knifepoint.

"Friendship," Mom repeats, and it's laced with such incredulity that even Dad thinks it's time to step in. He gently takes Mom's arm, as if he's going to lead her back into the living room.

I barrel down the rest of the stairs. "Hey, JJ, come on up," I say. "We'll keep the door open," I add for my parents, lest they think anything nefarious is going on. Plus, the door is already open.

"I wasn't concerned," Mom says coolly.

Oh my *God*. "Mom!"

Dad is visibly trying to hold in his laughter. He is enjoying this way too much; Mom is almost out of pocket.

Mom holds her hands up and shrugs. "What?" she asks innocently.

We're probably going to have to talk about this later, but I am not upset to see JJ looking so embarrassed and uncomfortable.

My heart also swells a bit knowing that Mom is supportive of me and Amayah. If anything, it should be a wake-up call for JJ going forward, that you can actually accept the people you claim to love without conditions and expectations of how they should be.

"Good to see you both," JJ says to my parents, even though it very clearly hasn't been that good for him.

He follows me upstairs, where Amayah is now sitting on my bed. His eyes flick from the bed to her, and his eyebrows start to twitch.

"Want to sit, babe?" Amayah asks, smiling at me. *Babe?*

JJ winces. Ah. That's why she did it.

"Of course, hon," I say, plopping down next to her.

"Did you call me over here to rub *this* in my face?" he asks.

"Rich, given that *your* girlfriend has tried to mount a hostile takeover of BSU and is using your relationship and arrest as fodder for her prom campaign," Amayah says.

"Well, I asked her not to," he replies.

I bite my tongue. Then when I want to retort even more, I bite deeper. He asked her? He *asked* her? He rarely asked me anything. Our relationship featured an almost pathological number of passive aggressive "suggestions" that were really just vague ultimatums.

Has he grown and actually learned something about how to treat a partner, or did I somehow bring out the worst in him?

"We have questions for you," I say, trying to push the self-deprecating thoughts away.

"About my girlfriend? No thanks."

"About freshman year. About quitting football. About some of the people you were hanging out with," I reply.

"I can't do anything about the new Discord, okay? You're not even on there. Can we just drop it?" he asks.

Amayah and I exchange a look. We knew there was a new Discord, but JJ's involvement was murkier. He knows about it and what's on it. Interesting. And what does that mean for Ashley? Is he sharing her pictures, or are they already there?

Important questions, but not right now. Right now, we need to learn more about Cassidy, Grayson, and whatever connections there may be between them.

"It's not about the Discord either," I reply. "It's about Cassidy Burke."

I watch him to see if there's a change in his face. A twitch, a microexpression. Anything to indicate that she meant something to him, even if it was a long time ago.

He shakes his head. "Why would you ask me about Cassidy Burke? Are you trying to learn about Jason? Spoiler: What you see is what you get."

Is that a waver in his voice?

"Freshman year, when you were on the football team, were you hooking up with her?" Amayah asks.

JJ startles, his eyes going wide. "No. Why would you think that?" He looks to me, as though I'm going to save him.

"So you hooked up with her while you were with me and preaching the potential dangers of interracial relationships?" I ask.

"Fuck!" he says.

God, he's so easy to needle. I've never thought he was the one attacking the girls on the list, but this almost confirms it for me. Sure, he has the spurt of anger, but he's transparent. Three good interrogation questions, and he'd spill it all.

"Ah, is that what you did with—" I begin.

"Stop it, Ida. *Stop*. No. We're not going there," he replies.

"What's the problem, JJ? Your hypocrisy?" I ask.

"I never hurt her. Not even after what she did, I would never. I can be an asshole, but I'm not abusive. I'm not a killer. You really think I could... I wouldn't."

He's tearing up, and I can't tell if it's from being discovered or because he cares what I think about him. Well, there's no way it's the latter.

"What did she do? And what did *you* do? Then I'll decide what I think," I say.

"Let it go," he replies.

"No," I say.

"Tell us before we have to ask Ashley. I'm sure she'd have ideas," Amayah adds.

JJ flinches, and I have to wonder what their dynamic is. Ashley gives off tradwife vibes, but by the way he's reacting, I think she's more of a dominant force in their relationship than I ever was.

Good. He needs someone who can put him in his place. I hate that there's a girl willing to throw herself into that role though.

"JJ, she *died*. I'm being targeted. So is Ashley. So are eight other girls. We need to know everything so we can protect ourselves. So we can protect everyone. Including you, considering that you're now a suspect given what happened to Sally. If anyone else found out about you and Cassidy..." I let the rest of the statement speak for itself. If, say, the cops found out about him and Cassidy having some kind of relationship, he'd be public enemy number one, regardless of his involvement.

I'm sure guys like Jason Miller would be more than happy to make sure that JJ was well positioned at the bus they'd throw him under.

He closes his eyes for a few seconds. When he opens them, there's a kind of steely resolve, and I feel my stomach drop. He's not going to tell us anything.

"I've been wondering if... I don't know. Yes, I started the Discord, but I didn't make it what it became. And Cass—I wasn't the last person she pissed off."

Ominous.

"Do you know who is?" Amayah asks.

"Of course not," he replies.

"What did she do to you?" I ask.

He sighs. "When I was on the football team, I used to hang out with Jason, Grayson, Lauren, and Cassidy. She and Jason always had that will-they-won't-they thing going on, which was more on him than her. She and I had similar senses of humor." At the look on my face he adds, "Don't look at me like that. I have one of those."

"*Do you?*" Amayah asks.

He rolls his eyes. "Anyway, in one of their won't-they phases, we started hanging out. We made out a couple of times, until Jason found out and finally asked her on a date. Then she dropped me."

JJ has an ego, but being dumped, especially freshman year when he wasn't as jaded, wouldn't piss him off that much. There's more to this story.

"Still not answering what she did to you," I say.

"Well, while we were make-out buddies, she was all about fighting the power. She was...she was the one who suggested that I kneel. And then when I did, she was one of the first people to call me disrespectful."

Oh my God, I remember that. She was posting all these Instagram Stories about how we have to respect the flag and how, as the daughter of a veteran, she was offended.

And all along, it was her idea? The move that earned JJ his position within BSU, that radicalized him, was at the suggestion of the white girl he was hooking up with?

That getting out is more of a motive than anything. Forget Grayson. JJ's entire identity for the past three years has been that one incident and everything that happened afterward.

"And if people knew that, you'd look even worse. It'd ruin your reputation," I say.

"I didn't kill her," he replies. "If anything, I'm grateful to her now. She may have wanted to screw me over and get me kicked off the team, but if she hadn't, I wouldn't be where I am."

It's an oddly optimistic way to look at what blew up the entire social ecosystem he'd built, but I find myself believing him. As many qualms as I have with how JJ operates, I know that he's happy with who he is. And isn't that worth something?

"What about Grayson?" Amayah asks.

His eyebrows knit together. "What *about* Grayson?"

Given that I've now seen him in Grayson's orbit more in the past couple of weeks than I have since freshman year, the disgust in his voice surprises me. I knew they weren't on *good* terms necessarily, but I didn't think there'd be this much vitriol.

"There are some rumors—" I begin.

JJ rolls his eyes. "Those rumors have been around forever. They're unfounded. He thinks he's socially liberal, but he's not."

His voice is steady, but there's something in his clipped tone, the evenness of his response that makes me question him. But what reason would he have to lie about Grayson? Or lie for him?

I make eye contact with Amayah, and she nods. At least we're still on the same page. It seems like maybe she's the only one these days.

"It would be in his best interest to keep it quiet, though, if he were, right? He's always riding the fence between guys like Jason and guys like you," I say.

"Fence riding is a generous way to put it," JJ replies.

"Did he share the Discord? Freshman year? Did he start adding pictures?" I ask.

JJ closes his eyes for a few seconds. "Yes. And yes."

And, based on the timeline, those pictures were probably of Lauren. Grayson is officially at the scene of every crime. Both literally and figuratively.

Now, we just have to figure out what else he's been up to lately. And with whom.

CHAPTER 32

OBVIOUSLY, MOM WANTS TO BE THE ONE TO HELP ME pick out my prom dress, but we strike a deal. Amayah and I will preview a few at the mall, and then Mom will be a deciding vote for the final choices.

Spending my Saturday at the mall isn't exactly at the top of my list of fun activities, but spending it with Amayah makes my heart skip more than a few beats. Her fashion is so casual and cool that I think she's going to take me to some hole-in-the-wall boutique relegated to the back of the first floor of the mall, where they dump all the stores no one really cares about.

Instead, we're in a big-name department store, walking through their display of prom dresses. The enchantment of the moment fades when I'm confronted with a canary yellow monstrosity covered in ruffles and sequins. It's as if Big Bird rolled around in a bath of glitter.

I think I'd lobby for whoever's been attacking us to take me out if I had to wear that in public.

We stop in front of the largest rack of dresses. We're not alone; I see at least three other girls from Banneker flipping through the hangers.

Amayah chuckles to herself.

"What?" I ask.

"Your face is loud as hell right now," she replies.

I suck in my cheekbones and narrow my eyes. When Amayah barks out a laugh, I recognize that my attempt to look a little more neutral and discerning is not working.

"These aren't really..." I lower my voice. "My thing."

Amayah smiles. "I know. But you also had literally no input on what you'd want to wear, so we're starting big, seeing what features you don't hate, before narrowing in on some dresses you could actually like."

Oh, thank God. Though I feel hard-pressed to identify anything I don't hate in this display, besides the girl who brought me here.

"Well, what are you wearing?" I ask.

"I'm chivalrous, so I need to know your outfit first. And I'm totally not letting you see until prom. I'm committed to making your jaw drop."

"Well, you do that anyway," I say, grinning at her.

She takes both of my hands and pulls me into her chest. I stumble and nearly kiss her by accident. Then, I lean in to do it on purpose.

Just before our lips touch, there's a whir of movement. I pull back reflexively and try to ignore the hurt that flashes across Amayah's face.

One of our classmates is staring at us, looking more than a little surprised. But they're not the movement I saw.

That person is parked behind the rack of black blazers a few feet away. I can't make out any distinguishing features, and every time I think I can see, they burrow deeper into the clothes.

"Yep, it's how it looks," I say. I take Amayah's hands in mine and lean into her. "I think someone's watching us," I whisper.

"Yeah, you literally just spoke to them," she replies, louder than I wish she would have.

"Not there," I whisper. "*There.*" I dart a glance over to the rack.

Amayah's head turns way too obviously.

Whoever I saw there is gone, and I can sense Amayah fighting the urge to call me paranoid. She probably thinks that this is me being insecure about us being out and queer in public.

But I know what I saw. Someone was watching us. And this isn't the first time.

I shoot off a text to Lauren. **Lurker spotted @ mall. Suit section of Nordstrom.**

She responds immediately. **WTF?? Lurker under the bleachers at my swim meet 15 mins ago.**

I show the message to Amayah, who mouths, *More than one?*

Do you think I start typing. I pause, then delete. We're suspicious of Grayson, yes, but can I really ask Lauren if she thinks her ex-boyfriend is stalking me? Banneker is also thirty minutes away. Whoever was lurking here at the mall couldn't be the same person at the swim meet.

Could it be I delete it again.

I think mine was a girl, she says.

She offers nothing else, and I don't really know how to follow up.

I'll keep an eye open here. I couldn't tell w/ mine.

Have fun, she responds. **Can't wait to see what you pick.**

Whoever it was is gone, and it's not like I'm going to find them in a store this big, let alone in the entire mall. I have to wait until they pop up again, which seems inevitable.

Amayah pulls out an evergreen ball gown with a tulle skirt and a turtleneck.

I know that this is mostly a reconnaissance mission, but I still feel a jolt of insecurity. What if she's showing me things she actually likes, and I shit all over them? Would she like me less?

"Be honest," she says. "Features you like, features you don't."

Ironically, the thing I hate most about this dress is that it reminds me of something JJ would have wanted me to wear. Sure, he didn't dictate how I could dress, because that would have been red flag central, but he definitely made it known when he thought something was too much or too little. Too distracting for his lieutenant to be wearing.

"It's conservative," I say.

"Is that a good or bad thing?" She adds, "I'm not JJ. I'm not coming in with expectations."

"How did you—"

"I don't know that I ever saw your clavicle when you were dating him," she replies.

She's not wrong.

"I like the color, though it's not particularly springy. The tulle is a little frilly for me. The turtleneck could work, but I'd want the dress to be sleeveless." The words flow out of me like I've been hiding the *Project Runway* judge inside myself my entire life.

With JJ, we were always about the mission. Things like fashion, despite the fact that JJ arguably has more clothes than most people I know, were frivolous. I'm starting to see that he had different rules for he and thee.

Amayah holds out a black dress, no tulle, with a V-neck but the same thick ball-gown-esque skirt and a bit of sparkle.

"It's giving chic funeral," I reply. "I'm ambivalent on the ball gown. Don't hate the sparkle as long as it's subtle."

"What about the V-neck?" she asks, her eyes flicking down toward my chest.

I feel heat everywhere her gaze lingers.

"I don't mind it," I reply. "If you think I can pull it off."

She chews on her bottom lip. "Cruelty doesn't suit you." She's visibly starting to flush.

"Well, what's cruel about it?" I ask, sounding halfway breathless. "And how deep do you think I could pull off?"

She pulls out a pastel pink midlength dress with a thin V that seems to hit almost at the navel and raises her eyebrows.

We don't have a school dress code, and this doesn't actually show that much cleavage, but I'm pretty sure I'd end up in trouble regardless. Plus, there's no way that Mom, as a member of the PTA, would let this one fly, given what the other parents could say.

"Pink isn't my color. I like the length. I'd love that neckline on you instead," I say.

She snorts. "That neckline wouldn't do much for me, and that length would make me look shorter than I already am."

"Well, I wasn't thinking about what the neckline would do for *you*," I reply.

She fixes me with a look so intense that I could buckle at the knees right here. "Don't start something you can't finish," she murmurs, before turning back to the dress display.

God, I really want to get out of here. But she's showing no signs that we can be liberated from this endeavor anytime soon.

At the very least, we could make out in the dressing room. Throw a girl a bone, right?

Next is a canary yellow mermaid-style dress that flares out at the knee. I always thought that yellow washed me out. JJ insisted that it would look good, but I never tried it.

"I'll try it on," I reply. Not for him, but because seeing how it looks is a step forward for myself. It's bold, it's different, and those are things I'll have to be if I want to make it to the stage on prom night.

She pulls it off the rack, and we keep making our way through the dresses.

"There you are!" Mom walks toward us, already holding four different shopping bags despite the fact that we've barely been in the building for an hour.

As she approaches, I realize just how closely I'm standing to Amayah. Our shoulders are overlapping, and we have our free hands intertwined. I almost drop her hand, but at the smile that breaks across Mom's face, I remember I don't have to hide. There's nothing to be ashamed of here.

"Hey, Mom."

"I thought I'd see how the search is going."

"It's going well," Amayah says. "We're trying to figure out what Ida's style is. Casting a wide net."

"And what about your style?" Mom asks.

"I want to see what my date is wearing first," she replies.

Mom does a kind of shoulder shimmy, and I'm not sure I've ever seen her beaming more. She's visibly thrilled, and it makes me want to cry a little but in the best way.

"You two are going to look *incredible* together. Not to pit girls against each other, but no one could possibly compare," she says.

Her enthusiasm is contagious. We really are great together, and the kind of happiness I feel around Amayah has to be apparent to anyone around us.

"Thank you," I say. *It means a lot,* I think to myself, but I'm sure she already knows.

"Oh, you won't believe who I saw in that boutique over by the first-floor garage," she says.

I brace myself for her to say that JJ and Ashley are here shopping too. That boutique is the only black-owned one in the mall, and JJ definitely has gotten several of his dashikis there.

"Was she tall, pretty, and accompanied by a box-dyed redhead?" Amayah asks.

Mom raises her eyebrows. "Why would Simone have been with JJ? She was with her *boyfriend*." She says it playfully, just like a teasing Black auntie would. And like someone who thinks I already know.

A creeping sense of dread starts to build. Sure, Simone and I haven't been remotely on the same page lately, but it's only been a few weeks. I would have known if she had a boyfriend, unless she was very deliberately keeping him a secret.

"And what did you think of him?" I ask.

"I texted her mom for the deets. You kids still say *deets,* right? Anyway, she said they've been together since the end of summer. They're cute. He's tall too, and there's definitely something there, even if he does look on the paler end. They were holding hands, and I even saw them kiss."

"Did she introduce you?" I ask, my throat absolutely arid.

"Oh, she didn't see me. He looked familiar though. Maybe you hung out with him? Or he was friends with JJ? I don't know. He's an athlete; he had on his letterman jacket. The back said Davis. Hopefully not our esteemed PTA president's Davis."

There it is.

Grayson has had a secret girlfriend, post-Lauren. It's my best friend.

What do I do now? Simone couldn't really be behind all that's happened. Not her. She can barely kill a spider. She literally hates true crime as a genre and in actuality.

None of this feels like her.

But then again, I wouldn't have thought it was like her to keep secrets and lie to me. So what do I know?

Maybe I've never really known her at all.

Amayah sets the dresses we've picked out down on the nearest surface. There's no way I'm picking out a dress right now.

Mom keeps chattering, completely unaware that my heart has started beating out of my chest.

Amayah snaps photos of the contenders on her phone, so we can revisit, I assume.

Meanwhile, I text Simone. **We need to talk.**

@ the mall, grabbing sneaks. Lunch? she responds immediately.

See you there.

CHAPTER 33

I CORNER HER IN THE FOOD COURT, WHERE SHE'S standing in between the Cinnabon and the Sbarro, making her eternal calculus: sweet or savory, pizza or dessert. She always chooses both. It's a fake choice. Unlike the very real one I'm about to ask her to make.

"Okay, so garlic—" she starts.

"Who are you here with?" I ask, cocking my head to the side.

She looks around, as though she's trying to spot a hidden camera. As though I'm the one who has something to hide.

"What do you mean?" Confusion flits across her face, but there's a twitch, a nearly imperceptible movement of her features that tells me the real truth. She's scared. And I take a weird sort of satisfaction in that. She *should* be scared. After everything she's done to throw our friendship into jeopardy, I hope she'd still care enough about me to realize how horrible this is.

"Who are you shopping with?" I ask.

"I— Why?"

"Who the fuck are you here with?" I ask, my voice starting to rise.

A few people turn toward us, and Simone recoils before pulling me into a nearby corner by the Panda Express.

The smell of what passes for orange chicken mixed with the nearby bathroom makes me want to gag. Or maybe that's because of what I know about Simone and who she's been spending her time with.

"What is wrong with you?" she whispers.

"You're deflecting."

"Who are *you* here with then?" she asks.

"Amayah. See how easy that is?"

"I thought *we* were going to shop for prom dresses together," she says.

It's a tiny dagger to the heart. She's right. We always planned to shop together along with our moms. Until Amayah took over my prom campaign, that was the idea. At some point I think I forgot.

Guilt springs up inside me. She's been keeping a huge secret, but I've been pulling away too. I might object to her choice of boyfriend, but I can't pretend I don't know why she didn't tell me. At least not if it's new.

But wait… Mom said *end of summer*. That was before me and Amayah. I was still with JJ at that point, at least for a minute.

"I thought you would have told me if you were dating someone, especially if it started over the summer," I say.

"It started right when you and JJ were on the rocks. I didn't want to rub it in."

JJ and I were always on the rocks. It's not the best excuse.

"You didn't want to rub it in because you were happy or because you knew that JJ, and I by extension, would be upset that it was Grayson?" I ask.

"Yes."

"He's how you've known about who was going to be on the list," I say, remembering the reveal of the top choice. Of my reveal.

"Yes."

"He's the one who shared my old messages to JJ. Who made news of the channel public," I say.

"We haven't talked about it," she replies.

But by the hurt in her eyes, I know that he is. He's the start of all of this. But is he the end? Or could she be?

"What else don't you want to know about your boyfriend?" I ask.

"He's a good guy."

"Yeah, that's why you never told me about him, right?" I ask.

I'm horrified that I've started tearing up. We've both been avoiding this conversation. Confronting each other. Being honest for the first time in what feels like a long time.

She squeezes her eyes closed for a couple of seconds, and when she opens them, a tear falls down her cheek.

"He's religious and I—"

And there's the real dagger to the heart. The explanation I've been waiting for that makes it one million times worse.

"You wanted me to keep my sexuality quiet so that your new boyfriend wouldn't find out and judge you for it?"

She hangs her head. "I'm so sorry."

"You were my friend first. We were—"

"I was scared. I like him so much, and I thought maybe—people evolve, right? I was going to make him evolve."

"How can you like someone who would have to change their beliefs to accept your best friend? That's incompatible. That's—unless you believe it too. You're ashamed."

"Never! It was just out of nowhere, and I thought maybe it was a phase; I didn't want to… You and JJ were just always so… It's such a different direction."

I thought that JJ was heartbreak. Even though I was the one who ended it, we were on life support longer than I cared to admit. His rejection of me was a rejection of who I fundamentally am, even though I'm more than who I'm attracted to. Even though we were a mess. Even though he hooked up with other people. Even though he wouldn't put a label on our relationship.

I thought I could change him too. Make him believe that I was worth the commitment. And I couldn't. Simone saw that. And she went and found someone we both know to be more intractable than JJ. And, somehow, more hypocritical.

What kind of friendship is that?

"And now? What do you think?" I ask.

"I love Amayah; she's awesome."

"And the two of us together?"

Simone hesitates.

That's enough for me. I don't need her to answer, and by the time she tries to, I cut her off with a wave of my hand.

"I support you!" she says. "Love is love."

"Ask your boyfriend if he thinks that. Ask him who he's going to vote for when we turn eighteen. Ask him who deserves to get married."

"That's not fair! I'm not my boyfriend," she says. "You're not giving me a chance."

"You've had your chance for months, and this is how you choose to affirm me? To accept me? With fake platitudes and silent judgment? Keep your chances. I'm done."

She calls after me as I walk back into the food court.

I pretend I can't hear her. The same way she pretends that she's not cosigning her boyfriend's shitty views and actions.

If she can ignore the obvious, so can I.

CHAPTER 34

AMAYAH AND I SIT IN SILENCE BESIDE EACH OTHER ON the floor of my bedroom, halfheartedly flipping through the photos we took of potential dresses. Neither of us really knows what to say. In reality, what *can* we say? This is one of those moments when words fall short.

The full scope of the betrayal still hasn't set in, even though I'm ten times more heartbroken than I was over JJ. I loved him. I was in love with him. But I loved Simone more. Her friendship meant more to me than any other relationship. And now it feels like I'm the only one who felt that way.

Mom, driving us home, could tell something was up but didn't try to engage us beyond chatter about what we were thinking dress-wise. I'm certain that once she gets on the phone with Simone's mom, things will be different. But how?

Amayah leans her head into my shoulder. "It's sort of a shitty rite of passage to come out as a queer person and find someone you love isn't...the most supportive," she says.

"Who was yours?" I ask, as a tear finally plunks down onto my lap.

"My brother."

I didn't even know she had a brother, which doesn't inspire confidence in me as to where their relationship is now.

"Did he come around?" I ask.

She shrugs. "He deployed eight months ago."

There's no further clarification, and I don't think I need more. If he had accepted her, this would be the time to tell me.

There's a soft knock on my bedroom door. Mom is standing there, her mouth pursed into a tight line, and her phone clutched in her left hand. She looks flushed.

That phone call definitely just happened, and I don't think it went well.

Amayah pushes herself up. "I can head out—"

Mom shakes her head. "Of course not. If Ida wants you here, I want you here."

"We don't need to talk about it," I say, as Amayah sinks back down beside me.

"I understand that you probably don't *want* to talk about it, but we need to," Mom replies.

She comes and sits down with us. She smiles sadly when she sees the canary yellow dress on the screen. Oh God. The conversation must have gone *really* badly. Mom has always referred to this shade of yellow as "something you should only entertain on Easter Sunday when you're five."

"How many excuses did she make?" I ask.

Mom snorts and throws her voice up half an octave, in a perfect imitation of Mrs. Brown. "'At this age, the girls are just trying to find themselves. Why is Ida's experimentation any more valid than Simone's? The Bible *does* say it's Adam and Eve, if we're being technical.'"

Amayah groans loudly.

"Since when are the Browns religious?" I ask.

"They're Christmas and Easter Christians. I've literally never heard her express anything like this before. I think she's trying to be supportive of Simone, but it's—I don't care. If you suddenly decided you wanted to have terrible views because of who you were dating, I wouldn't be sticking up for you with my best friend. I'd give you your space to grow, but best believe I'd have a glass of wine and a lot to say," Mom says.

I realize, once again, that I should appreciate Mom more. She has always allowed me to figure out who I want to be, giving me guidance when needed but letting me make mistakes. She knew wasting my time with JJ wasn't the best idea, and she let me know, in her own way. But she didn't stop me. And I know she talked to Mrs. Brown about it, because Simone definitely parroted those talking points at me. Which feels especially rich right now. I get that we're all learning what we believe, but choosing a homophobe over her best friend? It couldn't be me.

It wouldn't be.

It reminds me of JJ choosing to date someone who allegedly has completely different beliefs, and holding it over all of our heads, like we're the unevolved ones. People can grow, but this all feels like regression to me.

Or maybe this is who they've always been. Maybe they've never really accepted me, and they needed that push to show it.

"So we've both lost best friends today?" I ask.

"I did cuss her out so...yeah, probably," Mom says.

She sounds so casual. Does it hurt less when you're older? Like life is short; none of this matters? Or is she putting on a brave face for me?

"We'll be okay," I say. "Right? Better off without them?"

"We'll be okay," she replies. "But that's not the only reason I wanted to talk to you. Both of you."

Uh-oh. What else could she possibly have to say? Does the PTA know what has actually been going on at Banneker?

"Both of us," Amayah repeats.

Mom nods. "It's come out, just a few minutes ago, that Cassidy Burke died after taking fentanyl. Her parents are insisting that she'd never take fentanyl independently."

"They think someone dosed her?" Amayah asks.

"Yes."

Amayah and I exchange a look. So whoever has been attacking

us girls had to have been at the party with Cassidy. And has to have access to fentanyl.

A doctor's kid? Or whoever secretly deals drugs? There's always someone.

"Who?" Amayah asks.

Mom closes her eyes for a couple of seconds. "Right now, the finger seems to be pointing at two people."

Just two? There have to be more people with access to fentanyl than just two people. In fact, I'm pretty sure someone like Jason Miller could find drugs pretty easily. He certainly has no problem finding kegs and Fireball to bring to house parties, from what I've heard.

"Who?" I ask.

"JJ and his girlfriend," Mom replies.

Oh fuck. JJ's mom is a pharmacist, and Ashley's dad is a psychiatrist at the local hospital. I see how they'd be suspects, but I don't believe they care about prom *that* much. They can't. Right?

My phone pings.

Lauren is sending me panicked texts.

Whoever has been following us has been spotted in her backyard, and she's home alone.

I tilt my phone to Amayah, who nods slowly before excusing herself as subtly as possible.

I can't let her go by herself. But how am I supposed to cut this conversation with Mom short without looking suspicious?

Mom's phone starts buzzing, and she glances at it. Her face

darkens. It's Mrs. Brown calling. Damn, how much more could Mrs. Brown have to say?

I guess that doesn't matter. It's a way to end this conversation. If anything, it will keep Mom busy for at least an hour because, God love her, she's long-winded, and Mrs. Brown loves to monologue too.

"You should get that," I say. "Maybe we don't both have to lose our friends."

Mom looks at her phone again. Mrs. Brown appears to be keeping her finger on that call button.

"And we have a couple of prom things to work on at Amayah's place," I add. "If that's okay. It shouldn't take too long."

Mom unenthusiastically nods, her eyes still flickering toward her phone.

She takes a deep breath before putting the phone to her ear. The moment she steps out of the room, I bolt up.

For good measure, I grab the nearest heavy thing I can find, which happens to be a participation trophy from my elementary soccer days.

Hopefully I won't need it.

CHAPTER 35

AMAYAH CUTS HER CAR'S ENGINE HALF A BLOCK FROM Lauren's house. I tuck the trophy into my armpit. The end is a little pointy, but my best bet would probably be to swing. I think. It's not like I typically find myself in this position.

Amayah reaches into her back seat and, adding to the lore of things I didn't know about her, she pulls out a violin case. Unfortunately, it's a soft one. She unzips it and grabs the bow.

At my raised eyebrows, she says, "Viola. Second chair. No big deal."

I don't know what second chair means, but I assume it's something good. And that bow looks sharp and springy.

I text Lauren, who immediately responds that she's in the kitchen, hiding down by the sink.

Amayah leaves the car first and motions for me to stay behind her. For a moment it crosses my mind that this is kind of hot. The girl I'm into is fully prepared to protect me in whatever this is.

Then I remember that, if this is like a horror movie, the queer girls die first, and the Black girls die even earlier. Now I feel sick and like my legs are stuck in quicksand.

Amayah tugs at my hand. "We've got this. You took a self-defense class."

I snort. We should have tried to bring our resident black belt, Ashley. Though she might let the murderer get me, and after how I've treated her, I don't know that I could hold it against her. Also, I'd be dead. So.

We creep around to the side of Lauren's house. It's a cute craftsman, the kind you'd see in any show about a suburban neighborhood where maybe there's something happening behind the scenes.

In fairness, Lauren does look like every scream queen from the 1980s and '90s. There's a reason she won last year's school Halloween contest with her Buffy costume. Here's hoping she has a few stakes she'd be willing to throw us from the window.

Amayah stops in her tracks behind a giant oak tree. I nearly crash into her, but she holds out her hand behind her back. My foot freezes right over a branch she somehow missed.

She points out in front of us, and I see that, maybe twenty feet away, there's a figure in the shadows.

I hold my breath.

I text Lauren, telling her we have the stalker in our sights.

Then Amayah inches forward, the bow out in front of her like a sword. I try to follow her and manage to avoid the stick in front of me. Instead, I trip over a hose, crashing into the dirt. The trophy bounces against the ground, the sharp top of it breaking off and scattering several feet away.

The figure's head snaps toward us.

"Fuck," Amayah whispers, reaching out to help me stand.

I take her hand and, in a fit of adrenaline, try to pull us back toward the other side of the yard. Back to the car. Back to one of our houses. Anywhere but here. I manage to grab the bottom of the trophy.

Amayah doesn't take the bait.

Or she realizes, way before I do, that we don't have time to get very far, because the figure is headed right toward us, holding the sharp edge of my trophy.

Oh my God. I can't let Amayah get hurt because I'm clumsy or a coward. I'd never forgive myself. Besides, Lauren texted *me*. Amayah didn't have to come. She's not running for queen. This is my responsibility, and I have to take it.

I shove Amayah out of the way. As she staggers to the side, I grit my teeth and assume the position we take when we're running sprints in gym.

One, two, three, four.

Before I can think about it too much, I charge, running full speed at the figure.

Amayah calls after me, and I can feel my phone buzz in my pocket. I assume it's Lauren, watching from inside.

The sharp edge of the trophy gets me in the abdomen, and I rear back, clutching at the spot.

My brain tries to calibrate. Okay, there's no blood yet; it just hurts like hell. The figure tries to run away, still holding that piece of my trophy.

My legs don't want to take me any further, and the panic of the moment hits me. But I can't let them get away!

My arm pries itself loose from my side and pulls back. I fling the base of the trophy as hard as I can at the back of the stalker's head.

Of course I miss. But I nail them in the shoulder, which slows them down, just not enough for me or Amayah to catch up.

They disappear into the darkness, and I sink to the ground. Fuck. It's over.

"You nailed them. There's going to be a nasty bruise for sure," Amayah says.

"Yeah, but they're still out there."

I hear a door swing open, creaking like nobody's business. We really are living in a horror movie.

Lauren comes running toward us, barefoot and shaking, her blond hair in wild tangles all around her.

"Oh my God. You literally—you ran them away." She throws her arms around me. "Thank you, thank you, thank you."

"They're still out there though," I reply, trying to pull out of her grasp.

"But you got them in the shoulder. We see if anyone at school is in pain tomorrow, right?" Lauren says. "You might have a future on girls' softball with that arm. Or fuck the gender binary, boys' football!"

"I am anti head trauma, so I'll sit that one out," I reply. "But thanks."

Lauren motions for us to come inside.

We follow her into her kitchen, where she's made hot chocolate. There's also a bottle of whiskey sitting out, and I wonder what the ratio is in the mug she picks up.

Before I can think too deeply about it, I grab the whiskey and waterfall a shot into my mouth. It burns and I nearly choke, but it slows the screams racing through my head. I'd rather feel the burn on the inside of my stomach versus the outside.

Amayah puts her hand on my shoulder, but I shrug it off. The idea of being touched makes me feel sick. I'm vibrating out of my body. This whole time, of course, I've understood that someone is after us, but it felt remote. Now it's real. As real as the pain blooming in my abdomen.

"Ida, we have to check your wound," Amayah says quietly.

"It's fine," I reply, reaching for the whiskey bottle again.

Amayah pushes it out of my reach. "You're bleeding."

I look down. She's right. There's a spot of red growing across my shirt. Fuck. I let Amayah lift the shirt, silently cursing that this is the first time she's done that. Not exactly the romantic moment I was hoping for.

She leans closer, and now I'm really hot, sweating, and kind of embarrassed, which makes me feel even warmer and also nauseated. None of this is what I wanted. How did I end up here?

"Can you get a clean, wet washcloth?" Amayah asks Lauren. I

guess it's a question at its core, but she says it with such authority that it's a command, and it's one that Lauren is quick to obey.

When she returns, it's with something so plush and pink that it makes me laugh to imagine my blood on it. Oh my God, am I delirious? I've lost so much blood that I'm also losing my mind?

Amayah puts the cold washcloth against my stomach, and I gasp at the shock of the temperature.

It's like ice, though I know, realistically, it can't be *that* freezing. I must have lost a lot of blood. In the books I've read, this is how it feels when you've been stabbed, or you're about to die, or you're—

"You're in shock, I think," Amayah says. "It's not deep. The bleeding is already slowing up. Do you have a first aid kit?" She turns to Lauren.

Lauren jogs out of the room and comes back a few seconds later lugging a red plastic monstrosity. When she pops it open, there's gauze, bandages, antiseptic; shit, I think there's a needle, like she'd do home sutures. Or maybe there's a sewing kit stuffed in there too.

Amayah acts like she's done this before. She warns me that it might sting while she uses an antiseptic wipe, but she says it so casually, right as she's wiping off the wound, that I barely notice the feeling.

She peels the wrapper off a bandage and rubs it on my stomach. God, this is *not* how I wanted her to touch me. Her hand stays on me for several seconds too long, and she stares into my eyes.

Then she presses her lips to mine, furiously, like it's both the first and last time she'll ever do it. My hands find my way to the sides of her face, and I kiss her back. It's like we're the last two people on earth.

Lauren clears her throat, and I remember that we are very much *not* alone in this room, let alone on this planet.

"Sorry," I say. But what am I really sorry for?

"No need. Love is love, right?" Lauren raises her eyebrows.

"Um...yeah. Got caught up, given everything," Amayah says. She meets Lauren's eyes and stays there, as if daring her to have a problem with us.

It's how I wish I could look at JJ, at Simone, at people like Grayson. There's a confidence in Amayah that I haven't entirely found yet in myself, and I admire it even if it scares me a bit. What if she decides she wants someone further along on their being out journey? I'm not ashamed of it, not at all, but she's my first relationship with a girl. What if I'm not doing it right? Will she leave?

"Of course. Do you guys want food...or...?" She laughs bitterly. "I don't really know how you're supposed to thank people for saving you?"

"I'm just glad we could help," I say. "But I should probably be getting home. Don't want anyone to worry."

I glance over at Amayah, who nods.

"Oh. Okay. I can drive you," Lauren says. "I feel like I need to do something."

I shake my head. "No. It's okay. We're good."

And when Amayah takes my hand, for at least a few moments, that seems to be true.

CHAPTER 36

THE NEXT MORNING AT SCHOOL, EVERY PART OF MY body feels wired, like I've pounded too many white chocolate mochas. My stomach still stings, and I have to remind myself to not poke at the bandage. The last thing I need is to end up in the nurse's office. Having to call Mom or Dad, who were already suspicious when I got home last night, would doom me to eternal grounding.

I stand by my locker before the first bell, trying to spot anyone who looks like their shoulder has some kind of injury. Given that I have barely any concept of that person's height (maybe tall—definitely not super short but could be average?) or gender (the clothes were baggy; it was dark), I'm really just looking for a wince, at best, some athletic tape.

I'm pretending to look for a textbook when I feel the presence of someone behind me. Okay, let me not pretend to be so intuitive. I smell hot sauce and grease emanating from someone's very warm breath.

"Got a second?"

God, has he ever heard of Listerine?

Grayson stands there, holding a piece of tinfoil that evidently contained some kind of scrambled egg and bacon concoction. There's still a bit of hot sauce by his mouth. I really have to question why I have any attraction to boys at all.

I could gag. I want to, desperately. But maybe he knows something. He's the closest I've been able to get to the guys who made the list. Actually, is that even true? Technically, he's been in my back pocket this whole time. He's given Simone plenty of clues, which she's passed onto me. But we've never had a one-on-one conversation. And unless he tells me he took a trophy to the shoulder last night, he doesn't actually want to talk to me. He's here for Simone.

"For you or for Simone?" I ask.

"She's really upset," he says, and his lips kind of smack together, revealing egg still embedded in his teeth.

"Okay. So am I," I reply.

"Well, you can understand why she wouldn't tell you, given..." He gestures to my entire being.

What does she see in this guy? Any handsomeness has to be cancelled out by his near-total lack of hygiene. And so far, his personality leaves quite a bit to be desired. How did he land Lauren too? He's a mediocre thumb of a man who somehow lands the hottest, coolest girls in school.

"Awesome. Fuck you." I slam the locker closed.

Simone's judgment must be clouded if she thinks this dude is going to talk me into anything close to forgiveness.

"You don't get it. We..." He groans for several seconds. "We're in love."

"You are so right. That is not something I can understand. Absolutely could not see her perspective."

"Why? Because Lauren's been filling your head with shit?"

Everything freezes.

I haven't talked to Simone about Lauren. So how does Grayson know? I swallow, trying to figure out the best way to respond.

"Lauren's been pretty open and honest with me. Unlike your current girlfriend," I reply.

"So you think it's okay for your new bestie to have spent years with me? Dinners with my mom? You know she was asked to be a student ambassador for Moms for Liberty, right?" he says.

"But did she do it?" I ask.

That seems to shut him up for a few seconds. It's not exactly a gotcha, especially given that his mom's weird conservative fetish came *after* he and Lauren got together.

"I'm not my mom," he replies, which both is and isn't an answer to my question.

"Speaking of your mom, how does she feel about Simone?" I ask.

He turns bright red, as if this wasn't the logical next question. What does Simone see in him? He's kind of a dumbass; I am not impressed.

I don't remember him being quite so brain-rotted when he and JJ were friends, but who knows? I wasn't paying that much attention to anyone not named Jeremiah.

"She appreciates anyone who works for their goals and doesn't make excuses," he says.

"So she doesn't know?"

God, he's getting redder, which I didn't realize was possible. It's almost incredible to witness, like some kind of scientific experiment in action.

"This is why JJ never took you seriously, even from the beginning," he spits out. "You're not the kind of girl he wanted to bring home to his mother. Who would want to introduce their mom to the girl who says she wants to—"

My ears are ringing. That wasn't one of the texts from freshman year. That was from this summer. One of the texts that JJ sent Simone to get her to keep me from running. One of the texts that…

I spot Simone at the other end of the hall, and I charge toward her, with Grayson at my heels, yipping for me to slow down. I've never been one to cause a scene, but this prom campaign has changed me. I may not be the prom queen yet, but I've discovered a flair for being a bit of a (righteous) drama queen.

When Simone sees Grayson behind me, her eyes widen, and she looks a little terrified. She's surrounded by several members of the girls' basketball team, as well as Bridget, who seems to be demonstrating some of the self-defense moves we learned.

Bridget smiles as I approach until she sees the look on my

face. She takes a step back, like she recognizes something she wants no part of.

"Let's not do this here," Simone says, making me snort.

She doesn't want her friends, her *real* friends, to see what she's been up to? Whose side she's on? Several of the girls in this group are queer too. Do they know who she associates with?

"Where would be the best place to discuss your cosigned homophobia?" I ask. "Or the fact that you showed my private texts, which you shouldn't have had access to in the first place, to your boyfriend? Or that you're willing to date someone who slut-shames your supposed best friend for what was a consensual relationship?"

The other girls start whispering, and more and more people are entering the hallway.

"I didn't mean—" Simone says.

"Which part? Which bigoted, sexist part did you not mean to be involved in?" I ask. "Which fucking part, Simone?"

"I just think… Can we go *anywhere* else?"

"Why? You took things that were private and special to me and told someone who you knew would hold it against me. I don't care about your image or your privacy. Hate how that feels?"

Her eyes are welling up, and I force myself to feel nothing. I'm not the one who should feel bad. Even though I do hate seeing her in pain. But this is pain that *she* caused. She and her asshole boyfriend.

"I didn't know he would post them. Or that he'd tell people you're bi; I—" She gasps when she realizes what she's said.

My heart stops. She's the one who outed me. And she just did it again.

"Fuck you, Simone." Instead of fighting it out, creating more of a spectacle, I walk away.

It's only when I make it into the girls' bathroom, safely locked inside a stall, that I put my head into my knees and sob.

It feels like there's no coming back from this. And even though I don't want a friend who could treat me like this, it doesn't take away all our good times. It doesn't take away the friendship we've had since we were basically in diapers.

But it sure as hell does taint it, probably forever.

Someone slips into the bathroom, and I see their crisp white Jordans moving across the floor toward me.

Simone slides down to the floor outside of the stall I'm in.

"It started at the summer bonfire for athletes," she says, as if *now* I'm supposed to care. "It was old Hollywood themed. I dressed like Dorothy Dandridge, and I felt...I felt good. And then I got there, and not one guy looked at me. It was like I was invisible. And girls like Lauren Buckley, who barely even tried, by the way, were surrounded. Even Ashley complimented me, and you know how stingy she can be. Halfway through the night, when I was ready to go, Grayson showed up. And he saw me. He complimented me, and we spent the rest of the night talking and... I don't know, Ida, I just wanted someone to like me."

"I liked you," I reply.

"Not like that."

No, not like that.

"So why didn't you tell me?" I ask.

"Because we've always clowned on him for being some dumb

jock, and I knew you wouldn't take him seriously, even though I know he's different. I fell fast...and then I met his mom, and I just—I thought because he was with me, I could change his mind. I barely go to church, but I started going to his, and they were railing on the gay stuff and sex, and all of it. And I know it's wrong, but I don't know—I could see the point? A little?"

I'm about to swing the door out and hopefully knock the wind out of her.

"You're not helping your case," I say.

"It scared me. But he told me he doesn't *really* believe all of it. Just some parts, but he acts more into it for his mom."

"Does his *mom* approve of his Discord activities?" I ask.

"She doesn't know. And I didn't either, at first. I was horrified! But, like, why would you send stuff like that? The photos he has of Lauren, I mean, *oh my God*. I just want her to have some self-respect. Right?"

At that, I do swing the door open, and Simone jumps up.

"If he does it to the girl before you, he'll do it to you too," I say.

"He's not homophobic; he's just traditional. Like JJ."

"*Really* not helping your case."

"I'm sorry," Simone says.

As I push past her, I not so accidentally slam my shoulder into hers. She lets out a small scream and clutches at her shoulder.

I didn't hit her that hard.

And where she's grabbing...

That's where I nailed the attacker's shoulder last night.

CHAPTER 37

AMAYAH HAS BEEN STARING AT ME IN SILENCE FOR THE past couple of minutes, her hand hovering over the lunch she surely intended to eat. There's a flash of panic inside me, wondering if maybe she thinks I'm wrong or, worse, insane.

Word of the confrontation spread fast. Being Black popular doesn't mean that good gossip can pass by the general population. And even I have to admit this is good gossip. If it wasn't my life, I'd be living for it.

Amayah takes a deep breath. "It'd make sense, especially the targeting of Lauren. Even though Simone has always seemed like a girls' girl. Minus what's been going on with you obviously."

"She wouldn't be the first person to throw away her morals for a guy," I reply.

"I'm not into guys generally, but I *really* don't get that one's appeal," she says. "Care to explain?"

"That's borderline biphobic. Even I don't get the attraction. I like guys, but him? I don't understand, beyond he's the one who made her feel seen at a vulnerable time."

I hate that for Simone. We all want validation, like, of course. But is it really worth all of this? Is it worth losing your friends? Abandoning your principles? And even though I know I'm not the paragon of good taste, at least in dudes, I feel a small sense of superiority. I let JJ get away with a lot, but I had a line that I held. Though, I guess, if they were real convictions, she wouldn't have let them go for anyone.

"I can't imagine that she'd actually hurt anyone. Maybe she's been intimidating, like to Lauren, or at the library, or with the note to Ashley, and Grayson is the one doing the actual attacking?" Amayah says.

"It's possible." I mean, I guess anything is possible, even if all of this feels so far away from the Simone I thought I knew.

"You know what? It also makes sense because, before last night, even though you've been followed or threatened, no one has actually tried to hurt you. The only time you were attacked was when you were chasing her. And Ashley, who we know she has a girl crush on, hasn't been attacked either. And fingers have been pointed at JJ, who both you and her boyfriend have reason to hate," Amayah says.

Oh my God. She's right. Even in the library, there's no way the shelf would have hit me. And Simone is the one person besides Amayah who would have known where I'd be. The library, the mall.

It fits.

But why? Why would Simone do any of this? Saying it was for a guy is way too simple an explanation, and a total disservice to her.

Amayah takes a reluctant bite of her sandwich and glances at her phone. She appears absorbed for a minute and then snorts at something on her screen. She hands me the phone, which is opened to Ashley's Instagram.

Ashley has posted herself doing a Black power fist, with the caption #saynotohomophobia.

I have to cover my mouth to hold in barks of laughter. She's incredible. Beyond bold. I almost admire it.

It's a direct shot at Simone, though, and by extension Grayson. And if there's retaliation going on, it stands to reason that Ashley is next.

Before I can think too closely about it, I send JJ a text with a heads-up that Ashley might have made herself a target with some of her recent activities. He likes the text immediately. I probably don't need to tell him. Ashley can clearly handle herself. But having backup is never a bad thing, especially after last night.

Amayah slaps her hand against the table, causing several of our classmates to turn to look at us. The whispers start.

I put my hand over hers, and the whispers rise to a steady buzz.

"What is it?" I murmur.

"A motive," she replies, sliding her phone back over to me.

On the screen is the PTA's web page. Elections for the next year are coming up, and each of the candidates has a page on the website. Mom's running again, because she's either idealistic or a glutton for punishment. So is Mrs. Davis, Grayson's mom. And her page is covered in all the worst buzzwords. She wants to end DEI and ban wokeness. Keep our bathrooms and sports teams segregated by biological sex. Her slogan is all about bringing morals back to Banneker.

She was the mastermind behind the failed morality standards that initially got Lauren ousted from the race. What a coincidence. As if her son wasn't the one who both received and posted those photos publicly. *Morality for thee but not for me.*

"You think that Grayson is going after the girls on the list as values enforcement for his mom?" I ask.

"I don't know that he's doing it *for* his mom, but I'm sure they're connected. The reason they're targeting the girls on the list has to be because of the pictures. They're trying to shame them. And maybe you and Ashley have been targeted less because you have fewer messages to play off of."

It makes a perverse sort of sense. Apparently, Cassidy sent Jason photos of herself from the school locker room. Bridget did a pinup-style shoot for her boyfriend the day she turned eighteen. Sally is an outlier, in an even grosser way. Rumors have started circulating that someone posted upskirt shots of her during a shift at the diner, *and* that she was having an affair with one of her patrons.

Who, we don't know yet.

The girl is barely out of the hospital, and people are already trying to justify why she might have been stabbed.

I don't care who she's sleeping with. Nothing justifies being *stabbed* while waiting tables.

The cafeteria door swings open, and Ashley walks in, JJ trailing behind her. She's gripping the sleeve of his dashiki, looking slightly murderous. She looks around the room, and when her eyes lock in on mine, she starts over to us.

Uh-oh.

Before I can plot an escape, she and JJ are standing in front of me, him looking sheepish, her looking pissed.

"I don't need you looking out for me. I'd rather die," she says. "Stop texting my boyfriend. Aren't you gay, anyway?"

"I'm bi," I reply. "And just trying to help. I promise I'm not interested in *JJ*."

"Well, you keep finding reasons to talk to him or be alone with him. At your house. At school. At meetings. Is that supposed to be a coincidence? Move on."

Amayah kicks me under the table, no doubt a reminder that I don't need to be the subject of another school-wide drama today.

"I can see how it would look that way, but JJ and I have a lot of history, and we work together for BSU. I have moved on. I'm in another relationship," I tell her.

Amayah smiles. We absolutely haven't defined what this is, but *relationship* doesn't seem too far off.

JJ grimaces. One of the things I found least attractive about him was that he was almost never willing to speak up for me. At the time, it seemed like he was letting me stand up for myself, but now I see it for what it was. He was abandoning me. He was leaving me to my own devices not because he thought I was capable, but because he just didn't want to deal with it.

Meanwhile, Amayah has never let an opportunity go by to defend me, whether we were acquaintances, friends, or anything more. And I deserve that. I deserve someone who will stand beside me. I deserve someone like her.

"With whom?" Ashley asks. "And do they know?"

"With me," Amayah replies, taking my hand.

Ashley's eyes widen. Has JJ not told her? "Oh. I—" She turns to JJ. "You didn't... Congrats."

"Thanks," I reply.

She pulls JJ away, toward the tennis team table, his face making it seem like he's a prisoner.

The other girls don't look particularly thrilled to see him, and the feeling appears very mutual. Though, not as mutual as the like between me and Amayah.

Me and Amayah. *That's* a perfect feeling.

CHAPTER 38

AS I SIT IN MY ROOM LATER THAT NIGHT, I HAVE A NAGging thought about the morality thing. Well, actually, several. Anything to distract me from the prom court nominations coming out tomorrow.

What I don't understand is the why. Specifically, why Cassidy. All the girls on the list have made some sort of morality faux pas, i.e., presumably, sent varying degrees of sexts. But! Doesn't there have to be some kind of ranking? Like of how "naughty" the texts were. And wouldn't that inform how hard they go after each girl?

So why is Cassidy the one who's dead? And if it's Grayson, with Simone on the side, why would the one person they kill be his best friend's girlfriend? Is it because she dumped Jason? Or was hooking up with someone else? Then again, so was he, not that that matters.

Wouldn't Lauren be the biggest target? Or even me? But I guess that would be too obvious.

It bugs me. Was it just that Cassidy was easy to get to? Or that she happened to be at the party, and someone slipped her one drink too much? But wait... She wasn't drinking. And there was fentanyl in her system. Fentanyl that could point to JJ and Ashley. But let's also be real. Who's the best-known procurer of substances for a party?

Jason.

It would be easy enough for him to have slipped it to her. Then again, I guess anyone could have. Big party. All it would take is turning away for a few seconds. Someone slipping something in her cup.

Something still doesn't feel right.

Sure, Cassidy could have been an easy target, but so could any of the other girls on the list who were at the party. And based on social media, there were a lot of other girls at the party. In fact, I might have been the only girl on the list who *wasn't*.

So where's the morality connection?

Ugh.

I don't want to do it, but I have to.

I need to get into the group. Or see the posts. Make it happen?

The question mark is honestly a courtesy. Unless he's changed his password, Malcolm X's birthday, I really could just steal his phone.

Why don't you ask your best friend? he shoots back, with an attached Instagram screenshot of Grayson and Simone.

What a fucking time to go public.

I guess with prom nominations dropping tomorrow, establishing yourself as half of a golden power couple is one way of grabbing attention. Grayson is technically running for king.

Gag me with a spoon. The idea of having to stand up there next to him makes me want to gouge my eyes out.

Should I ask your girlfriend? I respond.

My phone starts ringing almost immediately.

"Hi," I say.

"Skip the pleasantries, considering that you're basically blackmailing me," he replies.

"How about skip the dramatics?" I ask.

JJ groans for a solid five seconds before blurting out something that sounds like gibberish.

I realize probably three seconds too late that he's giving me his login information.

"Repeat? At a normal speaking cadence," I say. "Please."

"This idea of normality is just—"

"JJ, oh my God. Girls are getting *attacked*. Let me try to figure out what's happening."

"I don't want you to get hurt! I care. I have a heart. I'm a *person*," he says.

It's almost tender, except I think this is the first time he's ever told me he cares about me. At least in words.

"Do you?" I ask. "It'd be easier for you—"

"No, it wouldn't. Don't ever think that. You. . .you're my sparring partner. My BSU partner. My. . . I guess you're not mine anymore. But I can care, okay? I can want you alive and safe."

Tell that to your girlfriend, I almost quip. But I don't. And honestly? I think that's growth.

I grab the nearest piece of paper, which is an old bakery receipt, and a pen. As I'm writing, I realize that I can't, and don't want to, do this alone.

And I know who I should invite.

"Thanks, JJ." I hang up before he can say anything else.

An hour later I'm crammed on my bedroom floor between Bridget, Sally, and Lauren. They're the three who have been the closest to the attacker, and I'm hoping that between the four of us, we can figure something out about who has been doing this. Plus, they deserve to see what's been shared about them. We all do.

Sally still winces when she sits down, but she refuses to take a chair or even sit on the bed. Her hands shake a bit, and her eyes constantly dart back and forth, searching for danger.

I want to reassure her that she's safe, that no one can get us here, but I don't know. It could be anyone. It could be her boyfriend, the person she's loved since freshman year. What is she supposed to do with that? What are any of us supposed to do to fight back against an enemy among us?

Bridget has a scar above her left eye, from when she was hit. Which the administration still maintains she somehow hallucinated.

The gaslighting is insane. How many emails have gone out to

parents saying that there's no way these incidents are connected? How many times has it been implied that whatever happens to us, we pretty much deserve it for sending the kinds of photos and messages that get boys riled up? That make them act out of character.

That make boys hurt girls.

I go to the Discord site and type in the login information that JJ gave me. All four of us hold our breath as the page loads. We're in.

Now, because he's JJ, there are actually several groups and conversations to sort through as we try to figure out which is the one we're looking for. It's not like it's labeled *our girlfriends' nudes*.

Lauren leans forward and taps the screen. "There," she says, shuddering for a second. "It's some dumb thing the guys always say."

I roll my eyes when I see the group labeled *no homo*.

Click.

Thank goodness for small victories, the photos are blurred. Unless you click them. But maybe that's because of my privacy settings. Each one is labeled, though, with the girl's actual name. Posted by boys who are using screen names as some veiled attempt to be private. I fucking hate them.

I start to scroll, slowly enough that we can read the names.

Bridget cringes for a moment and points to the screen. Someone with the screen name reLAXbro has posted a photo tagged with her name.

"We don't have to—" I say.

"Do it. That's definitely Jason," Bridget replies. The picture fills the screen, and Bridget winces. "Yeah. It's Jason." She sets her jaw.

Lauren reaches out and gently touches Bridget's shoulder.

I grab my nearest notebook and turn to a fresh page.

reLAXbro—Jason Miller. Girls posted: Bridget Lewis.

We keep scrolling. Jason is pretty prolific in his posts. More of Bridget, several of Lauren, and many of Cassidy, which we don't click.

Another one of Bridget pops up, and she holds her eyes shut for a second. She then moves my hand out of the way and clicks the photo.

One of us gasps, and I honestly can't tell who it is. The photo is graphic. Really graphic. It's not like any of the others Bridget sent.

Bridget lets out a wounded yelp. "Oh my God," she whispers.

"It's not your fault," Lauren says immediately. Our mantra for today. For all of this.

"That's not me," she says. "I never sent that. It's not my body, even though—" She shudders as she points out a birthmark. "I have that, but this—"

"The fucking AI," Lauren says. "It's a deepfake."

Like the photo of Lauren in the locker room. How many of these are there?

Bridget tears up as we start to read the comments. No one seems to acknowledge that the photo is fake. Instead, there are increasingly gross comments about "her" body. About what the guys would want to do. About how they want to save the photo for later.

And there's Jason, acting like the big man on campus for having the photo.

Bridget shakes her head. "We need to find out who more of these guys are," she says, grabbing the notebook from me. "There." She points to another username.

Lotheatero, who doesn't appear to have posted in several weeks, commented a raised-eyebrow emoji on the AI post of Bridget.

Sally slams her hand down on the floor, confirming what we were already starting to suspect.

We click his profile, and his post history loads.

Every post is tagged with Sally's name. Lotheatero is Scott Hudson, her boyfriend of four years.

"I'm going to kill him," Sally says. When all of us turn to her, she holds up her hands. "Poor choice of words, given everything, but seriously? Why is this person going after *us*? Who cares if we sent the pictures? *They're* the ones sharing them and making new, worse ones."

"Honestly? It'd be justified," Bridget replies.

Sally motions for me to click open the photos. They're sort of sweet. Clearly pictures you'd send someone you really trusted, with whom who you had a loving relationship. Someone who you'd never expect to share them, then be able to face you the next day.

There's one of Sally that Scott didn't post, but he commented.

You're fucking sick.

I click it and Sally lets out a screech. Someone made an AI post of her, covered in blood like *Carrie,* except. . .well.

You can guess.

Posted by user catchandrelease. I click and that's their only post. Hmm.

Clearly, based on his comment, it's not Scott. In fact, since this post was made, the day after Sally's attack, Scott hasn't posted. Almost like he realized his disgusting behavior contributed to what happened to her.

We keep scrolling and end up at more pictures of Lauren. Several from Jason, which Lauren reports she never actually sent to him. She sent them to Grayson.

Simone really found herself a winner, didn't she?

In fact, Grayson doesn't really seem to be on the thread. The photos of Lauren are mostly from reLAXbro.

Lauren squints at the screen as we pull up several photos of her. These from different usernames.

"That asshole," she says. "He posts under different accounts. Single posts only. Like no one would know it's him."

We start finding more single posts. Jesus. How much time can one person have? Then we find one tagged with my name.

This whole time, I never wanted to believe JJ could still be doing it. Sharing my messages. But this one is new, from within the last couple of days.

"We don't have to look at it," Lauren says quietly.

No, we do. They've shown me theirs, laid out the betrayals for me to see. It's only fair that they see mine too.

I click and almost relax for a minute. At first glance, it's not a photo I sent. It's AI. Then I let myself take it in. I'm not alone in the photo. It's me, JJ, and Ashley. JJ is fully clothed, watching.

I feel bile rise up in my throat.

Who made this?

It's time-stamped, which makes me feel even sicker. It's from literally minutes after Ashley confronted me in the cafeteria with JJ. As in, someone had to have posted this on school property.

That's something we can bring to the administration, but at what cost?

I turn to the other girls. They seem to be putting together the same puzzle pieces that I am. There are barely any rules about any of this. Least of all the AI part. But posting this on school property? We can get them on the honor code.

If the administration believes us.

Sally is the one who shakes her head. "We're the ones who'd get in trouble," she says quietly.

Lauren's head whips around. "Why?"

"Because this would be considered pornography. And we're the ones accessing it. Even if the boys got in trouble, we could too."

Shit, she's right. I feel so hopeless. We know who has been posting. We know *what* they've posted. But we can't do anything about it. We just have to sit in the knowledge that people we trusted were willing to betray us, because no one else will protect us.

I hear Mom shout an expletive downstairs, and then her footsteps bound up the stairs.

I slam the laptop shut as she appears in the doorway, which I'm sure doesn't look suspicious at all.

She doesn't seem to notice. She has zeroed in on the other three girls.

"What's up, Mom?" I ask cautiously.

She sucks in her cheeks. Oh, she's *pissed*. But she also looks kind of sad.

"I'm really sorry," she says.

The four of us exchange looks.

"Why?" I ask.

"An email just went out from the PTA. One that I absolutely do not condone. But it enforces the morality clause for the prom scholarship. And it features a list of girls who are reported to have violated it. All of you are on it. They say because of inappropriate messages or pictures; I don't know."

She hands me her phone.

Grayson Davis's mom has written a scathing creed about how this generous award should be reserved for girls who represent the best of Banneker. And she lists all the girls in the running who do not meet that standard.

Including Lauren on the list feels particularly petty, given that she's been out of the running for almost the entire campaign window. It has to be because of Grayson and their past relationship. I'd love to know if she sees Simone as a better fit, morally.

Simone isn't on this list. Neither is Ashley.

In fact, Ashley is the only girl on *the* list who isn't included in Mrs. Davis's diatribe.

What the hell does that mean?

CHAPTER 39

APPARENTLY, THE EMAIL CAUSES ENOUGH OF A STIR that the PTA has decided to call an emergency meeting less than twenty-four hours after it's sent. Even though it's outside of school hours, the gym is packed with both students and parents.

The PTA stands in front of the bleachers, though notably, Mrs. Davis is the only one near the lectern. The other six members, including Mom, are off to the side, looking like they'd rather be anywhere else.

The principal also looks less than thrilled that this is happening. Considering that his office has been full of parents, students, and even alumni all day, this whole crusade has become a massive headache. He stands at the edge of the bleachers, his head buried in his phone.

Mrs. Davis clears her throat. "What a turnout!" She sounds

like a politician, as if people are here in support of her. "Thank you so much for having me."

One person claps. Several boos then break out across the room.

The person clapping is Grayson, who is sitting in the front row, with Simone next to him. She has her hand resting on his leg.

"Gross," Amayah whispers, clocking them too.

What a way to publicly declare your relationship.

"On behalf of the PTA, I'd like to thank you all for coming. This year's prom campaign has turned into quite a show," Mrs. Davis says. "What should be a beloved tradition has devolved in recent days. To help maintain the integrity of the prom court, and to encourage competition, the PTA, led by me, offered a monetary incentive."

As if the money was her idea. What next? She's the one who donated the funds? Please.

I see Mom whisper something to the parent next to her, whose shoulders shake with laughter.

"As a Banneker prom queen myself, I know all too well the importance of that crown," Mrs. Davis continues. "And I know the sacrifices girls make to get it. I didn't have carbs for the month leading up to the dance." She laughs and looks around the room, as if expecting us to join her. Maybe she doesn't realize our generation isn't broadly supportive of disordered eating for a school dance?

Amayah rolls her eyes.

"I bet you could make a killer campaign ad out of this," I whisper, squeezing her hand.

"I'm literally planning it in my head right now. Basically meditation," she replies.

Mrs. Davis coughs. "Anyway, all that to say, I value what the prom court represents. And that was the spirit of my email. I said that I spoke on behalf of the PTA, but the other members would like me to clarify that I spoke in my capacity as an individual, not as the PTA president."

A figure shoots up from the center of the room. It's Lauren, and in the bright lights of the gym, I can see that her face is beet red.

"And what do you have to say, as an individual, about slut-shaming a bunch of teenagers for your own agenda?" Lauren asks.

Mrs. Davis glares at her and turns her head slightly off-center so that Lauren is in her periphery.

"The way that some of the students have conducted themselves is upsetting to me, as a woman, and as a mother. My intention with the email was to make clear what kind of behavior should be considered acceptable. But I should not have done that in the PTA's name, which is why I will be taking a leave of absence as president," she says.

Several people in the crowd cheer.

Mom starts to take a few steps forward. Oh my God, is she finally going to be president?

"You can't just ignore me. Your son is the reason for a lot of these so-called 'conduct violations,'" Lauren says.

"Nelle Carter will be taking over as interim president until elections can be held," Mrs. Davis says. "And in my personal capacity, I would like to endorse Simone Brown for prom queen.

She's an outstanding young athlete who has behaved admirably, and kept her clothes on, unlike so many others. Thank you."

Mrs. Davis walks off to the side of the gym, as a chorus of boos grows louder and louder. The principal is clearly trying to calculate whether to address the clothes comment, given that this woman is literally talking about children, but he decides against it.

Mom approaches the podium, her eyebrows knitted together. What an introduction. How on earth is she supposed to respond to that?

Grayson has already started walking toward his mother, pulling Simone behind him like a hostage. All the eyes in the room seem to be following them.

"I look forward to serving as PTA president," Mom says. "And, in my opinion, anyone who wants to run for prom queen can run. Morality be darned."

Cheers echo throughout the gym.

I try to spot Lauren, but she's out of view, either seated or gone.

I still can't believe that Simone left with Grayson. It didn't seem like he was loosening that grip. Is he, with his bacon grease–smelling skin and shitty right-wing views really worth all of this? Is he really worth her friends? Her reputation?

Out of the corner of my eye, I see Ashley stomping out of the gym, with JJ at her heels. As a self-styled paragon of morality in the race, it is probably a blow not to be endorsed by Mrs. Davis. Not to her chances, more just to her self-image.

Mom takes one last look at the crowd and nods before stepping back.

The principal starts talking, but no one really cares. Everyone starts milling about the room, gossiping about Mrs. Davis, Grayson, and Simone. A couple of people name-check Lauren and Ashley too.

"We should try to find Lauren," I say to Amayah.

Bridget materializes next to us. "Agreed. That was rough."

Given that she's a full head taller than either of us, Bridget scans the crowd for Lauren's particular shade of blond while Amayah and I start for the exits. Maybe we can head her off before she leaves.

Before we can move, the room is plunged into darkness. There's one terrifying second where everything is quiet. Then, people start screaming.

Amayah takes my hand as the panic speeds through the room. The hundred-plus people contract into each other like the ventricles of a heart. A very warm heart with no oxygen to spare.

The scoreboard flashes on. Home: 2, Away: 0.

"So, it's not a power outage," Bridget says slowly.

"But what the fuck does that two mean?" Amayah replies.

Finally, the crowd stops moving, everyone seemingly entranced by the scoreboard. I start to have a sinking feeling in my stomach.

The lights flip back on, seemingly brighter than ever. I hear one loud gasp, and then the screams start.

As the center of the crowd expands back toward the walls, I see that, unfortunately, my instincts were spot-on. Ashley is crumpled before the podium.

I scan the room for JJ. I don't know if him being nearby is better or worse. Being at the scene of another crime *and* being her boyfriend is bad. But not being here, and people having to seek you out? Maybe worse.

Amayah nudges me and cocks her head toward the side of the room. JJ is running to the podium.

Jason Miller, of all people, grabs him by the arms to hold him back.

JJ screams, sounding like something primal. It's the most passion that I've ever seen from him.

The principal points to him, and at the same time, the school lockdown alarm begins blaring. Shit, this could not be going any worse.

Jason begins pushing JJ to the front of the room, like an executioner leading his victim to the guillotine. Okay, so it's getting worse.

No! This isn't right. JJ never would have hurt Ashley. Not like this.

Amayah squeezes my arm for a moment, and I realize that she's trying to hold me back too. But then she loosens her grip.

She's willing to let me go to him.

In the end, I don't have to. Mom rushes over to the two of them and motions for Jason to let JJ go.

Jason shoves JJ at Mom's chest. She catches him and then puts herself, physically, between him and the principal. When the principal tries to move toward him, holding his hands out like he's approaching a bull, Mom shakes her head.

I can already hear the police sirens outside.

Just before the officers burst into the gym, there's one more scream.

Ashley slowly lifts her head. She's bleeding from a wound that looks like the result of her hitting the side of the podium.

She lets out another single yell as she tries to stand, but falls back to the floor.

JJ scrambles out of Mom's grip and runs to where she lies. He puts his arms around her, leaning his head into hers.

The police have their guns trained on him, fingers balanced on the triggers. As if there aren't a hundred other people in this room and endless opportunities for ricochets.

Ashley's mouth moves, but she's impossible to hear given all the other noise.

Mom snatches the microphone and shushes the crowd.

When the room is finally quiet, we hear Ashley repeatedly muttering "Davis," as Mom holds the microphone nearby and JJ rubs her back.

Then Mrs. Davis, Grayson, and Simone all appear in the gym doorway.

The principal points at them, and the police descend.

CHAPTER 40

THE NEXT DAY, GRAYSON AND SIMONE ARE BOTH absent, and there's a raging debate in the hallways over what Ashley could have meant by saying "Davis." There's the obvious idea that she was pointing the finger at Grayson or his mother. Or Grayson *and* his mother. Simone is sort of on the sideline in that maybe she knew, or maybe she just backed the wrong horse.

I wanted to text her last night, but what exactly could I say? *Did you or your boyfriend attack Ashley Beckett? Is your boyfriend's mom trying to take out anyone she sees as immoral to clear a path for her ideal prom queen?*

It's far-fetched, but right now it's the best lead we have. We know that Grayson was there for both Cassidy's death and Sally's attack. He's certainly strong enough to have whacked Bridget. He has access to the list, so it makes sense from that perspective. But why? Him being the morality crusader is more than a little rich, given that he's posted a ton of the photos in the Discord. And I don't know that we can go for the Freudian angle—that he's saying that he's doing it because his mom asked him to.

It's just weird.

I feel like I'm onto something. The Discord, and feeling some kind of way about it, has to be a motive. But is it really the motive for the Davises?

I don't even want to go down the other path. The one Amayah's implying but is too afraid to actually say.

She thinks Simone's behind this.

Her reasoning is solid. I mean, more solid than anything I have. What's bothering me, though, is…why are they so bad at this? It's great that they haven't killed anyone else. Was Cassidy's death intentional? Was it a fluke? An opportunity?

Sally is standing by my locker between first and second periods. I'm sort of shocked she's even here today. Seeing another girl attacked so publicly has to be traumatic.

"Hey," I say. "How are you holding up?"

"Hanging in there," she replies.

"What's up?" I ask.

She hands me a piece of paper. It's a list of names. Jason, JJ, and Grayson are all featured. So are Bridget, Lauren, and several other girls from the list, as well as at least twenty other Banneker students.

"These are all the people I could think of who were sitting at the counter the day I was…you know. Someone had to have planted the knife. It was stuck in between two broken tiles, sticking out so that if anyone leaned in, it'd stab them," she says.

"Is there anyone who you think would have wanted to hurt you?" I ask.

She shakes her head. "It just happened to be me. But it could have gotten anyone who happened to lean there."

"Was there a chair?" I ask.

The first bell rings. I should be making my way to class, which doesn't feel particularly important right now. I have another three minutes.

Sally looks around the rapidly emptying hall. "There are stools. But I didn't have to move to the side like I usually do. The knife got me in the stomach. Which means, no, someone moved the stool."

"When?" I ask.

Sally glances behind her again. "I'll have to think about it. I've got to go."

She walks, still gingerly, down the hall.

I clutch the list. One thing stands out to me. Simone isn't on it. She couldn't have been the one to place the knife.

That doesn't mean that she didn't do something else. That she isn't in on it with Grayson. But maybe the chance is slightly lower. I can hope. Our friendship may be rocky, but I still find it so hard to believe she could be a part of this. And if she is, then our friendship is really over.

The second bell rings.

Fuck it.

Who needs class? I'm going to the hospital. I've heard from all the girls who've been attacked except for one. And I've spotted my ride.

JJ, with his head down, is shuffling toward the library. It looks like he's ditching too.

He's also trying his hardest to avoid making eye contact with me.

"Come on. You know you see me," I say.

"Busy," he mutters, trying to continue on his way.

"Nope. We're skipping. Come on. Let's go."

Finally, he stops walking. When he looks up, I can see dry red splotches under his eyes and a sliver of dried snot underneath his nose. He's heartbroken.

He really loves her.

"Go where, Ida? I'm over the games. I don't want to—"

"To the hospital," I reply. "I want to visit Ashley. How's she doing?"

"I promise she doesn't want to see you. And certainly not us together."

"Two things. You and I need to talk about what's in that group. And she and I need to talk about what she knows about her attacker," I reply. "Now let's go before we get in trouble for being out of class."

When we were together, I was never the mischievous one. If anyone had a crooked eyebrow, a wayward idea, it was him. I trusted him then, and I need him to trust me now. So does Ashley, to be honest.

JJ groans. "Fine. I'll drive."

"Well, no shit, I don't have a car."

"You barely have a license," he says.

"Licenses aren't earned on a continuum. We have the same qualifications," I reply.

"I've seen you three-point turn into several different curbs. We are not the same."

God forbid a girl have terrible spatial awareness. The car and I were perfectly fine. At least I don't go five below the speed limit on I-95 during rush hour.

"I've seen you take like ten minutes to pull backward into a parking space for no reason," I reply. "We are not the same."

"Yeah, because if you tried to back into a parking space, you'd obliterate the bumper."

I smile at him, then reach for the pocket where I know he keeps his keys. "Let me try with yours."

He jumps back. "Hell no. Keep up, short stack." He and his stupidly long legs are halfway to the back door of the school before I can even register where he's headed.

I have to jog to keep up with him, and when I reach him, slightly out of breath, he tosses his keys in the air, then catches them.

"Congrats. You're good at catch," I say.

"You're one to talk. Haven't you been taking self-defense classes? And you're out of breath with *that* jog?"

"I took *one* self-defense class, and my ex thought any cardio other than walking was unbecoming for a lady." I keep my face completely immobile.

"I *never* said that. You're the one who didn't want to go on morning runs," he replies, pushing open the door. He hesitates for a second before holding it open.

"Who wants to go running at five a.m.?" I ask.

"Me," he replies. "And Ash."

Nicknames? I swear this guy barely ever called me just Ida. It was always "Ida Carter," like we were in a college lecture hall.

"Oh, I'll bet she's faster than you too. How does your fragile masculinity handle that?" I tease.

He grins. "I like it."

"I'm glad. And I'm happy for you," I say.

We reach his car, an old beat-up red Mustang, and he holds the passenger door open. It always sticks when you try to pull it, and I could almost never get it to open on my own.

"I'm happy for you too. Amayah is cool. And she pushes you instead of holding you back," he says.

I pause before stepping into the car. "You didn't hold me back."

He shakes his head, and there's sadness in his eyes. "Yeah, I did. I should have supported your campaign. You'd be a great queen. You're a leader, even if I never let you be. And I'm sorry."

"Thank you," I reply.

After that, what else is there to say? We're both silent the entire way to the hospital. There's still so much I want to talk to him about regarding the group and the list. But it somehow doesn't feel like the time.

As he takes what feels like a lifetime to back into a parking space in the tightly crammed parking garage, I realize that he never told me how Ashley is doing. She controls her image so thoroughly, and her friends have closed ranks. The only things

I've seen on social media are speculation, which she hasn't debunked yet.

"Is Ashley— I know she can't be—She's..." I sigh. How the hell do I ask this?

JJ winces. Of course. He never likes when someone talks while he's trying to park. It messes up his mojo or whatever.

I mime zipping my mouth shut and throwing away the key while he straightens up. And by straightens up, I mean adjusts the back of the car by *maybe* a centimeter. Perfectionism is a disease.

"She's okay. Eighteen stitches in her forehead, a concussion, and a shattered kneecap. She's being released tomorrow, most likely," he says. "They're mostly just monitoring. And trying to decide who has to tell her she's not allowed on the tennis court."

That's a position I really don't envy. The girl lives and breathes tennis, and she has a tennis scholarship at Yale in the fall. I'm willing to bet she'd pull a rib out and use it to practice serves if she thought that would help her bounce back quicker.

"Did she tell you what happened?" I ask.

"Not yet. She's not allowed to have screens, and she didn't want to see me with her stitches so prominent. Her mom had to convince her to let me come." He turns the car off.

"You know, speaking of screens... Someone, maybe Grayson, but I can't be sure, posted an AI photo of you, Ashley, and me."

I don't have to describe it for him to pick up on exactly what I mean. I swear there's a little flush in his cheeks.

JJ lets out a bitter laugh. It's distorted, not his real one. "Yeah.

He wanted to date Ashley right after we got together. When she turned him down, he started the group and made the AI posts."

"More than one," I say. I stopped looking after the one.

"Yep."

"Did you know he's dating Simone?" I ask.

He nods and stares down at the steering wheel. Knowing him so well is really working against me right now. This isn't something he just found out. This is something he's known. Maybe even since he and I were still together.

"I think he might have something to do with the attacks," I say. "Maybe his mom too. The morality thing."

JJ rubs the back of his neck. "I can see why you'd think that. But then, why Ashley? Morality-wise, she's pretty unimpeachable."

"But she rejected him."

"Months ago, and he's with Simone. The other ones make sense, as terrible as that sounds, but Ashley's the outlier," he says.

I realize that I'm still holding Sally's list, crumpled in my hand. I pass it to JJ.

"All the people who were in a position to put the knife in the diner," I say.

JJ squints and then reaches into his pocket for a pen. Of course it's a fountain pen. As he presses the paper against the center console, I can see ink bleeding through.

There are actually ink stains all over his car, and even on some of his dashikis. It was always one of my favorite details about him, even though I found it almost unbearably silly.

"It was a steak knife from the diner," he says, handing the

paper back to me. "Nothing else was on it. Sally said the only thing they found on it was her blood."

"So someone had to have either taken it from the back, or ordered a meal, like steak, that needed a knife, then left it there?" I ask.

"I crossed out the vegetarians and the guys I was with. No one was sitting there. I purposefully left the space open when I realized there wasn't a stool."

Okay, so that narrows things down, a bit. But not enough.

"But were you with the guys all day? Couldn't one of them have been there earlier and planted the knife?" I ask.

JJ sighs. "I guess."

So we're back where we started. The order idea is compelling though. Maybe the diner keeps the receipts, and we could narrow down who might have ordered a steak that day.

I'm about to say as much, but JJ swings his car door open, and his feet hit the pavement before I can open my mouth.

I follow him as he takes long strides toward the entrance doors.

We show our IDs at the security desk, and after a call to Ashley's room to verify, we're sent up with sticky name tags as guest passes.

A security guard seems to be lackadaisically walking back and forth in the general vicinity of her room, but it's not what I expected. After Cassidy and Bridget, we had private security brought into the school. Ashley doesn't even have a cop outside her door less than twenty-four hours later?

JJ seems to read my thoughts.

"I offered to stand guard, but she said no," he says. "She said that even with a broken knee, she could take out an intruder."

I snort. That does sound like her. She'd probably wield an IV pole like a battering ram.

JJ walks into the room first, and I can hear the shuffle of his feet as he rushes toward Ashley.

"Hey, baby," Ashley coos. Then, her tone hardens. "Where is she?"

I take a few steps inside, staying close to the door, as I let it close behind me. Maybe I shouldn't have come. I knew she wouldn't be thrilled to see me, but that sounded downright vitriolic.

"How are you feeling?" I ask.

She glares at me. Honestly, I'm shocked she even let me up. I half expected her to say I was the one who attacked her just so I wouldn't be allowed through security

JJ comes over toward me. "Ash, we're here—"

A television remote flies at my head with alarming precision. JJ catches it in his right hand just before it hits me in the face. He really would have been a star on the football team. Those reflexes are a talent.

"See, I can take care of myself," Ashley replies.

I don't point out that she *is* technically in the hospital right now. Not her fault, obviously, but like…it wasn't unreasonable for JJ to want to protect her.

"What was that for?" I ask.

"For having the gall to come here," Ashley replies. "What on earth could you want? Trying to rub it in?"

Rub *what* in? There isn't anything to gloat about in this moment. And anyway, I'm not an asshole. I'm also not the reason she's here so...

"Come on, that's ridiculous," JJ says.

Ashley's head whips so fast that it makes her flinch. When JJ tries to open his mouth again, probably to tell her to be careful, she holds up her hand.

"I've had to hear about how this girl is *so* dedicated to helping figure out who's been attacking us. How she wants to be a protector. And it doesn't even occur to her that after the list of disqualifications came out, I'd be a target. No prewarning from the daughter of the new PTA head. Thanks a lot, *sis.*"

All I can do is nervously let out a chuckle. She's blaming me for this? Even for her, that seems beyond rational. Clearly, Ashley knew she'd be a target. We were all working with the same information.

"I didn't have a heads-up, and I would think that not being on that email was a benefit. The Davises have something to do with all of this, right? You said it yourself," I say.

Ashley's upper lip curls. "Sure. That's what you think? It has to be them, and not your little friend."

I look to JJ, whose jaw has slackened. Is this confirmation? Simone is the one who attacked Ashley? Well, that's it. Who else could she be referring to?

"I'm going to make it right," I say. "I'll take care of it. I'm glad you're okay. Bye."

I'm already ordering an Uber back to school as I fast walk out of the hospital room. If it gets here in the next ten minutes, I can be back in time for lunch, in time to brief Amayah and confront Simone.

JJ halfheartedly calls my name, but I know he'll want to stay with Ashley. I would too, if I were in his position.

I text him a quick thank-you, just as the Uber pulls up. Then, I take a deep breath. This won't be easy, but it's what I need to do. I'm ending this today.

CHAPTER 41

AMAYAH SITS AT OUR USUAL TABLE, POKING AT A chicken Caesar wrap. She barely got a word in when I breathlessly told her about what happened with Ashley in the hallway between last period and now. Now that I think about it, she barely tried.

However, she did text Simone inviting her to our table, since I know that a text from me probably wouldn't mean much. Simone will know that Amayah represents an olive branch. Or so she'll think.

Amayah doesn't have to tell me that she hates this idea. It's written all over her face. But I'm doing the right thing. The confrontation is happening in public, where Simone can't do anything. Amayah will be right here, and JJ and Ashley know about this too.

I'm not setting myself up to be hurt. And I made sure that Amayah made clear that the invitation was for Simone only, Grayson not included.

"It's going to be fine," I say.

Amayah takes a three-second exhale before making eye contact with me, her jaw tense. "I really wish you'd discussed this with me beforehand," she says. Before I can protest, she says, "Spilling your plan to me in the hallway between classes and then vanishing before I can respond does not count."

Shit. Is this our first fight? We kind of need to be a united front here. This isn't a divide-and-conquer situation.

"I'm sorry, I really am. I just want to end this. And before prom is best, right? Then we can focus on the campaign, finding our outfits, making out?" I cock my head slightly and smile.

She takes a sip of her water.

Okay. This is definitely going to be a problem. But it's not one that I can deal with right now. Especially not with Simone walking toward us.

Simone slides in next to me, and I instinctually scoot a few inches away, in case she tries another move like the steak knife.

Her face, which she was already struggling to keep from wavering, falls. She turns to Amayah, who takes a bite of her wrap so big there's no way she's participating in the conversation while she chews.

"I can go," she says. "If it's going to be like this."

"No," I reply. "We want you here."

Amayah snorts. For someone who has been so incredible at playing it cool the entire time I've known her, she's really letting it all hang out today.

"Amayah? Do you have something to say?" Simone asks.

Amayah swallows. "Absolutely not. This is between the two of you."

"I really think it would help you to talk with Grayson. You'd understand where he's coming from. And his mom is actually really impressive; did you know that she was the first woman to become a leader at their church?" Simone replies.

"Is that because their church just started allowing female leaders three months ago?" Amayah asks. Then she shakes her head, as if reminding herself that she didn't want to be involved in this and goes back to her wrap.

Simone's jaw clenches.

So that's a yes.

Am I supposed to be impressed by that? I swear, a few months ago we made fun of people who bought into bullshit like this. If the price of love is abandoning your morals, then I refuse to pay it, and I can't imagine why Simone would either. But maybe this is what happens when you feel pushed to the side. When someone who typically only finds girls like Lauren beautiful falls for you, after years of rejection, maybe it rewires something in your brain.

"Why am I here?" Simone asks.

"Because we invited you," I reply.

She rolls her eyes. "Well, I think we're done here." She starts to stand.

"Are you done attacking the girls on the list?" I ask.

She sits back down, her eyebrows knitted together. "Excuse me?"

Amayah closes her eyes for a moment, before taking another bite of her wrap. Her silence could not be any louder.

"Are you *done* attacking the girls on the list?" I ask.

"What the fuck are you talking about?" Simone's voice is loud enough that a few people from nearby tables start glancing over at us.

Causing a scene, once again. It's one way to get noticed, though I don't know that fighting with your best friend in the cafeteria is the winningest prom strategy.

"It's been confirmed by one of your victims," I say.

Her eyes widen. "What?" she whispers.

I think the statement speaks for itself. I try my best to make continued eye contact while my thoughts swim. I've known Simone for most of my life. I know what she looks like when she's been caught doing something she shouldn't. We've been in that position together way more than once. This isn't it. Something doesn't feel right.

"You disappeared right before Ashley was attacked. Did you do it?" Amayah asks.

Geez, why is she jumping in now? I was being a little coy about my sources. I don't want to put more of a target on Ashley's back.

"Uh...no," Simone replies.

"Not exactly convincing," I say.

Simone scoffs. "Okay. If attacking Ashley means her coming up to me and calling me a kiss-ass for getting Mrs. Davis's endorsement, and me calling her a fake-ass bitch who was only down with the culture when she could benefit from it, then sure. I attacked Ashley."

Amayah drops her food onto her plate and shoots me a look like, *See, I was right.* I am not looking forward to whatever conversation we're going to have to have later.

"You know what I meant," I reply. "So you admit you fought with Ashley."

"With *words*. And then I went to the girls' bathroom to cry. What about it?" Simone replies.

"And Ashley followed you there? And that's where you—"

"I didn't physically attack her. I was in the bathroom; I heard her scream; I ran out. That's the whole story."

But that can't be the whole story. We know more happened, *and* that my friend was in on it. Who else could Ashley have been talking about? It's not like I'm swimming in close social connections.

Amayah hits her hand on the table, and Simone and I both whip our heads toward her.

"This is ridiculous, you two. Ida, you're going off hearsay from a girl in the hospital who hates you and I'm sure would love to mess with you. Simone, you're letting a guy you've known for five minutes make you homophobic enough to reject your best friend. Can we all just stop?" Amayah says.

"I'm not homophobic! And neither is Grayson!" Simone says. "If anything, *she's* rejecting *me*."

"Oh yes, compare you wanting me to keep my sexuality a secret so as not to upset your conservative boyfriend and his mom, with me not wanting to be around said conservative boyfriend and his Mom for Liberty," I say.

"We're in love! I've wanted a guy like Grayson my whole life, and you suddenly decided that you liked Amayah. You've known her for how long?"

Amayah's face darkens, but this time she doesn't pipe up. Her eyes have a faraway look, and I wonder if this is the same conversation she had with her brother before he deployed.

"I didn't decide to like Amayah; I just do. I've liked girls before her. I might like girls after her. And guys. It's not a phase; it's who I am. You throwing away all your principles for a mediocre white dude with bad beliefs? Hopefully a phase," I reply.

We're getting nowhere, and I don't want to keep going in circles. Something happened with her and Ashley. Something happened *to* Ashley. These things could be connected, or they could be separate incidents. This conversation isn't going to help me find out.

Speak of the devil, Grayson storms over, his face an ugly, splotchy shade of reddish purple.

He snatches Simone's arm. "You don't have to deal with this. I can't believe you let these people talk to you like this."

I raise my eyebrows at "these people." Historically, I know what that means. So does Simone, based on her wince when he says it. But she lets him get away with it.

"You don't have to deal with *this,*" I say, gesturing to Grayson. "I can't believe you let your boyfriend post nude photos of his ex and generate AI photos of me and Ashley. All while being *so in love* with you, right?"

"*What?*" both Amayah and Simone exclaim.

"Liar," Grayson snaps.

"Would you like me to show her the accounts? I'd be happy to," I reply.

His mouth flops open and closed like a fish choking on air.

Simone's eyes fill with tears. "You told me you'd stop," she whispers.

Amayah shakes her head, looking as ill as I feel.

Simone seems to be trying to match her basketball winning streak with betrayals of our friendship, and she's doing an excellent job.

"Fuck you," I say. "Both of you. I can't believe you knew this entire time. And you let him. You let him violate all of us, for what? Was it worth it? Have fun at prom. I hope you look back on the photos and hate yourself."

I storm out of the cafeteria. I don't really expect anyone to follow me, maybe Amayah, but I don't even have faith in that right now.

CHAPTER 42

AFTER SCHOOL MOM AND I ARE BACK AT THE MALL, staring at the three dress options Amayah and I narrowed down. At pickup, Mom wiggled her eyebrows for a solid thirty seconds, trying to get me to text Amayah and invite her out with us. I did, just to satisfy her, but Amayah, unsurprisingly, did not respond. Mom seemed to buy my excuse that Amayah has been working on some kind of prom installation for BSU, and I wasn't exactly jonesing to offer additional information.

Mom, who has the same overactive face that I do, is trying very hard to be expressionless as she gestures between the three. The first is an ankle-length canary yellow sheath dress with slightly puffed short sleeves. The second is navy blue with a sweetheart neckline and a pleated skirt down to the floor. The third is a deep red A-line with cap sleeves and sparkles. Mom definitely likes the yellow the best, since it's bold, but she's open to any of them.

The navy is the most traditional, which feels comfortable, but the whole point of my campaign is that I'm not the "traditional" choice. So shouldn't my dress reflect that?

Mom smiles slyly. "Well, which color would you want to see Amayah in? She's matching you, right?"

"That question feels like a trap." The answer is red.

Mom, ever the mind reader, whips the red dress off the rack. "Try it on."

There's no use in fighting her on this, so I head into the dressing room area. There are already at least three girls from Banneker here, and I try to avoid eye contact. I've had enough attention for a lifetime. If I actually win prom queen, I'm going to need to go into hibernation until the start of college to recover.

I step into the dress, and my first thought is that it's too long. Which it is, just a bit. I squeeze my eyes shut. I'm not ready to see the full picture yet, and anyway, there's no way I can zip it up by myself.

There's a soft throat clear outside. "It's me," Mom says.

"Come in. I need help zipping."

The curtain moves, and I feel Mom breathing behind me. She starts to zip, and it sticks for a second. I'm about to say something, but then she gets it up the rest of the way.

Mom clears her throat.

I turn to face her. "Mom? Are you okay?"

There are tears in her eyes. "You look beautiful. A little hemming, but otherwise…I think it's perfect." She points to the mirror.

I turn around and gasp. This is the moment. The one you see in all the romantic movies when the lead realizes they look like a princess. I never thought it was real, at least not for someone like me. But right now...wow.

The sparkles gleam against my skin, making it look like an even richer shade of brown. The silhouette hugs the shape of my body, just enough to make me feel like everything is being held into place, but without feeling like the dress is trying to squeeze my organs. This dress makes me want to go see Amayah. It makes the words of a victory speech swirl in my head. It's conspicuous, and shiny, and everything I wouldn't have chosen to wear to prom a year ago. Or a relationship ago.

This is it.

"What about shoes?" I ask, sounding more breathless than I intend to.

Mom grins. "Oh, this is my moment. Shoes and jewels. I've got ideas."

I reluctantly change back into my regular clothes so we can venture to another area of the store to explore accessories. I've never been a shoe girl, but right now, I'm jazzed. Show me the heels, the flats, the strappy sandals, the pointed toes. I'm ready.

Mom folds the dress over her arm as we make our way to the shoe section.

I feel my phone buzz. When I take it out, someone is trying to AirDrop me a photo. Nope. I've learned my lesson.

I move to put the phone back into my pocket when it buzzes again. And again.

Jesus Christ. How many times can this person try to AirDrop me? I look around the store, trying to see if anyone is conspicuously on their phone or watching me.

Okay, a lot of people are on their phones, so that's not going to work.

Mom looks over at my screen and snatches the phone. She accepts the photo before I can even protest.

The noise she lets out is primal. I'd hate to be on the receiving end of that.

She tilts the phone over to me.

It's that fucking poster again, the one with the noose that started all of this. But this time, it's on the floor, and there's a figure leaning over it. I try to place the location. Tile, lockers... Amayah was right! We should've stormed the boys' locker room. Then the figure, though slightly blurred, becomes apparent, thanks to his stupid hat and the identifiable jersey.

Mom and I exchange a look. Each of us could have a field day with this for very different reasons.

Do I relish in reminding Simone that her boyfriend is nowhere near as evolved and sweet as she thinks he is? Well, yes, honestly, especially after today. Is Mom going to be thrilled to tell the rest of the PTA that their disgraced leader raised the kid who drew a noose on his classmates' poster? Oh, for sure.

But who sent this to me? And why now? That incident is old news at this point. And how can we connect this to what has been happening with the attacks?

Mom is already composing an email.

I take my phone and save the photo. If I have to go tit for tat with Grayson on blackmail photos, so be it.

I'm taking Grayson down by whatever means necessary.

Okay. Not whatever means, because I'm not a murderer or assaulter, but everything else should be on the table, right? Within reason. And laws. But maybe bending ethics a bit.

I send the photo to Amayah, who responds immediately. **On it.**

Here we go.

CHAPTER 43

"YOU'RE A BITCH."

A glob of spit flies past my ear at my locker. Well, I made it five minutes in the school building before being confronted about the events of yesterday. After I sent Amayah the photo, she swiftly had it on our prom campaign Instagram, along with quotes from my original BSU statement.

It has gotten the most engagement of anything we've posted so far, and according to her, both Ashley and I surged in the prom queen polls.

And from the disgusting loogie decorating my locker, the athlete contingent is particularly invested in these recent revelations. Jason Miller and several of his friends glare at me.

"Okay," I reply. "Thank you for your feedback."

"Grayson is dating a Black girl, just like you," Jason says.

"I'm aware," I reply.

Plenty of racists date Black people. This really isn't the flex Jason thinks it is. Dating a Black girl doesn't absolve you from drawing a noose, a pretty obvious, absolutely unnuanced historical symbol of anti-Black racism. Especially not in response to a situation *you* created. Simone was completely terrified by that poster, and it was her boyfriend who did it.

Or was she actually upset? Amayah seemed to think she was overreacting or lying. Could Simone have been in on that too?

No. That's too much.

"You can't take a joke? The poster was a joke." Jason takes a step closer.

That distinctly animalistic quality of his incisors hits me once again, along with his teenage boy halitosis.

"What part of it was a joke?" I ask.

Jason sneers. "You don't know what a joke is?"

I blink at him several times. "No. I want to know what part of a white boy, or group of white boys if you'd like to admit involvement, drawing a noose, a.k.a. something that was used to lynch Black people, was a joke. Explain it to me."

Jason's face starts to turn red, and a vein in his forehead begins to pop.

A steady flow of people who probably just wanted to put away their backpacks or grab books from their lockers before first period have pooled around us. It feels very telling to me that they're watching but not intervening. No one is chiming in to agree, or better yet physically coming in between me and Jason.

Witnessing can only do so much. Sure, people have to see what's going on. But once you see it, what do you *do* about it?

Right now, it seems like nothing.

I look at the guys behind Jason. The ones who I assume helped him with the list. Or posted about their girlfriends and their hookups in the Discord. "Can any of you explain?"

When no one responds, I shake my head. The first bell rings, and most of the crowd still lingers.

At least they didn't take the easy way out, I guess?

But I will. I'd rather sit through a quiz than this, which is really saying something.

I start down the hall, and Jason grabs my arm. He squeezes tight.

I yank out of his grip. Bridget, my sister in self-defense, bursts out of the throng of people, her field hockey stick raised.

"Back the fuck up, asshole," she tells Jason.

"What are you going to do?" he asks, reaching for me again.

Bridget swings with tactical precision.

Jason ducks, and the stick makes an elegant arc just to the side of where his head was. "Crazy bitch."

Bridget swiftly returns the stick to her side as the assistant principal comes running. She makes her eyes huge so that she looks like some sort of innocent kewpie doll, but there's still a fire in them.

"Get to class," the assistant principal snaps at all of us. His eyes flick over Bridget and her field hockey stick.

Jason opens his mouth, and Bridget fixes him with a look

that I almost wish could kill. It'd be a vicious way to go, and he'd totally deserve it.

Bridget gives me a nod and power walks in the opposite direction of the crowd, toward the locker rooms. Bless the athletes who have to bring their equipment to and from school every day. Well, if those athletes are using said equipment for good.

I decide to bring my backpack to class, so I can avoid touching my locker before I find a cleaning wipe. Plus, having to spin my locker combination with all the adrenaline coursing through me would inevitably end in failure.

Jason's friends have dispersed, so it's just the two of us, unfortunately headed to the same class.

"You should mind the company you keep," he says.

"Rich, coming from a racist by association," I reply.

"I hooked up with Bridget," he says.

"Yeah, you have a reputation for that. And then uploading their photos."

I try to walk faster, but that doesn't help, given that Jason is at least a foot taller than me, and an athlete. If I had to avoid everyone this guy hooked up with, I probably would only be able to talk to like three girls in the senior class.

"It was recent. Like a month ago," he continues.

I stop outside of the door to our classroom. Whatever unburdening he wants to do, he certainly doesn't need to be doing it with me.

"Okay?" I reach for the doorknob.

He leans in closer, and I do my best not to gag. This guy does not need to be this enmeshed in my airspace.

"Cassidy was pissed when she found out. The night of the party. She confronted Bridget. I didn't see her after that."

He pushes past me into the classroom, leaving me with the impact of what he's saying.

Bridget might have been one of the last people to see Cassidy alive.

CHAPTER 44

AMAYAH SLIDES HER FRIES INTO THE MIDDLE OF OUR lunch table. We haven't talked about the whole episode with Simone, but she did get an order of fries for us to share, *including* the barbeque sauce she knows I love to dip them in.

"It's weird, right? That Bridget never told us?" I ask.

She shrugs. "It doesn't exactly make her look good. I can see why she wouldn't mention it, especially since half the school thinks she faked her own attack or tripped into a locker."

Fair. She does have a point there. And it's not as though Jason Miller is a particularly credible reporter. He definitely has reason to point the finger somewhere else.

"So what do we do?" I ask.

"We're two weeks out from prom," Amayah says. "We focus on the campaign and let the authorities do the rest."

"But they're not doing anything," I say.

"And that isn't our problem. Ida, we're kids. Like you told JJ at the start of all of this, let the adults handle it. Let's focus on what we can control."

She's not wrong, but it feels... I don't know. This doesn't feel over. And it feels like my partner in all of this is starting to either lose interest or turn a blind eye. What would be the reason for that?

"And what can we control?" I ask.

"Your dress? Did you pick?" she asks.

"Yep."

She raises her eyebrows. There's a flash of—hurt?—in her eyes. Like she wanted to be there for the ultimate choice. Or she's upset that I didn't tell her. As my date, or as my campaign manager?

"Color match?" she asks, holding her voice steady, though her eyes are focused slightly to my left.

"Crimson red." I reach over and cup my hand under her chin.

She sighs. "Don't try to distract me," she murmurs.

"Distract you from what?" I ask, leaning forward over the table.

She takes the bait and kisses me so deeply that I feel tingling all the way down to my toes. My head starts swimming, and I can hear my breathing becoming shallower.

Amayah pulls away and pops a fry in her mouth. "Now who's distracted?"

I raise my hand. "And I might be experiencing catastrophic loss of oxygen to the brain."

"Good. You've been doing entirely too much thinking about things that don't involve kissing. Or red dresses that you're going to make me wait to see you in. Even though, as your campaign manager, outfit approval is kind of important, right?"

"Ah, but you're not coming to prom as my campaign manager. You're coming as my date. And I absolutely refuse to let you avoid the moment," I say.

I grab a fry too, trying to emulate her coolness and definitely failing, per usual.

"What moment?" she asks.

"The moment when you come and pick me up, and I descend the staircase. And you gasp, or faint, or swoon. I want it all."

"Challenge accepted. I'm counting on a swoon from you too. Maybe I'll even have to catch you if you get lightheaded," she replies.

Mission accomplished. I am officially very, very much not thinking about the list, attacks, Bridget, or Jason. I have a one-track mind, and she's completely in control of it.

I slide the fries to the side of the table and lean in against her ear. "Can we please go break the morality clause?"

She groans. "If we get caught, then the campaign—"

"I could be attacked tomorrow. Later today. Screw the campaign, and screw—"

Amayah moves her head away from me. There's a fire in her eyes but not the kind I was anticipating.

Oh God. I said the wrong thing. I said a lot of the wrong thing, didn't I?

"Don't joke about that. And let's not screw the campaign I've worked extremely hard on. Trust me, you're not getting attacked," she says.

How can she be so sure? There are several people watching us right now. Kissing in the cafeteria would probably trigger some sort of moral panic from a certain segment of the student body. Maybe I've just made myself a target.

"You'll protect me?" I try to bring back some of the flirtatiousness we just had.

"You can protect yourself," she replies. "And we can focus on winning that crown and the money. We can make history."

"Yeah. Sorry. I'll keep focused. But after prom? Once we know if we've won?" I ask.

"Then I'll burn every pillar of morality with you," she replies.

Oh, thank God. But really. How am I going to focus on the campaign? I just want to get to the end of the dance. Get to wherever I can with her.

My phone buzzes. I check and it's Simone. I've been tempted to block her but have decided against it only out of morbid curiosity. After everything, from the posters to the pictures, to the positions she's taken on my relationship, what could she have to say to me? And why would she be bold enough to try?

Grayson was suspended over the poster, and she has tried to keep a low profile since their relationship exploded into public view. It seems like even the basketball girls are icing her out. To be fair, image-wise right now she's a huge liability. Even Amayah, who has tried to keep an even keel, subtly recommended that, regardless of whether I want to work on our friendship, I avoid being seen with Simone at least until after prom.

Utility closet by the gym. Come alone.

I tilt my phone toward Amayah, who snorts. "Is she trying to make out?"

My jaw drops. "Is *that* where people go to hook up?"

Amayah shrugs but gives me a secretive smile. Good to know. But also, who has she been there with?

Another text comes through. **Do NOT bring Amayah.**

I roll my eyes, but something stops me from showing Amayah this one too. It feels more specific than simply coming alone. She doesn't want Amayah involved.

Fine. I'll bite. I take a handful of fries and push back in my seat.

"I'll wait outside for you. If you're in there for longer than ten minutes, want me to bust in?" Amayah asks.

"If we hit five, I feel like it's a hostage situation," I reply.

"Noted."

We stagger our exits. Anyone who sees what direction we're headed could probably make a guess as to where we're going. But technically, we're not breaking any rules. Even though I really want to.

I've never actually been over here. I can barely find the door, and Amayah, popping up behind me, has to point out the entrance. The entrance, which is tucked behind several rolling carts of rubber balls, is not exactly easily accessible.

I duck and squeeze between the carts. It's an acrobatic exercise, which explains why this is the designated place for athletes to hook up, probably with each other. The door is on the shorter side, making me feel like Alice in Wonderland. Hopefully, this visit doesn't involve croquet mallets.

Simone is standing in the middle of the room, surrounded by deflated basketballs, old bookcases, and what I swear are wooden tennis rackets. Jesus, how long has this stuff been here? She squints, trying to see behind me.

"You told me to come alone," I say.

"And where's your girlfriend?" she asks.

"Not here. As requested. Where's your boyfriend? Oh right."

She sucks in her cheeks and takes a deep breath. I know she wants to cuss me out or take a shot back, but she won't. Can't compare being in a same-sex relationship to being with a racist. Or if she can, I'm really going to need to get out of here.

"I think it's important that you know who she really is," Simone says. "I don't have an issue with you being...whatever you are...but Amayah? She's not right for you."

Oh, this is rich as hell coming from her. A Black girl who affirms my beauty, intelligence, and identity isn't right for me, but a boy who draws nooses on her group's poster is right for her? Horseshit.

"Well, I think we're good here. See you never, Simone," I say, turning to go back through the labyrinth.

"You're going to want to see this," she says.

See what? The apple basket that the boys' basketball team used sixty years ago? What could she possibly have to show me.

I spin to face her. “What?”

She points to an old whiteboard to her left. It’s covered in scribbles, drawings, initials, and names.

“People write their hookups here. The people who know about this room. Who use it,” she says.

“Okay.”

“Including some of your new friends from the list,” she says.

“Makes sense.”

What kind of gotcha does she think this is? Yeah, I know that the girls on the list hooked up with our classmates. That they did it in the school also isn’t a shock.

She uses her finger to underline one of the portions of the wall. Then she taps a name.

I don’t really want to play this game, but whatever. Who cares. I move closer to her, feeling my shoulders tense. It would be really easy for her, or Grayson, or anyone hiding in the shadows to attack me.

She’s pointing to *Bridget L.* Okay, at first glance that looks like Bridget’s handwriting. *Okay?* Next to Bridget’s name is *AM*, written in calligraphy.

My heart stops for a moment.

Simone takes a deep breath. “Amayah Murphy,” she says.

“Nice try,” I reply, hoping she can’t hear the waver in my voice.

“There’s a date,” she says. “September second of this school year. Ask her about it.”

Even if that’s true, Amayah and I weren’t a thing in September. And who she hooked up with before me is none of my business.

A connection with Bridget doesn't give her an excuse to hurt any of the girls.

As if she can read my mind, Simone says, "She and Bridget could be working together."

"So could you and Grayson. Or Grayson and Jason. There are so many different ways this could go," I reply.

"But Amayah never told you."

"I never asked."

Sure, it's weird. But that was at least six months ago. It doesn't mean Amayah has anything to do with the attacks.

"One or both of them could have been at the scene of every attack. We know Bridget was there with Cassidy. Amayah was with you and Lauren, and Bridget could have been the person in the yard. And both of them were at the diner when Sally was attacked."

Good job, Nancy Drew. You made some connections. I'm about to roll my eyes and leave when something sticks in my brain.

"I never told you about being with Amayah at Lauren's house," I say.

"What? No, you must have."

"I fucking didn't, Simone," I say, backing away.

She tries to run toward me, and I shove her back by her shoulders. I'm not particularly successful, given that she's much stronger than me, but she staggers back when I press a particular part of her shoulder.

The same part I nailed with that trophy a few nights ago.

I turn on my heel and try to rush for the door. But I'm not

fast, and this room isn't exactly conducive to speed. Like some stupid horror movie cliché, I slip and have to grip the nearest old bookshelf for stability.

Simone reaches out for me, nearly catching my sleeve, and I slide onto the ground, avoiding her grasp. On all fours, I scurry as quickly as I can toward that unbelievably short door. For good measure, I push over a rack of deflated balls, hoping it will give me an extra few seconds while Simone tries to dodge them.

The door swings open, and Amayah's hand reaches in. She pulls me out and slams the door shut, nearly knocking it into Simone.

I gulp air as I stagger into the hallway.

Simone comes barreling out behind me, and Amayah throws her body in between the two of us.

"Stay away from her," Amayah says.

"You too. You *and* Bridget," Simone says. For someone who was just chasing me around a glorified storage closet, her pursed lips and hands on her hips look more triumphant than I'd expect.

Amayah freezes, then turns to me.

I try to keep my face as neutral as possible. "Apparently, Simone's big gotcha is that I'm not the first girl you've kissed. While mine is that she let slip that she somehow knows about what went down at Lauren's. Except we never told her, did we?" I ask.

Relief flits across Amayah's face. "No, we didn't," she says, turning back to Simone.

"And why do we think Simone would know about that, if we didn't tell her?" I ask.

"If she has something to do with the attacks that have been happening? She certainly has motive via her new questionable personal connections," Amayah replies.

Simone glares at us. "Think what you want about me, but I know the truth. And I know about you," she says, making pointed eye contact with Amayah. "And I'm sure a lot of other people would love to know too."

"Well, if outing people is the kind of reputation you're after, have so much fun," Amayah replies.

Simone lets out a strangled noise that sounds like a mix of offense and indignation. But Amayah's not wrong. I've never heard anything about Bridget being queer, and Bridget certainly didn't divulge that information to me at any point. Is outing people Simone's new hobby? How wonderful.

The bell rings, signaling the end of our lunch period.

I take off down the hall before either of them can follow me. Luckily, we don't share any more classes that day.

Unluckily, there's a BSU meeting after school.

Fantastic.

CHAPTER 45

SINCE OUR BREAKUP, I'VE TAKEN TO SITTING SOMEwhere in the front of the room but not at the podium with JJ. Today, I'm at the podium, trying to avoid both Amayah's and Simone's attempts to talk to me.

JJ, who is already standing in front of a crowd when I walk in, raises his eyebrows when I slide in behind him.

He turns to me. "I thought you were done being behind me," he murmurs.

"I'm always behind you, in support," I reply.

"You know what I mean."

"Drama," I reply.

He shudders. While he loves being dramatic, he hates drama as a general concept. I'd love to see how he's been with Ashley, given that she is consistently at the center of tennis drama (which is apparently quite brutal).

JJ checks his watch, as though there isn't a wall clock directly in his line of sight, and then clears his throat.

"I'd like to start this meeting with prayers for one of our own, Sister Ashley Beckett, who is making a speedy and full recovery that we hope continues," JJ says, bowing his head.

Everyone else follows suit, though I catch Amayah with one eye open, focused on me.

"Hear hear!" Paul says after a few seconds.

JJ's sharp exhale is audible to the entire room. Interrupting is a no-no. Especially not a prayer.

"Some decorum, please," JJ says. "I would also like to take the time to make BSU's stance on and commitment to our queer brothers and sisters clear."

He has the wherewithal to not turn and look at me, but he's the only one, even though there are at least two other queer people here right now. Well, shit. They're looking at me too.

"I have made the mistake of appearing to be against our LGBTQ+ brothers and sisters, both publicly in this club, and personally in my relationships. I am not homophobic, at least not intentionally, but I do profess to be ignorant and prideful. And, as the leader of this organization, I want to make it clear that if you are homophobic, and you perpetuate homophobic actions, you are no longer welcome here." He looks directly at Simone.

Oh. He's really going in. I should feel grateful, right? And I do, a bit. Some of this feels a little too late, given everything. But at least he's doing something. At least he's standing up for me, for my community, when my best friend won't.

Simone gets to her feet. Bad idea. There's no way she's going to say the right thing, or anything remotely close to the point of JJ's statements.

Paul tugs at her shirt for her to sit back down, his mouth contorted into a preemptive grimace.

"Having questions and believing that we can all evolve and grow beyond our teenage selves doesn't mean that we're—" Simone says.

JJ shuts her down with a swish of his hand. "It's none of our jobs to decide whose selves are valid or true. And we can't hide behind religion, morals, or relationships, claiming those as a shield for our bigotry."

JJ spares a glance back at me, and I nod. He's right, and he's holding firm.

Simone takes the opportunity to sit, looking properly shamed. But our attention is directed to the doorway.

"A wonderful speech, sweetheart. Several people were gathered in the hallway, admiring your words," Ashley says, hopping in on her crutches. Her eyes are shielded with sunglasses, presumably because of the fluorescent lights, but I can still see dabs of highlighter and bronzer on her cheekbones. Even concussed and on crutches, you'll never catch Ashley slipping with the contour.

JJ flushes with pride, not at the idea of other people liking what he said, but at *her* compliments.

It's sweet, and I feel a wave of envy. This is how I would have felt about Amayah a few hours ago. Now I'm questioning all of it.

The timing of our relationship. The things she hasn't told me. The things she has. What does any of it mean? Do I matter to her? Am I a means to an end?

I won't let myself go to that place. The place that says she could be involved in any of this. That would break my heart more than Simone, and that's the scariest thing that I can think of.

"Prayers work fast," JJ says, grinning at Ashley.

"Not as fast as I do," Ashley replies, and indeed, she's quite speedy on those crutches.

"Glad you're back," I say to her.

She sucks her teeth for a few seconds, staring me down as she approaches. "Couldn't let you pretend to be first lady with your outfit *that* wrinkled. Did you crawl through a cave?" She gives me the slightest of smirks.

Was that…a friendly roast? Could Ashley and I become friends? That seems impossible, given everything, but there are certainly worse friends to have. She's loyal, quick on her feet (both literally and figuratively), and able to cut to the meat of just about any issue. I've actually started to admire her.

"Just the storage closet," Simone says, standing up again.

Oh, come *on*. She had a freaking out! Shut up!

Ashley chuckles. "Okay. I don't think we need to air out Ida and Amayah's love life, but to each her own."

Paul snorts and ducks his head into his computer. Great. That whole exchange will be immortalized in the meeting notes.

"They weren't there together. Ida was with me, learning about how Amayah hooked up with Bridget Lewis and kept it a secret. And that perhaps they could have something to do with the attacks. Including yours, Ashley," Simone says.

Paul raises his hand but starts talking before anyone calls on him. "Maybe avoid trying to invoke the trope of the devious bisexual. We don't know what conversations Amayah and Ida have had, and it's none of our business. Wouldn't you agree?"

"I would," Amayah says.

"Seconded," JJ replies. "Topic closed."

Simone's mouth snaps open and shut. She looks as horrified as I feel, which, good. What does she think she's doing? Plus, if Amayah was secretly a murderer, it would be a really bad idea to continue trying to name and shame her in public.

"Should we discuss our response to the new revelations regarding the noose on our poster?" Amayah asks.

It takes everything in me not to bark out a laugh. What a way to turn the situation around.

Speaking of turning around, Simone does just that. She walks out of the meeting, loudly slamming the door behind her.

"I'll be releasing a statement, and I've already had a private conversation with the perpetrator," JJ says quietly.

"I'd like to review said statement," Amayah says. "*We* would." She looks at me.

"I trust whatever you want to say, JJ," I reply. "But I'd love to give feedback, if you're open."

Ashley covers her mouth, but I can hear the lightest of snickers behind her hand.

Paul is still typing, but with a clear grimace. Could this

meeting get any more awkward? My girlfriend has been accused of murder by my best friend, and now it's clear that the two of us are out of step with each other for the first time in months.

"Of course," JJ replies. "I'll send it to you both tonight. Next on the agenda, I'd like to talk about prom, and how we'll be supporting candidates affiliated with our organization." He keeps talking, very delicately expressing his enthusiasm about both Ashley's and my campaigns.

Ashley settles into the chair next to me. I half expect her to swipe at me with her crutch, but she doesn't. She leans her head into me, and I momentarily worry that she's going to pass out on my shoulder.

"You misinterpreted my warning," she whispers.

The rest of BSU claps as JJ holds his hand out to us, as the potential prom queens.

Ashley takes my hand in hers and waves both in the air. To be fair, she has warned me about my friends, being too close to JJ, and using the same prom campaign slogans as her, so I'm not fully sure what she's referring to.

"Which one?" I ask.

"Your friend," she replies.

"Still vague."

She's enjoying this. But, given everything she's been through, I don't think I can fault her for that.

Ashley sighs, and this time, she puts her head on my shoulder. "You thought I was talking about Simone, right?"

She said *your little friend*. How many friends does she think I have? Plus, she and I have a very small overlap in our social circles. Who was I supposed to think?

"Were you not?" I ask.

She shakes her head. "Though she *is* moving in a way that isn't very friend-like," she says. "Free piece of advice. I was talking about one of your newer friends."

She doesn't say friend in that annoying, knowing-but-in-denial sort of way that people refer to lesbian relationships, so I assume she's not talking about Amayah. Shit. Is this another reference to Bridget?

"I've already heard some rumblings about Bridget. Did she have something to do with your attack?" I ask.

Ashley's eyebrows furrow. "Not that I know of. I was talking about my runner-up," she replies.

"Your runner-up?" I start racking my brain for anything I know about the tennis team roster before it hits me. She's not talking about sports. Or prom.

She's talking about her runner-up on the list. The number two. Lauren.

CHAPTER 46

I SIT ON ASHLEY'S REVELATION FOR TWO DAYS, TRYING to figure out what to do with it. She didn't give any additional information, and I'm trying to fit what I already know about the attacks into the idea that Lauren was the perpetrator.

Ashley told me she already told the police, but nothing has happened. Are they investigating? Who knows. She sounded sure, but she doesn't have any evidence.

I feel so sick over all of it. Lauren was the one who recruited me to help her track the girls on the list. Was she using that intel to figure out who to target?

And now that I'm in this alone, given everything, I'm really at a loss. It just doesn't make sense.

I'm trying to connect the dots, literally, in my math notebook, when Mom knocks on my doorframe.

"Come on," she says. "You've been doing...whatever you've

been doing for long enough. Let's go to the tailor and get lunch. Have a little girls' time."

I'm about to protest. I need to stay here and think. But that hasn't gotten me anywhere yet. Maybe a change of scenery could help.

Plus, I can pump Mom for PTA information, to see if there's some missing piece I can add to my fucked-up puzzle.

"Okay," I say.

Thirty minutes later I'm standing on a small podium in front of a full-length mirror, with pins sticking out of the hem of the dress. It takes my breath away once again, both how it looks on me, and the ribbon cinching the tailor wanted to do around my waist.

Mom circles me, pointing out a couple pins she thinks could be adjusted. When she slips in something about the waist and the tailor loosens the ribbon, I mouth *thank you.*

I'm stepping down to head back into the changing room when the tailor's front door swings open.

"Oh my God, you look stunning!" Lauren and her perfect gleaming smile stride toward me.

My heart starts to pound. Her hair is in a messy bun, and she's holding her dress in one hand and shoes in the other. But who knows? Could this be her moment to knock me off too?

I take a deep breath. No. Mom is here. The tailor is here. There is no one else to pin this on. Plus, she's had so many opportunities to come after me, and she hasn't, minus that day in the library. And even that doesn't sit right with me. There was no way that the shelf could've hit me. It seemed like more of a warning shot.

Or…

Maybe it was to look like she was coming after everyone equally. The note was supposed to point to Ashley. Maybe it was similar to when Amayah and I chased that figure outside her house. We only saw Lauren after, though she texted us before. Could she have been the one running away from us before disappearing back into her house?

"Thanks," I say.

Mom smiles at her. "Hi. I'm Ida's mom." She holds out her hand.

"Lauren Buckley. A newer friend," Lauren replies. She looks back to me. "Amayah won't know what hit her."

How could she be the person behind all of this? I thought she was… Just why?

"Hope so," I say.

Mom gives me a curious look but thankfully doesn't say anything about it in front of Lauren.

"Mrs. Carter, thank you for speaking out with the PTA about Mrs. Davis and her shaming of us girls. It was really—" Lauren's voice breaks. "It meant a lot."

Oh my *God*. I'm an idiot.

Okay, no I'm not. But I did have the wrong angle. Morality was right, of course. But what if it wasn't someone trying to impose morality on girls for sending sexual messages? What if it was someone trying to get revenge on the people who slut-shamed them the most?

Cassidy was one of the first people to call Lauren out after the PTA imposed their morality clause. She posted several times before her death. And Ashley, most recently, has held herself up as the opposite of Lauren. Someone who would never send *those kinds* of photos. But Cassidy is the one who's dead.

Why?

"Of course, hon," Mom says. "I'm glad we were able to help."

Am I sweating? I swear Mom is giving me the side-eye, and even Lauren seems to pick up on my uneasiness.

"I'm going to go change," I say, almost to no one.

When I get into the changing room, I'm shaking. What can I do? What *should* I do? My fingers won't settle enough for me to unzip this dress.

There's a rustle behind me, and I leap several inches in the air.

"Sorry, sweetie, I didn't mean to scare you," Mom says. "I thought you might need help with the zipper again."

My mouth feels like it's full of sand. I manage to nod.

She unzips the dress and holds my hand as I step out of it. She gathers the dress in her arms to bring out to the tailor.

Do I tell her? Would she believe me? Would that put her in danger? Fuck.

She starts to walk out, then pauses and pulls the curtain closed.

"What's going on?" she whispers. "Something is up between you and this girl."

"It's the whole list thing. We've been working together, trying to figure things out."

Her eyebrows creep up. I need to stop underestimating mom intuition. She's looking at me like she knows every single thing I've avoided saying.

"Working together," Mom repeats. "But not anymore?"

I shrug. "I've been putting pieces together."

Mom sucks on her teeth, takes a second, then nods. She walks out of the changing room, and I hear her saying something to Lauren, but I can't tell what.

I snatch my jeans off the floor, throwing each leg into them. I nearly trip as I try to hop and pull them up. I'm still pulling my shirt down when I stumble out of the changing room.

Mom and Lauren look at me as I walk out. Mom smiles. "Can you believe Lauren is going stag to prom?"

Lauren chuckles. "Not all of us can bounce back after a long-term relationship ends," she replies, her cheeks flushed.

"His loss, I'm sure," Mom says.

"Well, he's very much moved on," Lauren says, shooting me a knowing look. "Keeping busy with sports and art."

I almost snort at "art." I really liked her. She's quick, and she's fun. Why does she have to be a killer? Is all this really worth the revenge?

"Art? Is his work featured in the school?" Mom asks.

"That would be illegal," Lauren replies, letting out a strained laugh. "Ida, do you want to grab coffee after this?"

Um, not at all.

"Mom and I have plans. Rain check?"

Mom clicks her tongue. "We can grab lunch some other time. Hang out with your friend."

I open my mouth to protest, but that would look weird. Who wants to hang out with their mom over one of the most popular girls in school? I mean, me. Very much me, even on better days than this. But this might be my only opportunity to confront her. We'll be in a public place. If we go to the diner, it's also a place where she's already staged an attack, *and* they've upped security since.

"Amazing, just let me get this fitted," Lauren says, walking into the changing room.

Mom takes my arm and pulls me to the side by the door.

"I'm going to call you in a few minutes to ask you about that thing you needed me to pick up. Make sure to answer, and then, if you happen to miss the end call button, I'll make sure to stay nearby," she says quietly.

"Okay."

Moms always come through.

Lauren emerges from the dressing room, her entire face turning pink to match the peach of her Grecian style dress.

She looks beautiful, girlishly innocent.

I hope that by prom she still is.

CHAPTER 47

LAUREN LEADS US TO THE DARKEST BOOTH IN THE diner, tucked back by the bustle of the kitchen. Unless we were to yell, no one could overhear us.

Mom calls just as we sit down. “Yeah. Yeah, it’s at CVS,” I say loudly.

“I can barely hear you!” she replies. “Could you—” The call drops. Terrible service.

Damn it.

I lay the phone on the booth next to me, silently hoping that a bar comes through and I can dial Mom back. Something, anything, to make sure I’m not alone here.

In the meantime, I hit my audio recorder and hope for the best.

“You don’t have to be weird around me, you know,” Lauren says. “I know about your friend and Grayson. I don’t hold it against you or anything.”

Oh my God, *that's* why she thinks I'm being weird? I should go with it, but I'm so flabbergasted that she hasn't figured out what *I know*. Or, at least, what I think I know.

"Sorry. It's awkward," I say. Not a lie.

"For me too. Like, I hear he's still posting photos of me. Real and fake. While dating someone else. Fucking psycho behavior," she replies.

So why not try to kill him instead?

God, that's dark. I don't want Grayson dead. I mean, I don't want anyone dead. Grayson would be the least offensive option if I had to choose, but damn it, I'm not choosing.

Hold it together. Do not let her see you sweat. Except it's really freaking hot right outside this kitchen.

A waitress who isn't Sally flits by asking for our orders. We both order coffees, and I silently thank some higher power that she didn't bite the bullet and order food. I want to be able to leave as soon as possible.

"It's gross," I say, taking a sip of my water.

"I don't get why someone would want to be with him after that. She knows, right?" Lauren asks, looking at me expectantly.

"I assume," I reply.

"You don't talk about it?" she asks.

"Talking isn't really our forte right now."

She sighs. Is she seriously this worked up over *Grayson*? Does this man have some sort of pheromone situation going on?

"It was her outside my house, you know," she says.

I nod. "I figured."

"She was at the party; you don't think she'd—" She lowers her voice. "She wouldn't kill Cassidy, right?"

Oh my God, why the hell would she ask me that? *She* killed Cassidy. Is this not vastly overplaying her hand?

"No. She wouldn't," I say.

"She confessed to me that it was her at my house. Grayson told her I was still sending him pictures and said that she should scare me off by pretending to be the attacker. Like, what is wrong with him? And she stayed?" Lauren presses the heels of her hands into her forehead.

Does she not have other friends she can talk to about this? Why am I here? Is it the Simone of it all? Lauren seems distressed and confused, but she can't be, unless I'm wrong. Which I can't be.

The waitress drops off our coffees and a small cup of milk. Some of the milk slops over the side onto the table. Lauren wipes it up with a napkin before the waitress can even reach for the cloth looped to her apron.

"How long did you stay with him?" I ask.

She recoils. "Oh. Well. I'm dumb too." She lets out a cracking chuckle. "Sorry. I shouldn't call your friend dumb."

"She's not dumb. She's just acting that way right now," I reply.

"Who pretends they're going to attack their new boyfriend's ex without vetting the evidence?" she asks.

I'm going to scream. What isn't clicking? Does she have amnesia? She sounds so serious about her questions too.

"Who attacks several girls, killing one, because they called her a slut?" I ask.

Lauren blinks several times and opens her mouth to speak. Instead, she takes a sip of her coffee, which is still hot, and winces.

"What are you talking about?" she croaks.

"That reaction tells me you already know," I say. "You're the one who has been attacking the girls. You killed Cassidy."

"She wasn't dead when I left her," Lauren says.

Oh, come on. That's not true! She had access to the pills; she had access to the party. She had motive.

"Excuse me?" I raise my eyebrows.

"I'm not a monster!" she exclaims. "I went to talk to Cassidy to ask her why she'd repost that photo, the one of me they used for the list. She got it from Jason's phone. We fought. I pushed her, and she hit her head. But she was alive. I didn't give her anything; I just left."

"Why would I believe you?" I ask.

"Because I'm not a murderer! And I don't do drugs. I'd never have on me. But Grayson would."

I sigh. I want to believe her, I really do. But she's not denying any of the other allegations.

"But you were responsible for the other attacks?" I meet her eyes.

She nods. "They'll all be fine."

"Fine? Fine? You sat in my house with Bridget and Sally and acted like you cared! You—"

"I do care! I want to know what happened to Cassidy as much as anyone," she says.

"So you aren't the one who gets blamed."

She dumps a packet of stevia into her coffee. "So? *I didn't kill her.*"

I throw a few dollars down on the table. I have my confession, and no other reason to stay.

"If you follow me, I'll call the police," I say.

"I'd never hurt you," she replies. "You're the only person who didn't treat me differently. You were kind to me. You didn't act like I was a whore. Thank you."

"Are you done?" I ask.

"Yeah. I was done after Sally, but then that stupid PTA meeting. It was impulsive. I just wanted to know what happened to Cassidy. The police are calling it an OD, so I'm in the clear, as long as you don't tell."

I snort. Sure. I'm not going to report a series of crimes against my female classmates because she asked nicely? Please.

When I make it out of the restaurant and around the corner, I stop the recording. But when I try to play it back, I can barely hear anything over the clatter of plates. There goes my only piece of evidence. Damn it.

CHAPTER 48

MOM SITS WITH ME IN THE CAR TO CALL IN AN ANONY-mous report to the police about what I think I know. She didn't lie to me. She was literally sitting on a bench half a block away from the diner.

The police take my statement, but without any evidence, they don't seem particularly inclined to look into it further. They think Cassidy's death is solved, at least, per the newspapers. And with so much speculation about who is to blame for the other incidents, it seems none of the theories are given weight. If nothing else happens, this will all become a fluke, an unfortunate series of pranks or scare tactics that will be forgotten someday. It doesn't feel right, but it feels real. Violence against girls can easily be explained away or ignored.

As we drive home, neither of us really knowing what else to say, my phone buzzes with texts.

If it's Lauren, I'm going to throw the phone out of the window. Honestly, there's no one I want to talk to right now.

I have three texts from Amayah, two from Simone, and one from an unknown number.

I open the unknown number first.

Got your number from JJ. It's Ashley. 209 Wexler Blvd. ASAP.

"Um, Mom?"

"Yeah, sweetie?"

"Can you take me to 209 Wexler Boulevard?" I ask. "I've been invited."

The texts from Amayah and Simone are them letting me know that Ashley wants all of us at her house. Amayah wants to know if I know why, and when we're going to talk, just the two of us. Simone is more solemn, reporting that Ashley wants to meet with us and saying that she hopes we can have a productive conversation.

"Invited by whom?" Mom asks.

"Ashley Beckett. She's dating JJ," I reply.

Mom turns to look at me, nearly missing that the light in front of us is turning red. She slams the brakes. "Sorry," she says, even though she's lead footed anyway, and this happens a lot. "Are you serious?"

"I don't know why, but I'm interested," I say.

Mom sighs, turns on her left blinker, and when the light is green, she whips the car in the opposite direction of our house.

"You have to be careful," she says. "You're already so involved in this. But Lauren would be a complete idiot to hurt anyone again. And she's not an idiot, right?"

Who is she trying to convince? Me or herself? We're both definitely hoping that this is all over, at least the attacks. Whether Lauren will be held accountable is another story.

"I will be. Plus Ashley has a black belt," I say.

"Ashley also has a broken knee," Mom points out.

"Oh, trust me, that's not stopping her," I say.

I text JJ to ask if he's coming to the meeting. If I need a buffer between Ashley's throwing arm and a remote, I'm not confident that Simone or Amayah are stepping in.

Nope. It's for the girls, he responds.

I send a prayer-hands emoji, which he reacts to with a **haha**.

Okay, dude, you could at least reassure me that your girlfriend isn't plotting to make a sacrifice out of me.

Mom pulls into Ashley's driveway. Her house is surprisingly modest, with a bit of quirkiness on the outside. A genuine historic green Queen Anne with maroon shutters that has a plaque saying it is from 1895. The lawn is impeccably maintained, and there are freaking rosebushes and tulips dotting the sides of the property.

Mom parks the car and moves to get out with me.

"Mom, this isn't a playdate. You don't need to meet her parents," I say.

"Not hers," she replies.

Oh my God. Amayah's parents? My denim shorts are distressed, and so am I. I can't meet them looking like this. Or when our relationship is this awkward.

I look out my car window and almost breathe a sigh of relief. It's not Amayah's parents but Simone's. Then I remember where Simone and I are in our friendship, or lack thereof, and that feeling quickly dissipates.

"You sure?" I ask.

Mom smirks. "Sometimes a *fuck off* is more powerful in person." She pushes her door open.

I follow her lead and come face-to-face with Simone, who is standing next to my side of the car.

"Hey." Her face is blotchy, and she's digging her nails into her palms.

I give her a once-over. "You're allowed out of the house without a male chaperone?"

"He dumped me," she says. "He doesn't think he's over Lauren. And I wouldn't send him pictures."

Part of me wants to apologize to her or commiserate. Call him an asshole. But I also kind of blame her for it. She chose to date him, knowing everything he's done. Even after all his actions came to light, she stood ten toes down. Why should I feel badly for her?

"Good riddance," I reply.

She lets out a sob. "But I love him."

"Maybe don't?" Amayah walks up beside me.

I turn to look for her car, but I don't see it. God, she's good at just appearing. I try to lead the way to Ashley's door. Anything to get away from it being the three of us.

"I'd say you dodged a bullet, but it seems like you're still digging the bullet out after a self-inflicted wound," I reply.

"Good one," Amayah says, squeezing my hand.

I pull my hand from hers and ring the doorbell. We're *so* not there yet.

Simone snorts and wipes her face. "Glad we're all lucky in love."

"Not as lucky as me," Ashley says as the door swings open. She's bedazzled her crutches with purple rhinestones, and she's made sure to affix a small sketch of JJ to her cast.

Honestly, he should stay with her forever. We're only seventeen, but is he ever going to find someone who rides as hard for him as Ashley?

She motions for us to come in, and I am floored. Every fixture looks somehow both period appropriate to the house but still fresh. All three of us slide off our shoes by the door, and Ashley nods in approval.

She leads us to the living room, where there's a gorgeous navy-blue sectional stretched out in front of a seventy-inch television.

Amayah is the first to sit, tucking her feet underneath her.

Simone hovers behind the couch, like she has to be ready to run out of the room at any moment.

Ashley hops over to the edge of the couch and perches so that her legs are elevated and she's leaning against an armrest. She keeps her eyes fixed on me, to see what I decide.

I walk around the couch and sit as close to the middle as I can.

"The symbolism," Ashley says. "Perfect."

"Why are we here?" Simone asks, her voice still rough from the sobs.

"Because I invited you," Ashley replies sweetly.

"Why?" Simone repeats.

Ashley opens her laptop and places it on the coffee table in front of us. She pulls up a video from her text messages. She presses play.

It's JJ, but not recently. From when I was not-so-secretly in love with him. Freshman year.

Oh shit. It's the locker room vandalism video. Somehow, he looks so much younger, even though he was beefier. Throwing helmets, slamming shoulder pads into the wall. He kicks three benches over. Pulls a sink down from the wall in the shower area. Swings said sink into a collection of lockers.

Amayah whistles. "I didn't realize he was so strong."

"Why do you have this?" I ask. "When did he tell you?"

Ashley glares at me before taking a very deep breath and forcing her face to relax.

"It was sent to me anonymously on Discord," she replies. "It's none of your business when JJ told me."

Simone doesn't react. So she knows where this is from. *Who* this is from.

"Why? Why now?" I ask.

"So I'd keep quiet about Lauren Buckley."

Another sob escapes Simone's mouth, and she claps her hand over her lips. So Grayson really isn't over Lauren.

Amayah shakes her head and looks at Simone, disgusted. "You're not going to, of course," she says.

"Yes, I am," Ashley replies.

"Why?" I ask.

"I thought you, of all people, would understand," Ashley replies. "I love him. I don't care what happened before me. I care about his future, and I want to be a part of it. I'm not going to let JJ's past ruin that future. And I'm going to recover. So will the other girls. I'm moving forward."

Ashley closes the laptop, and her gaze travels between the three of us, defiantly daring us to say something.

"It's not your decision to make. Cassidy is *dead*," I say. "You have an obligation to—"

Ashley holds up her hand, and I instinctively flinch.

"Lauren says she didn't do it," she replies. Before I can begin to protest, she continues. "And I don't have any obligation to anyone other than myself and my boyfriend. This video, the one from the diner, and the fact that JJ dated Cassidy and has access to fentanyl? It would be so easy to point the finger at him. Who do you think the police would believe? What about a jury? It is not my job to put myself and the people I love in danger, physically or mentally, when I don't believe there will ever be real justice."

She's not wrong. At least not about the circumstances. But morally? I can't get behind this. It's not like I have much of an option though. I've done what I can do, unless I try to pursue this further. I'm not a detective. I'm not going to find some hidden connection and break the case wide-open. I have one witness who won't come forward and a whole bunch of conjecture. And does that outweigh the risks to JJ? To the safety of us all??

"Grayson carries drugs around," Simone says quietly. "Jason takes them from him all the time."

"Do we know for sure?" I ask.

"That they gave it to her? No. She could have taken it herself. We're never going to know," Simone replies.

This just seems so unfair. That someone is dead, and we won't know exactly what happened. That three girls were harmed, but the person who did it will get away with it.

I hate it, but I'm resigned to the fact that I can't do anything about it.

Amayah scoots over to me and takes my hand. "It's not okay," she whispers. "None of it is. But you've tried. You spoke out; you fought for all the girls. Can that be enough?"

"I don't know," I say.

"You should try to move forward too. All of you," Ashley says. "Especially you two." She gestures to me and Amayah.

"So I'll leave JJ alone?" I ask.

"Because you two love each other and are better together. That's the only way you could even come close to beating me as prom queen. Plus, you're cute," Ashley says.

"What about me?" Simone asks.

Ashley fixes her with a withering look. "You should try to move forward with yourself. Figure out why you fell for a guy like Grayson. Figure out why you were willing to sell your friend out for a side of homophobia."

Amayah closes her eyes, and I watch her try to suppress laughter that still manages to come out.

I really, really do like her so much. And I want to understand why she didn't tell me about Bridget. But honestly? Ashley's right.

The past is the past. And I want Amayah as part of my future, both at prom and beyond.

So maybe I will move on. Move forward.

See where this takes us. And hope that someday, somehow, guys like Grayson and Jason will get what they deserve. And girls like Cassidy, Ashley, Sally, Bridget, and even Lauren are able to find protection from the systems in place, without resorting to violence themselves.

I can hope.

CHAPTER 49

TWO WEEKS LATER, MOM IS PUTTING THE FINISHING touches on my lipstick when the doorbell rings. I nearly bolt up out of the chair, and Mom gently presses my shoulder.

"We're almost done; your dad can get the door," she says.

I try not to groan as I hear the front door swing open and Dad say, "And what are your intentions with my daughter?" before letting out a booming laugh.

So embarrassing.

"There," Mom says, backing away so I can see myself in the mirror.

She has given me a mostly dewy, natural-looking, soft makeup, with a dramatic eyeliner wing and a deep red lip. My hair is twisted and clipped into an updo, with a couple of tendrils framing my face.

It's perfect.

I grin and wrap her in a hug. "Thank you, Mom."

"Amayah won't know what hit her," Mom says.

"I'm counting on it."

"Be safe," she says. "In all ways."

I gag, but nod. Mom and Dad are letting us go to an after-prom party and have extended my curfew to a shockingly late two a.m. With everything that has happened over the past few weeks, from the pictures, which they now know about, to the attacks, which seem to have stopped for now, I thought they'd pull me closer. Instead, they're letting me spread my wings further. Some of that might be attributable to Amayah, who they like significantly more than they ever liked JJ.

Mom jogs ahead of me to the stairs, where she clears her throat loudly. "You look wonderful, Amayah." Then she clears her throat again. "Now presenting your future prom queen, Ida Carter."

Dad starts clapping furiously, and I kind of want to die but also love it.

I grip the railing, but in a casual way, as I descend the staircase in heels that are surely getting kicked off the second we get to the venue.

Amayah gasps, just loud enough for me to hear.

I almost trip when I see that she's wearing a blazer and skirt combination in the same color as my dress. The blazer is fully buttoned, and my mind immediately travels to the idea of changing that later tonight.

Amayah holds her hand out as I reach the last step. When I take it, she tugs me into her.

"You look beautiful," she murmurs, before planting a kiss on my lips.

"Just trying to keep up with you," I whisper, before returning the favor for twice as long.

Dad clears his throat, and Mom shushes him. Then a camera flashes.

We pull apart, and Mom begins directing a full-fledged photoshoot. Next to each other, holding hands. Sliding our matching corsages onto each other's wrists. Doing the traditional cheesy prom pose with each of us in front of the other, arms wrapped together.

Once she starts trying to get Dad to add props—the fake flowers from the kitchen vase and a Banneker High emblem from Dad's old letterman's jacket—Amayah and I make our excuses. We have a dance to get to, after all.

Mom relinquishes us and snaps pictures as we walk to Amayah's car. I literally hear her squeal when Amayah holds the passenger side door open for me, then holds out a hand to help me in.

That one is definitely ending up in the family Christmas card this winter. And maybe the one she gets of me waving out the window of the car, like we're going to a royal wedding.

Oh my God, the family Christmas card is going to be so embarrassing.

I'm good with that.

We pull up to the local country club, which is hosting the dance, on the earlier end of the arrivals, since I'm willing to bet that a sizable amount of the student body is still pregaming with wine coolers and cheap vodka at someone's house.

As we walk in, hands knitted together, I wonder if it's possible to smile harder than this.

The photographer is occupied with another couple. It's Ashley and JJ. Ashley is giving pointers on how to get her best angle. As if she has a bad one. Her dress is sleek and black with a deep, yet unrevealing V-neck. She has on one gold heel, and her crutches are lying just out of the camera's frame, which means she is strategically leaning on JJ for support.

For someone who swore he'd never go to a school dance, he looks pretty thrilled to be standing next to Ashley.

He notices Amayah and me waiting and whispers something to Ashley.

Ashley looks over at us and grins. She motions for us to join them.

My eyes widen and I wonder if this is a prank. But why would it be? So we do. And as we join them, I discover Ashley makes me laugh. And she's really good at figuring out how I should stand to get the best view of my dress.

After we get a few solo shots, Amayah and I venture into the room. There are simple white flower arrangements on each table and sparkling lights decorating the ceiling. Someone has made what must be hundreds of golden paper cranes, which hang across the walls. It's simple but perfectly beautiful.

The box for prom queen votes is placed right next to the

dance floor. Amayah makes a big show of writing my name and dropping her ballot inside the box.

Then she whisks me off to the dance floor just as a Top 40 pop tune begins to play.

I'm breathless and mid-twirl when I spot Lauren in the corner of the room, looking glamorous and demure, as if she's as innocent as she pretends to be.

She makes eye contact with me and nods.

I turn my head.

Simone walks in, in a classic magenta one-shoulder column dress that perfectly showcases her arms.

Behind her, Grayson follows, but I can't tell if they're arriving together.

And it's not my business. At least, I really, really don't want it to be.

As the night passes, I'm focused on Amayah. Even though I can see her glancing at the prom queen projections from time to time, I find that I barely remember I'm running. None of it seems important anymore, minus the fact that it matters to her.

When it's finally time for the announcement, she grips my hand more tightly than she has all night. When history is made, I hear her exhale in disappointment before she begins to clap as Ashley makes her way to the stage.

The crown, however bright and tacky, looks perfect on her.

I lost. But honestly? Looking at Amayah, I won. And I'm okay with that outcome.

Why get over your cheating ex when you can get even?
Don't miss Alex Travis's
The Payback Girls

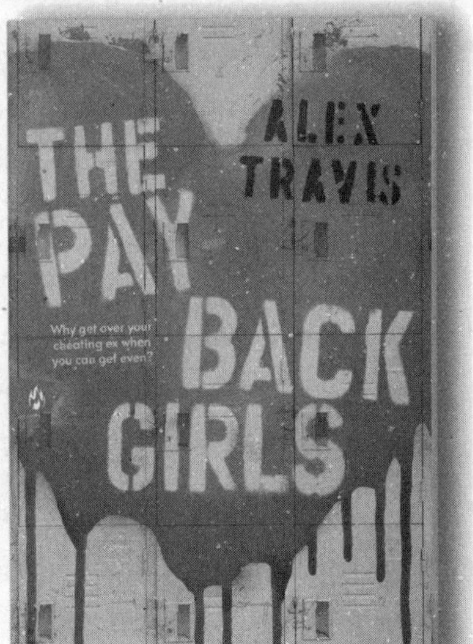

ROBIN ELLISON HAS NEVER MISSED A SHOT. BE IT HER swing or her stance, when she makes contact with a ball, it is game over. This is perfect for her role as star forward of the Burke High School field hockey team. It is decidedly less perfect when it happens before a pep rally and the ball is the student government president, Bria Kelly's, head.

Sitting in the stands, wearing Nate's jersey, I am sick to my stomach. The cold metal bleacher is digging into my butt, even on this unseasonably warm November day, and I'm catching whispers of Nate's two exes getting into a fight in the tunnel leading to the basketball court. Could it really be true though?

Both Robin and Bria are incredibly image conscious. Bria, especially, has a knack for making sure things are seen the way she wants them to be. If Robin is the queen, then Bria is the kingmaker and destroyer of the crown, wrapped in a five-foot-two package of more ice than fire. Her extra-long acrylics are sharpened into stilettos. I fully believe she'd slit a throat, probably mine, given how she looks at me in calculus.

Someone in the row in front of me cheers as Robin jogs out onto the court, holding her field hockey stick up in the air. The cheerleaders follow her out, barely waving their pom-poms.

They're all trying to move as far to Robin's left as possible. Oh my God, did they actually see the fight?

"I hear he rotates, one girl each night. Each has their own special place, so they never overlap," someone says. "Nate Walker's hoe-tation, except none of them know about the others. Until now."

The band's tuba player comes in too early on the "Stars and Stripes" march, and the noise booms out of the tunnel before the first drummer can even make it out onto the court. It almost drowns out the sound of a walkie-talkie screeching with feedback. The band pauses.

"Keep them on the court, I'm on the way with security," a voice echoes from the tunnel. Someone, I assume the band teacher, has their walkie way too close to their microphone.

Robin grits her teeth, leaning forward like she's going to lunge back into the tunnel. Bria holds up her hands as she exits the tunnel behind the band like she's trying to negotiate with a raging bull. Unfortunately for her, she *is* wearing red, and I'm almost certain red is all Robin sees. Every time Robin moves, the microphone pinned to her lapel rustles.

From what I understand, Bria, as president, is supposed to present Robin with an award, since the field hockey team raised the most money for the annual town charity auction. Robin even auctioned off one of her field hockey sticks from her state win, scoring ten thousand dollars for the local food bank.

"Robin, be serious," Bria says. "We're in *public* now."

"Since when have you ever cared about that, B?" Robin seethes.

The vice principal sprints through the gym doors, nearly

tripping over the foot of the field hockey cocaptain as he steps onto the other side of the court. He's followed by the school resource officer, who's gripping his utility belt. Oh shit, did Robin *actually* hit Bria in the tunnel?

I squint, trying to spot Nate in the crowd of basketball players forming around the vice principal. A few guys are still behind the banner planted in the middle of the court. Did Nate see what happened? Is he going to break them up before it happens again? Is anyone going to break up this fight?

"Ms. Ellison, that's enough!" the vice principal shouts, charging to the center of the court.

Robin's field hockey teammates, who are standing just out of the line of fire, have an IMAX-level view of the conflict. None of them look particularly surprised. So either Robin has a history of using her field hockey stick for alternative purposes, or they knew something was going on with Bria.

"I didn't do anything! Ask *her* what happened," Robin says, pointing at Bria.

"Didn't he cheat on Robin with Bria? What is this, last year?" someone in the row above me says.

I recognize the voice. It's Jess. She and the rest of the basketball girlfriends didn't save me a seat, but of course they want me to overhear their commentary.

"Only actual couples can cochair the charity dinner. So shouldn't it be Meg? Or is she too new?" another girl asks.

"Well, *I* heard that Nate and Robin never even broke up," Jess says. "So he's cheating with Bria *and* the other one."

I accidentally lock eyes with Robin, who is glaring into the crowd as if she's looking for someone. But who?

"I don't *care* who her parents are. Are you going to discipline her or not?" Bria snaps as the vice principal freezes a few feet shy of Robin.

Robin is still staring at me. She clocks Nate's jersey almost immediately, and her mouth tightens. Robin never misses. And now she's swinging at me too.

Bria's gaze follows Robin's. She rolls her eyes and gives me the finger.

I feel my eyes filling with tears. I force them back.

Robin's face scrunches in fury, and she pulls back her stick while everyone gasps in unison.

The vice principal takes a step away from her, gesturing to the school resource officer.

Robin swings as if she's going to hit Bria's perfectly symmetrical and meticulously highlighted face. She drives her stick into a patch of weeds, sending dandelions flying inches away.

Robin smirks as Bria flinches.

The school resource officer reaches toward Robin.

I imagine this is what spectators felt like in the Colosseum. It's exhilarating and horrible. I've never liked Bria, but she looks truly terrified, like she really thought Robin was going to hit her. Potentially for the second time today.

"Touch me, and my family will sue the school," Robin says to the officer.

Her father is a state senator, and her mother is one of the most well-respected civil rights lawyers in the country. I fully believe she'd sue and win, particularly given that relations between the Black students and this particular SRO are already tense.

The SRO pulls his hand back and shrugs at the vice principal. This vice principal has barely been on the job for three weeks, and he's already lost control of the situation. Our previous one would have dragged Robin and Bria to his office before they even made it onto the court.

The assistant boys' basketball coach, Coach McGregor, nods at the vice principal and grabs Robin around the waist while one of the football coaches grabs Robin's wrist. One of her teammates pries the field hockey stick out of her hand.

Noah Walker, photographer for the school newspaper, is intently taking pictures from the sidelines. I can only imagine what that headline will be on Monday.

Noah is only eighteen months younger than us, but everyone knows him as Nate Walker's baby brother. He and I have made small talk, but he's so painfully shy that it's apparent he'd rather be anywhere his brother isn't. Nate draws attention. But Noah seems to be holding his own up front.

"Are you kidding me, Noah?" Robin says, loud enough that her voice floats into the stands. "Maybe if the coaches had their eyes checked, they would have seen what actually happened before lying on the walkies." She tries to wiggle out of the coaches' grasp.

Noah shrugs and takes a few steps back, shielding the lens of his camera, as if she can reach him while being restrained.

I look back to the banner. Nate is peeking around the side, watching the show.

Bria catches him, and she covers the mic pinned to her lapel while she says something.

Robin's face falls. Coach McGregor drops her, and Robin staggers forward on the linoleum, trying to get her footing. She holds up her empty hands, as if that means she's less likely to lunge again.

"Ms. Ellison, you'd better start walking to my office before someone carries you there," the vice principal yells.

His threats ring hollow, now that he's let this go on for what feels like forty-five minutes. I check my watch. It's barely been five.

"This isn't how it was supposed to go. And why would you drag Meghan into it?" Robin asks, pointing at Nate.

I hear my name echo, like a thousand Robins are repeating "Meghan." My ears begin ringing. If I cry here, the crowd might enjoy it. If I were just a spectator, I might find it fun too. It really is incredible drama when you're not at the center of it.

Nate reaches out and covers her microphone. He says something that the rest of us can't hear.

Bria marches over to the banner, leaning into her handheld microphone. "And I'll never forgive you. You could die, and I wouldn't give a flying f—"

The field hockey coach blows her whistle, drowning out the rest of Bria's sentiment. Funny how they react faster to foul language than a fight.

"Over a *guy*?" the field hockey coach says to Robin. "Seriously?" She motions for Robin and Bria to follow her.

The rest of the field hockey team glares at Robin. If she gets suspended, their chance of winning the playoffs will be in jeopardy.

"*I'm* the victim here," Bria says into her mic as they walk. "I should be allowed to give my speech, then decide whether I plan to press charges for what happened in the tunnel."

Robin's head turns so that she's facing Bria. "For *what*? I *didn't fucking hit you*."

"You just told him it wasn't supposed to be like this. So you knew. You knew he was screwing me over again," Bria replies. "So don't underestimate what I *would* do."

?? I text Nate. **Tell me they're lying.**

The way my stomach turns, I know they aren't. He cheated. He cheated on all of us.

"See, I told you they were violent," I hear someone say.

"Take the girl out of the hood, but you can't take the hood out of the girl," Jess adds, loudly enough for everyone in the stands to hear.

No one in a ten-mile radius of this school has even driven past what could be considered the hood. Assume, assume, assume. That's all anyone does about any of us Black girls. Even I'm guilty of it. I have all sorts of assumptions about Robin and Bria that I'd never dare say to their faces.

Robin and Bria are whispering to each other as the field hockey coaches finally lead them into the building. Robin gestures to Nate back on the court and me in the stands. It's then that I realize my hands are still frozen, shielding my face from what's happening, not the sun. And now the entire senior class is staring at me.

I fix my face. My hands drop to my sides, and I smile out at the crowd. Time to practice large-scale diplomacy in a war zone. I'm covered in glitter that will take two hours to scrub off; I can't possibly embarrass myself further.

"Brutal," the girl next to me says.

"Hmm?"

"You really didn't know that you were one of many?" she asks.

Nate finally walks out, his eyes trained on his shoes. He doesn't look at any of us, not even Robin and Bria being led away. The vice principal follows them. He shakes his head when the basketball coach whispers something to him, glancing toward Nate. My heartbeat thuds up into my throat. Is he really going to pretend that none of us exist? This is just business as usual, apparently.

"Whatever Nate has done in his past isn't relevant to our relationship now," I reply. Classic politician's wife response. I'm not looking the other way; I'm just focused on the road ahead. Hopefully it's not paved with the blood of the most popular girls in school.

ACKNOWLEDGMENTS

Thank you to all the people who have read this book, or one of my others, and who have shared my stories, given kind words, and helped me keep this dream of mine going. I hope that you enjoyed this latest adventure and these characters.

To my agent, Dorian Maffei, working with you has continued to be incredible, and I can't believe that we've done so much together. Thank you for championing my work, your incredibly thoughtful feedback, and your guiding hand throughout the publishing process. I could not have imagined a better agent, and I'm so lucky to have you in my corner.

To my editor, Annette Pollert-Morgan, you do such a wonderful job of leaving me room to grow and explore ideas, while shepherding me in the right direction. Working with you has been so fun and such an opportunity for growth. Thank you so much for these two books and hopefully more to come.

To the entire Sourcebooks team, you all are the best. Lia Ferrone, publicist extraordinaire, you make events and promotion absolutely seamless for this avowed introvert. You are so excellent at what you do, and I am so grateful for it. Plus, you're a fun hang. (Y'allWest was a time!) Karen Masnica, thank you for keeping so many plans organized and letting me in on all of the cool ideas you all have to get my stories out into the world. I am so grateful to you and the whole marketing team, including Delaney Heisterkamp. Jenny Lopez, thank you for always keeping me in the loop and still answering so many questions all the time. To the incredible copy editors, Thea Voutiritsas and Carolyn, who probably have the most questionable Google histories checking up on some of the details of this book, thank you so much for your care and attention to this story. This team was also so gracious and flexible as this deadline was pushed so I could give birth and attempt those early days of motherhood, and so sweet in sending books (some of which we are reading seemingly dozens of times a day right now) for Riley to enjoy (she really, really loves them).

Mom and Adrienne, thank you for being so supportive and loving and marketing my books wherever you get the opportunity. I am constantly in awe of everything you all are doing and the strength and generosity you bring to all of us. I am so proud of you both and all that you've accomplished, and you're both proof that Black girls may cry sometimes, but we also rise to the occasion and bring others up with us. Dad, I miss you every day and wish you were here to see this. You'd be working the phones like no other to make sure that this book made it into as many hands as possible. Mom, Dad, and Adrienne, I love you all, and I am so grateful that you're my family.

Sean, I love you and the life we've built with our girl. Watching you become a father has been the greatest gift, and having you bring Riley to as many events as possible and keep her entertained so I can do this job and talk about my words makes me so happy. You're the friendliest face in any audience and the best partner and dad there could be. We're so lucky to have you.

Riley, my love, you cried frequently while I wrote this book (many times while snuggled up into my shoulder like the perfect Velcro baby you were), but we made it happen together. I hope you know that your feelings are valid, and mama will always be here to wipe your tears. I may be a writer, but there aren't words that could ever possibly capture the depth of my love for you. You are a revelation and a miracle every single day. I would trade literally anything for just one smile or laugh from you. As I watch you grow into the strong-willed, funny, smart, sweet, one-of-a-kind wonder of the world that you are, I am so glad that you chose me to be your mama. I love you, I love you, I love you.

Getting to be an author is literally a childhood dream come true and wouldn't have been possible without the support of so many independent bookstores. One More Page Books in Arlington, Birch Tree Books in Leesburg, Scrawl Books in Reston, Fountain Bookstore in Richmond, Resist Booksellers in Petersburg, and Solid State Books in DC are all wonderful bookstores, and I hope you'll support them and your own local bookstores.

ABOUT THE AUTHOR

Alex Travis was born in New York and made her way to northern Virginia to begin her daytime career as a full-time school psychologist. She has a BA in psychology from the University of Pennsylvania and a PhD in school psychology from the University of Maryland. Alex wrote her first book at the age of eleven and has been losing herself in fictional worlds of her own creation since then. Alex makes her home in Virginia with her family, an outrageous collection of Funkos, and too many books to count.